the
missing
piece

BOOKS BY CATHERINE MILLER

99 Days With You
The Day that Changed Everything

Waiting for You
All That is Left of Us

The Gin Shack on the Beach
Christmas at the Gin Shack

the missing piece

CATHERINE MILLER

bookouture

Published by Bookouture in 2020

An imprint of Storyfire Ltd.
Carmelite House
50 Victoria Embankment
London EC4Y 0DZ

www.bookouture.com

ISBN: 978-1-83888-989-0
eBook ISBN: 978-1-83888-988-3

For my brother, Brian, for all the support.
If you know him, tell him to call me.

Part One

The Right Atrium

The right upper chamber of the heart that receives deoxygenated
blood from the vena cava.

In other words, it is the start…

Chapter One

Keisha

On average, I take my pulse twenty-eight times a day. For accuracy's sake, and I do have a penchant for accuracy, this week's average is twenty-eight point seven.

It's my preference to check my heart rate at least twice an hour while I'm awake and that increases when I'm stressed. Like when I'm on public transport or attending work meetings or when my housemate is cooking. It seems sensible to monitor it more closely when my day is in a greater state of flux or when Lucy is once again trying her hardest to set fire to our home. Peril never seems closer than when she is attempting to burn rice or dry boil noodles or cremate breaded chicken.

I know on days when my average number of pulse checks is over thirty that I need to take heed of how I'm doing. It's funny that while the heart governs every function of my body, it's not how many beats per minute that concerns me, but how many checks I've done. That's what tells me about my state of mind. Anything above thirty, I need to pause and take stock of my life.

Anything above thirty-five means I'm no longer in control and my anxiety is instead.

I hover my two fingers over the black outline of the floral heart on my left inner wrist. The tattoo is inked over my pulse point. It's not there for the purpose of aesthetics as many think. It's not a symbol of my life's work in cardiology. It's to make this moment quick. It means I can easily find the place to hold my fingers and trace what I need to feel.

As I press my skin towards the bone, I connect with the radial pulse. The surge of blood moving rhythmically under the skin provides instant reassurance.

I'm never sure why this is exactly. It's without doubt that I know I'm alive. The action would be impossible if I'm not. So why does feeling that pulse, even though it's an obvious fact that my heart is doing its job, make me relax?

Deep down, I know why. I know why the presence of a pulse is a reassurance against the memory where there isn't one.

I glance at my pink leather Swatch watch, the colour so different to my skin tone, and wait for the second hand to meet twelve. It's then that I count.

One. Two. Three.

The beat is steady as the hand drums around. It's nearly the same as my heart rate, which is further reassurance.

At times when I'm not busy, I go for a whole minute to get an accurate read of my heart rate. But most of the time, like now, I can't indulge in a full check and instead opt for fifteen or thirty seconds, multiplying it as appropriate.

I flick a look towards the door of my favourite café, knowing that the view is favourable from this, my usual seat. No sign yet. I'll risk a thirty-second check.

Eighteen. Nineteen.

As I count, time slows down as my heart rate seems to pick up. It's a momentary bubble of what should be calm, but is often panic. I'm attempting to appreciate the most carnal function of the human body. I'm assessing arguably the most major organ inside me. But with each pump of the heart that I record, I concern myself with how it is functioning. How is it coping under the stress I'm inducing? Is it really worth it? Why wouldn't I protect my heart more by not putting it through this?

Resting heart rate: 68 bpm. Above my personal average, but not surprising given what is about to occur.

By my usual standards, this shouldn't be my favourite café. It has far too much sparkle for starters. Tess, the owner, has a penchant for unicorns and adding shine. The entire décor is something that can only be described as candyfloss vomit. I'm not sure if the amount of pastel in here would kill or cure a migraine because the number of unicorn-shaped objects in here (salt cellars, plant pots, mirrors, frames, umbrella stand) keep multiplying, providing far too much distraction from that particular research project.

As I'm already here waiting, it's too late to back out now, although I flirt with the idea every time I do this. Not that Tess will let me. This is the experiment over which our two worlds meet.

The café door dings, notifying Tess of a new customer. We're both alert to the fact that this might be the person we're waiting for.

Despite the décor, I love this place for a lot of reasons, but Tess is the main one. The place is named after her: Tess's Treats. Although Tess's Unicorn Menagerie would be more apt. I come for lunch every day and on the days she isn't too busy, she sits with me. I don't have to be lonely here. I think we might even be friends.

The person entering is the one I'm waiting for. He's shorter than his dating profile claims. He's at least two inches out on his supposed five foot eleven. It irks me that he hasn't been more accurate on this fact. I've never understood the need to exaggerate (or lie to be more specific) about something that can easily be clarified by a tape measure.

I behave myself by not getting mine from my bag.

'Hi, Keisha? I'm hoping I've got the right person, but as you're the only one here it seems likely.'

Without doubt my dating profile is more accurate than his. My five foot eight, black hair, green eyes, mixed race, slim build, is a true portrayal of myself beyond the headshot.

I stand, and extend a hand to shake. 'Hi, Phil.'

'Yeah, right, okay.' Phil reciprocates the handshake awkwardly. 'I nearly didn't find this place.' He glances round as if he's never been in a unicorn-themed café before. He's nervous and I wonder what his heart rate is. From what I can tell, it's certainly higher than mine. I take my seat again. I've already purchased my coffee to save the inevitable argument of going Dutch.

'Do you come here often?' he jokes, still awkward.

'Two hundred and thirty-six times this year,' I say, realising I shouldn't add the fact that thirty-eight of those occasions were for dates like this one. 'It's close to my work.'

He laughs as if my accuracy is a number plucked out of thin air for the sake of a joke. 'Did you want anything? I'm going to get a drink.'

'I'm good, thanks. I didn't want to take up a table without ordering something.' My mug is half empty already. I'm glad. Already I know he is not the one. My finger has been on my pulse point the whole time and there is no heart-rate jump in response to meeting this man. I peel my fingers away after gathering all the information I need.

'Where do you work then?' Phil joins me at the small wooden table. This is my regular spot because I can see the world pass by. It's upcycled along with all the other furniture in the café. This one has pale-blue paint with an extra coating of glitter. Tess insists on adding sparkle wherever possible. 'I'm guessing it must be the university if this is your lunch stop.'

It's a bad starter-question and yet so many dates set off like this, as if they want to hit the jugular from the very beginning. I always wonder if some of them have a list of approved professions they're willing to date (lawyer, teacher, CEO = yes, circus acts = a firm no) without any concern for whether that person can make them smile, or shares their values: things that will actually help provide longevity in a relationship. I want to tell him where he's going wrong, but I've found my earlier dates didn't take kindly to feedback.

'What music do you like?' I'm not going to answer his question. I don't know him from Adam and if he's happy to lie about his height then he may have an unholy number of other distasteful habits. Stalking is the one I'm always fearful of, hence why I never let anyone know where I work or where I live. A somewhat complex stance when attempting to conquer the field of dating.

'Oh, I see. Dodge the question. You can tell me the answer later.' Phil winks as he says it. He's not my type. He has glasses that belong in an eighties movie, and a goatee that doesn't suit him and which he's failing to maintain at a reasonable level. He has a nervous habit of rubbing his beard and poking his glasses back up his nose, all with one hand in a sweeping movement. He's doing it so often I'm having to quash the urge to ask him to stop. In his dating profile he looks cool and quirky. Two words people have used to describe *me* in the past. I thought perhaps quirky was going to be enough – clearly I'm wrong. 'You're as beautiful as your profile,' he says.

I don't reply, instead taking a sip of my coffee. I often get told I'm beautiful, striking even, and I never know how to respond to the compliment. The way he delivers it this time is too soon. We've just met. Winking should be reserved for month two of a relationship.

'Okay, music I like…' he says, filling the awkward silence. 'I've always enjoyed Blur and Gorillaz even though they're old hat these days. I guess it was my era and I haven't grown out of enjoying listening to them. What about you? What's your favourite music?'

'The rhythm of my own heart.'

'Is that a song title or a band? I've not heard of them. Let me look them up on Spotify.' Phil grabs his phone from his pocket and spends an unacceptable length of time searching for something he won't find.

I brush my fingers over the ink heart on my wrist. The temptation to take a reading is high. The need to feel the music that Phil will never discover is compulsive and resisting its pull is nigh on impossible. He brushes his goatee again, pausing in between the movement to wrangle his finger up his nose before slipping it to his glasses. He glances at me, hoping I haven't seen.

I have.

'I'm going to use the ladies.' I'm not sure why I feel the need to tell him when I imagine it is often the reaction his nose explorations cause.

He seems to have lost all communicative abilities since his phone has come out. I note he's made it onto the Facebook app in his search for a band that doesn't exist.

'Ah, yeah, sure,' he comments, flinching at being caught doing much more than looking up a band. It makes me wonder if he has gone as far as creating a status to document this disastrous date. At least it isn't all on me today.

Tess is waiting in the alcove of the kitchen as she always does on these occasions. She has one thumb pointing up and the other down awaiting the verdict. Even her apron has unicorns on it in her quest to cheer the world.

I press a finger on the thumb that is pointing downwards and Tess makes a faint uh-huh noise. 'Knew it,' she whispers.

'Is it open?' I glance towards the exit that's behind the industrial kitchen space.

'Of course. Debrief tomorrow. Usual time.'

I know this isn't the adult way to go about things. But this set-up has saved me many hours of anguishing conversations that simply weren't going to go anywhere. I check that Phil isn't looking this way, but he's so preoccupied with his phone that he's unable to pay any attention to his actual surroundings or the company he was briefly in.

It helps alleviate the guilt I feel as I slip past the cookers and preparation benches to get to my secret exit. Tess is crossing through number thirty-nine on our whiteboard grid. Thirty-nine red crosses on a chart of one hundred.

Tess thinks that love can be found everywhere. That it is not a case of sitting around and waiting for *the one*. She reckons that if you date enough people, eventually you'll find someone compatible. She is the driving force behind these dates.

My theory is that I'll feel it. That my body will respond. That my heart will jump in acknowledgement. I don't believe it's possible for it to be forced.

As I pass the bin area and head out the back gate, I linger in the short alleyway and place my index and middle finger over their source of comfort. I don't locate my pulse straight away but as soon as I do I feel my breathing ease.

I do a thirty-second reading. I want to be quick. I need to get on my way before my thirty-ninth first date realises I'm not coming back.

Resting heart rate: 74 bpm.

That's far too high. I'm clearly not cut out for this. I've been dating, not exercising.

I jot the information down in a small ring-bound notepad every time – if not immediately, as soon as I get the chance. I've never been without twenty-eight recordings per day. I pop the book of information back into my pocket – the one that is closest to my heart.

Walking away, I wonder if I'll ever know. Will I ever find out how the heart responds when it falls in love? Because a heart that walks away from every single date doesn't seem to be one that's cut out for love. Anyone would think it's unwilling to try.

Chapter Two

Clive

It was at 2.36 a.m. on a Tuesday at his house when Clive Ellington's world turned upside down.

Or was it 5.21 p.m. on a Wednesday at his allotment?

It might have been Colonel Mustard in the library with a candlestick for all he ruddy knew. He'd like to be clear on the facts, but what were the chances of that when he didn't even know where he was?

His senses were rising, but only gradually. There was an unfamiliar sound: a buzzing he'd never heard before. And there was an unfamiliar smell: mustiness muted by bleach. And an unfamiliar space: a compact single bed with metal railings at the side. And that rush. The whoosh of movement even though he was sure he was lying still. He was strapped in as if he was wearing a seat belt even though he definitely wasn't in a car.

It had taken seconds to know this wasn't home, but it was taking much longer to work out where it was. He'd been at the allotment, hadn't he? Or had he been?

It was then that he remembered. The knowledge of what had happened coursed through him. The horror of what he'd come across. The memory ripped through him, causing a pain in his chest as if his life was about to end.

His life *had* ended.

That's why he was here.

Bringing himself upright, Clive held a hand to his chest and tried to concentrate on breathing as he took in what he could.

'It's okay, Clive. We're on the way to the hospital. Settle yourself back.' The voice didn't seem to have a body. At least not one Clive was able to see.

Clive was still fully clothed, with his shirt open. Being in bed with a suit on was enough to confuse him. The gripping sensation tightened round his ribs as his mind flicked through everything that had happened that afternoon to Nancy – the love of his life – the other half of him that was no longer here.

'Help!' Clive said, meekly, knowing that this was perhaps the end and it was only survival instinct that was calling out, wanting him to be saved. The rest of him wondered if this was the opportunity to join Nancy. It was one he'd rather like to take. If she was dead, he wanted to be with her.

The pain of that knowledge pumped through him and became a physical agony that didn't let up, gripping his chest again.

At least he was in his best suit jacket, rumpled as it was, he thought, as he closed his eyes and prepared to meet his maker. It was better this way. He didn't want to save himself if the life he was leaving behind was one without Nancy. The thought was too much to bear.

There was comfort now in the pain he was experiencing. It was pushing him further towards the place he wanted to be. That was one of the last things he remembered thinking as his world went black and he felt his weight drop.

He'd never imagined feeling anything once he'd died and reached the other side. But as he made his way to heaven, it was done with a crash landing and absolutely zero finesse.

It turned out that Clive's version of heaven was down at his allotment. It was his nirvana before he'd died, where he was most content on earth, so it was no surprise to land up there. There was a certain harmony to be found on the piece of land that he'd cultivated. But being there reminded him of something unsettling. Something recent. Something that wasn't usually there.

In the afterlife there was an abundance of every crop he'd ever worked on – unlike the reality of his allotment most years. The runner beans were laden as were the peas. The gooseberries were ripe and the rhubarb crop seemed to be twice the size of last year. The gladioli with their mild scent, that he liked to grow for Nancy, were blooming so much he'd have to take a bunch to her each day.

Nancy.

There it was… That glorious hope.

All he had to do was leave the allotment and walk home.

They'd be together again and that truly would be heaven.

Only his legs wouldn't move as he was telling them to. Nor did the road he needed to walk down look as it should. In fact, it was all kinds of wrong. The view from his allotment was a haze. He could see his shed and his allotted space, but nothing was clear beyond.

He tried his legs again. It was a five-hundred-metre walk, if that.

It was no distance at all, and yet he'd never felt so far away.

'Clive. Clive, can you hear me?'

It wasn't Nancy's voice.

It wasn't any of his friends from the allotment either.

'Ack!'

The noise surprised Clive, especially as it came from him.

'It's okay, Clive. We thought we'd lost you there for a minute.'

You had, Clive thought, wondering what he had to do to go back. For some reason, even without Nancy there, the allotment called to him. It was as if it was the place he should be. The place in which he'd work this all out.

'I'm dead,' Clive heard himself say. 'Let me carry on being dead.'

'Not on my shift, sir. We'll have no one dying today.'

Clive opened his eyes, but he wasn't able to focus on the blurry medic standing over him or any of the other medical staff surrounding him. The only thing that did come into focus was the defibrillator trolley next to the bed he was on. Its bright-yellow colour and purpose was unmistakable with the large red letters on one side spelling out RESUS.

Death had been temporary.

It turned out he was very much alive.

Chapter Three

Keisha

Saying that I like my lab coat doesn't do it justice. The truth is, I *love* my lab coat. It's protective, practical and shields me against the world. I like that I don't have to think about what I wear to work too much because, well, lab coat! It removes any need to nod towards fashion. What a relief that is when my capabilities in such areas aren't built in. This item of clothing is partly responsible for the fact that on completing my cardiology degree, I remained at the university as a research associate. That and my desire to help eradicate heart disease.

We have a full day ahead of us at the research laboratory. We're collating results for two projects and alongside that I'm working towards my PhD. We have study participants for our cardiac research booked in for every timeslot. I like it this way. I prefer the days that are busier.

'Do you want an Oat So Simple?' Lucy calls from the small kitchen alcove.

'What's one of those?'

'It's porridge. You just add boiling water.'

Lucy's my closest friend. We live and work together, which for the majority of people is a recipe for disaster. Sometimes I think that it is but the rest of the time I know it works for us. Somehow, we need each other. Isn't it true that it takes two dysfunctional people to create one source of functional output?

'So do you want one?'

'I had some rice for breakfast.' I stop checking my lists to make sure she's not about to pour boiling water everywhere. Lucy's creased lab coat is far from pristine.

'That's not a normal breakfast, you know.'

'It is in some cultures.'

'I just need to add water up to the fill line, and leave it for two minutes.' Lucy holds the pot up to the light as if finding the line is a game no one is able to conquer.

For a second I fear she might try to fill the container from the kettle while it's above her head. I'm thankful when she does no such thing. It seems she is blessed with *some* common sense. Although most of that has come from experience rather than being a God-given gift. She must have learned her lesson from the microwave incident: the time she didn't read the instructions to pour out the chicken soup from the sachet with the metallic strip, causing sparks to fly as a result.

The two minutes while Lucy is waiting for the porridge oats to transform to something edible is the perfect time to take a reading. I save my carotid pulse for when I can't be seen by the general public. I worry what people will think of me if they catch me poking around at my neck. It's an easier place to locate and measure the heart rate, but people dish out odd looks if they catch me in the act.

Because I can feel Lucy's antics are causing my heart to race, locating my carotid pulse is easy. It is exerting itself more than usual, even though the overall rate isn't any higher than it was half an hour before.

These finer details are the ones that I enjoy most. Being so in tune with the rhythm of my heart means I'm able to identify certain fluxes without the need for machines. Even though my heart rate is the same, my central venous pressure is undoubtedly up. It's not every person who can walk along the street and declare their CVP is high. But, then again, it's not every person who wants to.

'This is not bad, you know. Bit hot, though.'

'I think you're meant to leave it to cool down for a bit.'

'I wanted to try it. You should try some too. It'll be better than your rice portions.'

'I'll try the porridge if you have rice one morning.'

Lucy pulls a disapproving face.

It will be interesting to see if Lucy not skipping breakfast for once has the desired effect of reducing the snacks she tends to go through between starting work and her lunch hour. It was only yesterday I found her happily gorging on a pack of mini savoury eggs that were supposed to be for her lunch. I decide I'll leave Lucy to monitor her food intake. It's only possible to conduct so many studies during the day.

'How was it then?'

'How was what?'

'Your date?'

'Oh, that.' Is it bad to have forgotten about it already?

'Yeah, that. Surely it wasn't another duff one?'

'I fear that's exactly what it was.'

'How come? What was wrong this time?'

'Two inches of inaccuracy.'

'Woah. Two inches is a lot. I take it we're talking about his height?'

'Naturally. And it wasn't just that. There was some unchecked nostril clearance. Some things are a very clear indicator that I'm not in the same room as *the one*.' He'll probably report the same about me, especially as I scarpered off, but whatever feeling it was that I was hoping to find, I definitely hadn't got it with him. I always find the whole dating thing far too awkward. It's probably why I've never managed to have a proper boyfriend.

'Ewww. I do wish you'd let me come with you one time. I want to be a fly on the wall.'

'We've talked about this. It's a no.' I already do far too many things with Lucy. Dating together is not about to happen.

The fact that Lucy and I have to take our lunch breaks at different times is a saving grace in many ways. Being alone means I get the opportunity to branch out and eat at Tess's café. It's the reason I have more than one friend.

'If you'd switch to some dinner dates like I've suggested,' Lucy carries on, 'I can just happen to be at another table. I might be able to give you some pointers.'

'It's still a no. It's bad enough with Tess keeping an eye on proceedings.'

The post-analysis with Tess is often the part I look forward to more than the date. I'll be doing that with her later.

The phone rings at the same time as the microwave beeps. I look over to Lucy and she opts to head to the desk and pick up the receiver. I respond to the beeps and go to the tiny kitchen.

The microwave is empty.

'What were you attempting to heat up?' I ask when I get back to the desk. Our first participants for a trial looking at the effects of a new beta-blocker should arrive soon and I need to do more preparation.

'My porridge.' She shows me the pot in her hand as if it's a perfectly reasonable explanation.

'But I thought you just had to add hot water?'

'Oh yeah. But I'd not realised at first and had put the time into the microwave already. I let it do its thing. It's the only way to get it back to zero.'

I gawk and have to tighten my jawline to stop it from slacking. 'There is a cancel button for that.'

'Is there? I like doing it my way so I get the numbers back to neutral. It's a quirk. I think I have a quirk.'

I'm not even sure how to respond. 'What was the phone call?'

This early on a Thursday it is likely to be a cancellation.

'It was our favourite doctor.'

'Dr Hutchins?'

'Yes. He has a takotsubo syndrome case for your PhD.'

'He does? And they're willing to take part in the study?'

'Yes, he thinks so, although he said it was a bit complicated. You'll be able to do the paperwork at the hospital soon.'

'Did you take the details?' Even if Lucy is prone to thinking that running an empty microwave is a logical idea, hopefully she's not lost the ability to take down the appropriate information when fielding phone calls.

'Of course. Patient details are here.' Lucy passes over a Post-it note.

'Do we have time to schedule it in over the next week?'

'There's always time. You can head up to the hospital tomorrow morning if you like.'

'Will you be okay covering the other appointments?'

Lucy and I have the same role. It makes no difference who gathers the information we need. But it's hard not to admit that I want to oversee things, to make sure everything is absolutely accurate. My fingers brush over my inner wrist.

'All I need to do is take the usual bunch of measurements,' she replies. 'I'd be able to do it in my sleep and ask the same questions every participant has to answer. I'm not about to bugger things up. Just because I can't cook, doesn't mean my ineptness rolls over to the rest of life. You shouldn't need reminding. Now book it in.'

That's the good thing about Lucy. She always knows when I need bringing down to earth. It's as if she can see my axis and knows when it's spinning off its centre.

I quit worrying about that for now.

I move my fingers away from temptation and onto my next task.

Ringing the ward, I book an appointment to see case study five. Only the fifth subject at the local hospital to qualify for my PhD study into takotsubo cardiomyopathy, also known as broken heart syndrome. A rare event that can occur after shock. It's not like the broken-heart emoji with the crack down the middle. It's when there is apical ballooning causing a sudden temporary weakening of the myocardium. The heart muscle doesn't crack, it blossoms wider than it should and can no longer pump as efficiently as a result: a swollen balloon. That's what a real broken heart looks like.

I speak to Dr Hutchins, who reiterates the fact that it's a more complex case, but eligible for the study all the same. The participant's interest has been caught by having to drink beetroot juice, apparently. My study is looking at the effects of nitric oxide (which beetroot juice is high in) on patients after takotsubo syndrome. The study's complexities are hard to explain but, in short, the drink looks like it'll make the heart healthier, helping with prevention and recovery, and I'm hoping to prove that.

When the call finishes, I start to worry about having to go somewhere that isn't our laboratory.

Because no matter how hard I try to live a life of routine and balance, there is always something pressing me to take my pulse.

Chapter Four

Clive

The past few days in hospital had been the unhappiest of Clive Ellington's life.

He always prided himself on being a jolly fellow, able to make the moodiest of people smile. That was until that moody mask belonged to him and he was unable to shift the blasted thing. No matter how hard he tried to find them, there didn't seem to be any positives.

There were a multitude of points causing him to be miserable and he'd happily list them all in some kind of bullet-point presentation, but no one wanted to listen. Why would they when he only wanted to rant on about how his wife had passed away and that he wished he'd joined her?

No one wanted to die and wake up to be a miserable old git, but that seemed to be what had happened, and he didn't like it. Neither did anyone else, he considered, as another lonely day stretched out before him.

He didn't like the numbers of checks they were doing on him now he was in the cardiology high dependency unit. They had various wires attached to him. They were worried his heart was going to give up at any minute.

They didn't seem to like his response that he wished it bloody well would.

Along with now being a widower, there were several things that were depressing him beyond measure, including the whole *not* being dead business.

First, they were insistent that he remained in something that he regarded to be a night gown. It came complete with a bum flap and looked truly awful. However much he tried to encourage them to allow him to wear his best suit, they weren't having it. In protest, he was wearing his suit jacket over the top. It was his favourite. It was a patchwork jacket and it was his best ever charity-shop find. One of a kind.

The only problem with insisting on wearing a jacket was that it was hot. Excruciatingly hot. He really needed to take it off, but this was his cross and he was going to bear it whether it was a stupid idea or not.

If that whole rigmarole wasn't enough, the second thing depressing him was that he was having to pee into a pot because they were monitoring his intake and output of fluid. They were actually measuring how many millilitres of drink he was taking on board and how much he was whizzing out the other end.

Rather than the usual technique of heading to the gents, there were all sorts of processes to follow. Ones that made wearing your best suit jacket rather complicated. He wasn't going to take it off though. If he let his guard down they were bound to see it as a win. Because despite the efforts being made to care for him, he did rather feel as if he were in a battle with the staff, especially the nurse in charge. They didn't understand him. He was trying to tell them important things, but the ward sister told him they were too busy whenever he tried to share his pain.

He didn't blame them. They had a job to get on with and counselling for more than five minutes wasn't part and parcel of the process. But that didn't help him. It didn't alleviate the depression that was beginning to overtake him. When people mentioned the plan for him returning home and he burst out crying, they weren't able to offer him answers. No one was able to remedy the situation he was in and that wrecked him even more.

For now, they just wanted to get him stable, the doctors kept saying, as if they knew that the chances of him ever healing from this were diminishing. It wasn't that his heart had broken once. It was breaking repeatedly. Every time he remembered what had happened, it was as if parts of him were shattering, as if his organs were made of glass.

Maybe that's what had occurred. Where he was once made of flesh and bone, he was now brittle, parts of him splintering at every opportunity.

He no longer knew how to paste a smile on his face.

The pocketbook of jokes he had memorised to make people laugh seemed to have slipped into a wet puddle and was beyond recovery. Even his manners, which he prided himself on, had nose-dived.

There wasn't much left of the Clive Ellington he knew.

He realised that the day he threw a bedpan in anger. He'd never known himself to be in a situation where he had so much pent-up emotion and nowhere to place it. Throwing things wasn't the answer and he was ashamed for having done it, but what else was he to do?

The Clive Ellington he knew had been alive.

This Clive Ellington was dead and yet somehow still living.

At least this Clive Ellington still owned the best jacket this entire postcode had ever known. And he was going to wear it. No matter what.

Chapter Five

Keisha

It's safe to say I'm not a fan of the unfamiliar. I'm never keen on going to new places. It brings about a kind of anxiety that is hard to explain. This is coming from someone who can't even claim to be at ease in their usual surroundings, so you'll understand that going to different environments isn't something I do willingly.

I've conquered this fear before. I have to remind myself this isn't the first time. I know this place. This will be the fifth visit I've made to Southampton General Hospital for the purpose of my PhD. On each of those occasions I have realised it's not been about dealing with a mere hospital. It is more like a whole *city*. It is a huge and daunting place that has more departments and specialities than I could ever possibly list without putting a person to sleep.

It should be an insurmountable experience coming here, but there is one thing that I find extraordinarily comforting about the place… It is *alive*. It has a pulse. There is a coming and going to it – a rhythm – that makes it seem as if this place has a heart.

There is a coffee shop at the entrance and I can't help but indulge in a hot chocolate and enjoy a spot of people watching, knowing that here there is every walk of life, every possible eventuality, wandering in and out of the automatic doors. I savour the two pink marshmallows that are on my saucer as relatively healthy allowable treats, dancing their spongey softness on my lips for a moment of pleasure.

I see doctors on their breaks, as they grab a bite to eat at the small store across the lobby. I see a middle-aged woman dabbing her cheeks as she flees the place. I see a father and daughter, a patch over the little girl's eye, as they select a gingerbread man and move towards the counter.

It makes me think of my father and his larger-than-life presence, as if he had to make up for the loss of my mother by facing life with twice the personality. I was so young when it happened that I don't remember her, but I wonder if I ever had moments like that with him. Whether, before he died, I was his little girl rewarded for being brave. I wish on this little girl's behalf that she gets to keep this memory. That this moment stays alive for her.

I wish it was like that for me too. Only all those memories have been blocked out, overtaken by another. It's only my father's dying that I remember with the greatest clarity.

I'm not the only one with death on their mind here. You can see it on too many faces. The patients, the relatives, the doctors, the porters. But there is also hope. The cures, the second chances, the new beginnings. The people drift in and out without saying hello to each other. Maybe a nod of acknowledgement, a smile in greeting. They're like the blood cells that are knocking alongside each other in this main artery of the hospital.

I wonder for a moment which department is the heart of the place. Is it the cardiology ward that I am heading to? Perhaps it's the intensive care unit where they are attempting to revive the sickest patients. Or the management suite where all the important decisions are made.

As I reach the end of my hot chocolate, relishing the delicious sweetness, I realise that perhaps there isn't one heart in a place as huge as this. I reckon the heart of this place lies in the staff rooms. It's hidden in a coffee cup every day as the people running this place restore themselves and find the strength to do it all over again.

The end of my drink also signifies the end of any procrastinating. I take my heart rate and revel in the beat, noticing its rhythm is not dissimilar to the beat of people coming in and out of the hospital doors.

We are both alive, this hospital and I.

The thought gives me the strength to do what I need to, even though it's the first time I'm having to venture to the coronary care unit. The other studies I run normally involve participants who are well enough to attend the laboratory at the university campus. My PhD study is different. It requires baseline readings from subjects while they are in hospital and looks to increase their nitric oxide levels in the recovery stage of broken heart syndrome in the form of beetroot juice. Whenever I try and explain the study in any depth, there are two responses: glazing over or the questioning gaze, wondering if I've gone mad. But there is genuine evidence to say the juice may help certain heart conditions and I'm hoping to go some small way to see if it helps with broken heart syndrome. If the study goes well then it is my ultimate hope that it will secure funding to test the theory on a much larger scale, understanding how to stop hearts from ballooning into breaking.

Even though the university and the hospital are linked, until starting my PhD, I've done my best to avoid Southampton General in every capacity. For a thirty-one-year-old I'm in good health and I do everything I can to keep it that way. Pulse-taking is just the icing on the cake. I use the university gym at least three times a week. I eat a balanced diet and ensure I rarely eat trans fats or anything that studies have shown are bad for the heart. I'm teetotal and even the notion that the occasional glass of red might be good for you hasn't altered my stance. I don't smoke. I avoid red meats. I am distinctly void of bad habits.

In short, I'm boring. I like to maintain the norm. I have a structure that I live by and like to remain within. I used to tussle with this, as if it was somehow a problem. But as I've become older I've realised there's a silver lining to being in my position. To knowing what I am comfortable with, and being comfortable with who I am.

Only there are times, like now, when it is impossible to avoid going to new places and meeting new people.

When I reach the CCU nurses' station, the staff are all busy. The wait gives me enough time to get anxious. I gently press in against the skin of my wrist, the folder I'm holding allowing me to do so unseen.

'Can I help you at all?' a receptionist asks me.

'I have an appointment with Mr Ellington.' I show them my ID.

'This way, please.'

I'm guided into a unit with four beds, each with monitors set up. They are recording each individual's heart rhythms. I'm familiar with their purpose and how they help, but I've never seen them in use with anyone other than a healthy subject. Here, in stereo, they are a cacophony and it feels as if my own heart rhythm is becoming irregular, knowing that the four rhythms I can hear aren't in sync.

The gentleman lined up to become case study number five is wearing a pair of orange trousers and an unbuttoned patchwork jacket, his chest bare, making it easier for the leads to be attached to his body. He hasn't noticed me yet at the end of his bed. He's busy struggling to open a jar of something.

'Blasted, effing thing,' he grumbles, and looks ready to launch the item across the room before he sees me. 'Well, don't just stand there. Help, would you?'

'I'm here for your appointment for the beetroot-juice trial.' I say it quickly, to stop him from thinking I'm a member of staff. The jar looks like it contains some kind of specimen and it's my kind of luck that he's trying to open it despite it being full. I haven't got the faintest clue what to do.

'You have two hands, don't you?'

I glance at my hands as if somehow my brain has neglected to remember that, indeed, I do have them. 'Yes.'

'So, if I'm doing this trial for you, it won't hurt if you use those two hands to help me. See, I just can't…' Mr Ellington tries to get a purchase on the jar again, his bulbous joints sliding despite his attempts to grip. 'It just won't…'

There's a golden liquid in the jar and for a long minute I stare as I struggle to catch up with what I've walked into.

'Would you?' he asks.

For the first time I see his eyes. They are blue. Marble-blue with tears forming, making them glisten like glass, as shiny as his bald head. I see them and I see beyond them, just for a fraction of a moment.

'What's in the jar?' I croak, feeling as if he might have seen into me, the way I've just seen into him. 'Because if it's pee, I'm not helping you.'

'Humph.' Clive half-laughs, half-grunts and the sound gets stuck in his throat and it booms louder from there somehow. 'What a ridiculous thing to say. I know this is the lowest ebb I've ever reached, but I'm not sat here cradling my own urine. My standards might be slipping, and I've no choice in these surroundings, but I'm not off my bloody rocker yet!'

'It does look distinctly like it could be urine,' I clarify, hoping that if I were to do a survey of the ward, I wouldn't be the only person to jump to that conclusion. I refrain from actually carrying it out.

'Come closer,' Clive suggests.

I take three steps towards him so I'm closer, but not too close. I don't take my eyes off him as I move, feeling fixed in his blue-marble gaze.

'See,' he says, as he shakes the jar for good measure.

There's a sloshing sound and I wonder why the staff have thought it wise to leave this man in possession of his glass jar.

I glance at the contents. 'What are they?' There appear to be approximately (I don't like dealing with approximates, but we'll class this as an emergency) twenty-five eyeballs in the jar. I'm pretty certain three of them are winking.

'Pickled onions. Best in England. Grew them myself and then my…' Clive trails off, staring into the jar.

'And you can't open the jar? And you'd like me to?' Relief floods over me now I know that I'm not dealing with a wee-in-a-jar situation.

I take the pot, lingering to examine the contents. There is a home-made label offering details of the onions' vintage. I have a lot of questions. Ones that I didn't ever expect to be contemplating. Like, how has this man got his pickled onions here? And is the catering so bad that this seems like a good snack option?

'Have you never seen a pickled onion before?'

Clive seems like he might be hangry. It's eleven in the morning, less than an hour to lunch.

'To be honest, certainly not home-grown and never up this close,' I reply.

'I found you a chair at last, lovely. Always in short supply here.' It's the receptionist returning.

'He'll be able to do it if you can't. Hand it over to him,' says Clive.

'I haven't given it a go yet.'

'I'll leave you to it,' the receptionist says.

I don't want him to go. I feel like a visiting relative rather than someone who's here in a professional capacity.

'Stop ogling them and open the jar already, would you?'

'Alright, Grumpy,' I say too quickly, the word out there like toothpaste squeezed from the tube that I'm unable to squish back in. So much for being the visiting professional. 'I'm sorry. I didn't mean to say that.'

Clive's expression becomes crestfallen. It's the saddest expression I've ever seen and I need to make it right again. In one move I take off the lid and am successful in not spilling the contents despite leaning away from the waft. It's a relief that the pungent aroma is distinctly vinegary.

'Oh, love. What must you think of me? I don't mean to be so miserable.' Clive sniffles and grabs a tissue for the tears that are descending, as if the onion odour has caught him.

I hope that's the reason. I know I should comfort him, but instead I place the jar and lid on the table and take up residence in the chair. I'm blushing, unsure how to respond and I can tell he is self-conscious too.

The tears continue and for the first time ever, I can see what I'm trying to learn more about. Here is a man with a broken heart. It's obvious before even taking a pulse.

Clive clears his face for a third time. 'I'm sorry. I know it's ridiculous to be crying over pickled onions.'

I suspect they might not be the reason he is so upset. There are many questions I should ask to find out more, but I can't process how. What do you say to a man sobbing over a jar of pickled vegetables? Instead I go with a well-practised patter of information. 'I'm Keisha Grant. Your consultant, Dr Hutchins, will have told you that I'm a research associate from Southampton University and you're a suitable participant for the PhD that I'm conducting looking at the benefits of nitric oxide after a cardiac event such as yours. He said you were happy to participate, if you feel up to taking part.'

'Ah, yes. I thought that was who you must be. It sounds very interesting. I always knew veg were good for you. Something about drinking beetroot juice daily, he said. Had my first lot this morning.'

'Yes, that's right. You'll have the same amount every day and we'll monitor your progress over the coming months. Are we okay to continue? I need to take some notes from your records and get some readings, but the monitor is doing most of that work for me. Then I need to ask a few questions and there are some forms to fill out. If you're not feeling up to it, we can always rearrange.'

'Would you like a pickled onion?' Clive finds a spoon and starts to fish them out one at a time, landing them on a saucer. Unlike his ability to open the jar, he seems to have this down to a fine knack.

'I'm not sure if I do. Like them, that is.'

'Well you must try one. I insist. If I'm going to be drinking beetroot juice daily, it seems only fair.' Clive pushes the small plate in my direction as if it's a dish of candy.

'Do you want to take part in the study?' Suitable candidates are few and far between. But I'm not sure that fact is enough to make me want to try the browned, pickled vegetable.

The problem is the diagnosis that the study requires the participants to have. It's rare to be able to identify it, because most people don't get to tell their story. A broken heart is a broken heart. Period. It isn't often that sufferers manage to get up and tell you about the event afterwards.

Clive bites into his onion and it gives out a very satisfying crunch. He chews away with ohhs and ahhs as he goes. 'I plan to savour all of these. I won't be offering these out to just anyone.'

I don't want to be rude so I take my offering and hope that holding my breath will help. I take a deep breath and cough with the fumes.

'Sarson's vinegar. My Nancy only ever liked the best.' With that, his eyes start leaking again.

'If I eat this, will you tell me why you're crying over pickled onions?' The question surprises me. It's not one from my official list and I'm not prone to spontaneity. But in this moment, I feel closer to knowing the answers than I ever have. Maybe this is the subject that'll finally teach me the answer to my question: What causes a broken heart, and is there any way for it to heal?

Chapter Six

Clive

Clive helped himself to a second *Allium cepa*. This shallot variety was his favourite to be pickled. He shouldn't be having two; he'd end up with indigestion. But he wanted to enjoy them over his remaining days and who was he to know how many of those were left? He was rather hoping not too many.

The problem was that the onions were taking him straight back to where it hurt. The memory that kept repeating. And now there was this young creature, who looked like a gracious gazelle and yet seemed uncomfortable in her own skin. Unconsciously, she was wringing her hands, one rolling over the other in an almost continuous motion. It was mesmerising.

Biting into the onion, Clive savoured the tang and tingle of the snack. When he had more than one his lips became kind of numb and he wished it was possible for that sensation to crawl across the rest of him.

'There's a lot to it,' he said in answer to the difficult question. How did he explain everything to this girl who'd appeared at the end of his bed? She was eyeing the onion she was holding with growing suspicion. 'Eat up, and I'll start at the beginning.'

She took the tiniest of nibbles, barely digging her incisors beyond the first layer. Her face with its freckles a shade darker than the rest of her skin curled in disgust.

'You'll need two bites and bigger ones than that to fully savour the taste.' He hoped he'd not wasted a pickled onion on someone who wasn't going to appreciate the full flavour.

'It's just so…' Keisha licked her tongue on her lower lip.

'Tangy? Take a bigger bite. At the moment I reckon you've just sucked some vinegar off the surface.'

Fair play to the girl, Clive thought as he watched her pop it whole into her mouth and chew, the grimace disappearing as she went.

'What do you think?'

'It's very… oniony? I'm not much of a foodie, sorry.'

Clive let out a soft chuckle. He was impressed she'd actually eaten it. He'd been offering them out to the nursing staff for days and none of them had taken him up on the gift.

'I don't think my allotment produce is on the wanted list for many foodies. Although it should be of course.'

Keisha nodded, still clearing her mouth.

'I'd offer you a drink if I were at home. They don't really let me play host here. Now, would you like to indulge me and listen to the tale of how I met Nancy?'

The nodding hadn't stopped so Clive took the opportunity to tell his story.

'I wasn't much of a dancer when I was young, but my brother Ken really was. Ken convinced me I needed to do something different, which was to go to an afternoon tea dance. My heart really wasn't in it. Not at a time of day when everyone would be able to tell what a bad dancer I was. At least if it had been darker and there was a bit more drink on the go then no one would have noticed the lad with two left feet. I sat on the side lines, tried to hide away. I was quite stunned when she came and asked me to dance. Even when I explained I wasn't really capable of such things, she still persisted. She told me that no one ever learned to do something by not starting.'

Talking about it made Clive's feet want to drum out a foxtrot, as if he'd awoken an ancient longing that was part of his DNA.

'And did you start?' Keisha asked, glancing at Clive's bouncing feet.

'Much to my brother's astonishment, I became a ballroom champion the following year.'

At least Clive thought he had been. The concept seemed to leave him as soon as he'd said the words. It was hard to think about the beginning knowing that it had come to an end.

'I've really had it being sat here.' Something took over Clive and he yanked off the wires that were caging him to his chair and the bed space. They were even making him use a commode so they didn't have to unplug his attachments. Once he was up, he knew it was time to dance again, to let the years flitter away, his feet skipping out the foxtrot. *Strictly Come Dancing* had nothing on him.

'Are you sure you should be doing that?' Keisha stood, clearing the way.

'This is just the warm-up.'

The bedside monitor bleeped loudly when the recordings flatlined. Clive ignored it as his feet completed a circuit of the four-bedded room, the old dear over the way giving him a round of applause.

'Would you like to dance?' Clive asked his young visitor. He wasn't sure what he was up to. It was as if he was hoping to capture the past. A moment he'd lost, but was now there in his grasp.

'I need to go,' Keisha said and, as quickly as possible, she left the ward, only peering back briefly with two fingers pressed against her neck.

Chapter Seven

Keisha

Beep. Beep. Beep.

Babum. Babum.

Beeeeeeeeeeeeeeeeeeeeeeeeeeeeeeeeeeeeeep.

Three days later and I still haven't been able to clear the sounds of the monitors from my head. It's like when you peer at the sun and it leaves the trace of a shadow in your vision, even when you've stopped looking in that direction.

If the beeping wasn't enough to remind me of the event, the pickled onion repeating on me is making sure of it.

I'm glad it's lunchtime and thankfully when I reach Tess's café there isn't a date waiting for me. I'm fed up with experiments. I want my life in boxes that no one can mess with.

'Number forty and forty-one are booked in,' Tess says, as soon as I arrive. She's always more excited by my love life than her own. 'Are you okay? You're never late.'

My lunch is on the table waiting. I always have the same meal on the same days and as soon as Tess sussed onto this, she started prepping them for my arrival. She prides herself on having the correct order and a flat white waiting for me. It's another of those things that pleases me greatly and seeing today's vegetarian chilli with white rice brings me comfort.

'It's been a bit of a day or two,' I say, easing myself in the chair with a great sigh.

'What has Lucy broken now?'

It was true that most of my stories of exasperation involve my best friend. The last thing being when she managed to snap a ruler when she was drawing a straight line. It didn't even seem possible.

'Not Lucy. A patient.' I take a gulp of the flat white. It's the lukewarm temperature that I love and the caffeine gives me the fortification that I require. I may not have many vices, but my lunchtime coffee is one.

'You tell me off if I call them patients. Don't you always tell me they're subjects or participants?'

'Fair point.'

Tess is an astute listener. She is always taking in more than I give her credit for. I've never worked out if it's a skill she's been born with or if it comes from years of running the café. After a failed sandwich-van business, which was more down to the failing relationship with her ex-girlfriend, Tess went on to set up this café. I think my first visit was within a week of it opening. Since then she's added approximately (and it's only an approximate because she adds to it weekly, sneaking in more when I'm not looking) two hundred and eight unicorns. I sometimes get the impression they make up for losing who she has always said was the love of her life.

'I had to visit this chap at the hospital, so he is a patient. If they managed to get him back to his bed, that is.'

'What do you mean?'

Beeeeeeeeeeeee... The never-ending sound pops into my thoughts again. I drink more coffee and plan to start chewing in the hope that it will quieten the noise, even if it is only in my imagination.

'He was a bit... well, "eccentric" is the best word I have to describe what went on.'

'Ah, well, that explains a lot.' Tess takes her place on my regular table, bringing her lunch with her. Some days are quieter here and the number of customers varies with the café being slightly off the beaten track. It's a hidden gem.

Tess's food always consists of what is surplus to requirements; whatever needs using up lands on her plate. Today it's yesterday's pasta-salad special with a side of pea and ham soup. 'Have you ever been in close proximity to anyone you'd describe as eccentric?'

'Not if I can help it. I think you know me well enough to know I don't like anything that's unpredictable. That doesn't just apply to humans.'

'So what happened to conclude that this man is unpredictable?'

'I didn't get any of the information I needed because he took all his heart monitor leads off and started dancing before I had the chance to.'

'Dancing! No wonder that took you by surprise. Did you join in?'

'No, I ran away.' I find myself surprised at being so honest. Tess and I are united by coffee and paninis and the occasional slice of cake. There is often no reason to talk about the bigger things when we seem to get along perfectly fine with the mundane of everyday.

'Will you still be able to use him as a participant?'

I scoop up some chilli onto a spoon, ravenous now. It's a tad cooler than usual, but I'm so hungry I don't care too much for the temperature. I shrug my shoulders to remain polite by not talking with my mouth full.

'Graham, the head of the department, and Dr Hutchins, his consultant, have said he sends his apologies and would still like to take part in the study. Apparently he has a particular love for vegetables and doesn't want to miss the opportunity to prove they have health benefits. I need all the participants we can get for the takotsubo study. I've said I'll go back, but Lucy is going to come with me this time.' My heart rate is up just thinking about the interaction.

'You don't sound like you want to.'

I eat more chilli and will the subject to change. 'It was an odd experience. I'm not sure how to explain it, but it left me feeling sad. They keep saying his case is complicated. I'm worried his story might break my heart the same as it did his.'

It hadn't been the pickled-onion shenanigans or the story of meeting Nancy or the wanting to dance that had made me sense that. It had been the look in Clive's eyes.

'He probably is feeling sad. I would be if I was stuck in hospital. Perhaps it rubbed off on you. But he was jolly enough to want to dance by the end of it. Maybe you visiting him and letting him participate in your study will do him some good.'

I nod, finding comfort in Tess's analysis. Generally I find it hard to read people. Especially ones that are crying one minute and dancing the next. 'I'll let you know how we get on. Now tell me about numbers forty and forty-one.' I'm glad to be able to move on the conversation, even if it is a subject I normally avoid.

This is one experiment where I'm not heavily involved in the admin. Tess is the orchestrator and has been more than happy to carry it out. And I'm more than happy to let her. The sooner we fulfil the conditions of this experiment, the sooner it'll be over. She's convinced I should be able to find love if I give it a chance. I'm optimistic that I can get through all one hundred without that happening. Perhaps then she'll let me give up on dating.

'Do you want to see the next candidates?' Tess makes it sound as if we are trying to find someone suitable for the next general election.

'I guess so.' There's not a hint of enthusiasm in my voice.

Tess goes and gets her phone, spending a few minutes accessing the app and finding the profiles she wants to show me. I use the time to wipe my plate clean and, as it's been a stressful week, I decide a second flat white is going to be in order.

'I knew we should never have downloaded the app onto your phone. You need to start using it for yourself at some point.' I smirk as Tess hands it over.

'Nah. I've told you before. I've had my first love and it didn't work out. My second love is this café. That's the only solid relationship I'm in need of.'

Tess is never going to change her stance so I know once we're done with this frippery she'll let me stick with my own stance.

I don't really pay attention to what the people in the photos look like. What interests me is where the picture is taken. Both backdrops are as boring as each other; both profile images are selfies taken on a sofa. It's a good job Tess is doing the selecting, otherwise not enough candidates would make the cut. Whatever happened to taking a photograph outside? To adding a bit of interest to their context? But I'm not going to complain. I want to get this done. One less experiment to worry about. And even though there is a small fragment buried deep within me that would like to be proved wrong, I'll also be glad to finish the one hundred and get back to a life of singledom. It's the only way I know how to protect my heart. To never let it fall in love in the first place.

Chapter Eight

Clive

Clive shouldn't have danced. He realised it within about thirty seconds of removing the wires. He'd scared the girl for starters, the loud beeping sounds making her flee.

But more than that, it had signalled something. If a man was well enough to dance around as if he was in a ballroom, then surely he'd reached the point that he was well enough to speak to the police.

The policeman who'd introduced himself as PC Doyle was waiting at the end of his bed and suggested they go somewhere more private.

'Do we have to do this?' Clive attempted one more plea.

'We just need to build a picture of what happened. Anything that you can remember may be of use to us.'

Clive swallowed, as if his grief could be pushed down, but he knew this was something that wouldn't go away by trying to ignore it. 'If we have to.'

The only upside was going somewhere else. He was fed up with these four walls where no one needed to know his business. With any luck he might suss out where the exit was.

It was disappointing to only be taken round the corner to what must have been the ward sister's office. Clive had been hoping for some kind of adventure and they'd barely had a stroll.

'Take a seat,' PC Doyle offered when they were in there. 'One of the nurses is going to join us.'

It was the ward sister. Clive didn't like the ward sister. She'd told him too often she didn't have time to talk to him and chastised him as if he were a child after he'd performed his foxtrot.

'Can it be another member of staff?'

'I am the most senior member of nursing staff on the ward. No one else is free at the moment to come and listen,' she said as she entered the room.

'You've been too busy to listen since I got here. So please go and swap. Just because you're in charge of looking after me doesn't mean you get to learn all the gritty details of my life as soon as a police officer turns up.' He didn't mean to be grumpy, but he was finding with certain people it was a necessity. He could imagine the ward sister discussing him with her husband over dinner even though it was against patient confidentiality.

'Is it possible to have someone else?' the police officer pressed.

It was nice to know at least someone was on Clive's side.

Once the ward sister was replaced with the male nurse who was far more attentive, Clive felt more at ease. Not that anything about this would ever be easy.

'I'm sorry to have been a pain,' Clive said when everyone was settled. 'It's, just, she puts me on edge. I'm sure she's a perfectly lovely person, but ever since she pointed out she had a degree, like it somehow made her superior, I've not been a fan.'

'I just need to hear your version of events, Clive. There's nothing to worry about,' the police officer replied. 'In your own words, can you tell me what you think happened?'

The problem was it wasn't clear in his head. He was able to recall the events, but he wasn't clear of the order. All he knew with certainty was how it ended. He wasn't sure how many days had passed since then. His guess was about a week.

Clive noted the box of tissues that had been strategically placed on the wooden desk. He teased a couple out knowing he'd need them at some point soon.

'Take your time.'

Clive nodded. 'I was pushing my wheelbarrow back from the allotment. I often use it to get my produce back home. It was full of broad beans, my first spring harvest. Whenever I have it with me I take the back route into the house to avoid dragging mud through the living areas. There's a side alley that takes me directly to the lean-to at the back. I was busy unloading for a while before I realised something was wrong.'

'And what made you realise there was something wrong?'

'Nancy normally greets me. Gets the kettle on before I get in. If not straight away, within ten minutes of being there. There was nothing that day.'

'Okayyy.' PC Doyle dragged the word, making it longer than it should be. 'When she didn't greet you, was there anything else that seemed different? Anything else that you noticed?'

'The inner door. The one between the kitchen and the lean-to. It was open. It isn't usually open. Nancy feels the cold something chronic and was forever telling me off if I didn't shut it.'

PC Doyle scribbled some notes. Referenced something else in his notepad before asking his next question. 'Was there anything else that alerted you to there being something wrong before you went through the door?'

Everything was a blur. It was hard to synchronise just one memory of a door that he'd passed through a million times before. Clive tried to think about the room. He'd built the lean-to himself about fifteen years ago, early on in his retirement. It was a more homely version of a shed and was essentially his sorting station for all the activities that occurred at the allotment. He had his own sink there so he didn't muddy the one in the kitchen and it was where he stored his boots and surplus potatoes. Nancy preferred it if he kept the house tidy. It was a room of functionality. It was Clive's domain, with its purpose being to ensure marital harmony. It had been in its usual haphazard form that day: paintbrushes in jars of turpentine on the side, carrots waiting to be distributed, sacks of potatoes near the kitchen, onions hanging near the door. The wooden lolly sticks he was using to write the names of the varieties he was planning to plant were where he'd left them, the new seedling trays waiting to be used. None of these things seemed to be out of place in the image he was recalling.

He didn't want to think beyond that. Why would he when it hurt so much?

'Nothing was amiss in the lean-to, but...' Thinking about it brought a chill to Clive. He'd tried not to think about it, especially since the horror of it all had landed him in hospital.

'This is all going to help.' PC Doyle gave an encouraging smile.

Would it? Clive wasn't sure how, when it was never going to bring back Nancy.

'There was a smudge on the door. A red streak, like someone had brushed paint on it accidentally.'

'When did you notice that?'

'You mean what time?'

'Yes, and at what point after arriving home?'

Clive felt old. He knew at seventy-nine that he was, that was a fact, but he'd always kept active. If his newly diagnosed heart condition wasn't enough to age him, this surely would.

'I don't know what the exact time was.'

'Can you give an approximation?'

'I don't wear a watch down the allotment and I only have a battery-operated clock in my shed there.' Clive didn't understand why he felt the need to explain these things. He wasn't guilty of anything. 'I didn't look at it before I headed home, but it would have been around three. The walk takes about ten minutes when the wheelbarrow is full and it would have been maybe five minutes after that. Why do you ask?'

'We're just trying to get a clear timeline. So we know what kind of time frame events occurred in.'

Events. The word jarred in Clive's head. It wasn't an *event*. Events were occasions to be celebrated: birthdays, Christmas, and sixtieth wedding anniversaries.

'You mean when my wife was killed?'

PC Doyle cleared his throat. 'We want to establish what happened.'

Clive began to choke up. He didn't like the grumpiness that kept surfacing, replacing his normal manners. He just wasn't sure how to remain polite when life had been so cruel. 'I know, I'm sorry. I think it's because this is making me feel like a suspect and I'm not. I'm really not.'

He cried some more at the thought that anyone would ever consider the possibility that he'd harm his darling Nancy.

'We know you aren't. But these questions are to work out what happened. Are you okay to continue or would you like a break?'

Clive cleared his tears away. He wanted to get this over and done with. 'Carry on,' he said.

'So, we've established you arrived home at approximately ten past three and it was about five minutes later that you noticed something was amiss. What happened after that?'

'When I noticed the red paint on the door frame, I went to have a closer look. I couldn't work out what it was or what would have caused it.' Clive's head was pounding. He could see the paint clearly when moments ago it hadn't been there. All the details he'd been trying to block out.

'What did you do next?'

He didn't want to go into the territory of what happened next. He wanted his memory to stay in the safety of his lean-to forever more. 'I called Nancy's name.' Clive's throat was dry with his wish of wanting to reverse time. If only he'd not insisted on sowing a row of radishes. If only he'd left it to the following day and spent the afternoon watching quiz shows with his wife.

'And did you hear anything?'

'Humming. Not from a person, from something electrical. I only noticed it when I started going into the house.'

'Anything else?'

'No, not until I went back to the kitchen.' The tears were overflowing now. He was full-on crying. Not in that dignified way where there was still some attempt at hiding the upset. Ever since that day he'd discovered her he was no longer capable of that kind of crying.

PC Doyle passed over some more tissues, but there wasn't much chance of them stemming the flow.

The nurse spoke up for the first time. 'Clive is due his next set of obs. I'll go and get the machines, if that's okay?'

'Is it half an hour already?' PC Doyle seemed surprised by the passing of time.

'It's a bit more than that.'

'I think it might be a good idea to wrap up for today. I'd like to continue with a few more questions tomorrow, if Clive feels up to it.'

'I think it might be for the best. Give Mr Ellington some time to recover.'

The nurse saw out PC Doyle before returning to Clive. The tissue box was empty now and Clive had taken to wiping his eyes with the sleeve of his jacket.

'Here's some more.' The nurse offered a fresh box. 'How about I get you some tea or coffee?'

'I thought we had to get back to do my obs.'

'Nonsense. The only concern I have for you currently is dehydration. We undoubtedly need to replace your fluids. Now, what's your poison?'

Clive took another tissue, amused by the young nurse's analysis. 'Tea. Milk, no sugar.'

'I'll make it – stat.'

Within moments the mug of tea was nestled in Clive's grasp, the nurse clutching one as well.

'Thought I'd take my tea break with you.'

The gesture didn't escape Clive's notice. It made another tear form.

'It's George, isn't it?' Clive asked. He'd been here over a week and even though he'd been told names it had been fleeting moments before one medical professional had been replaced by another.

'Yes, I'm George. I hope the tea's okay.'

'It's perfect. Thank you. Sorry for all the crying.' Clive wanted to say more but he didn't really know where to start.

'Never apologise for tears. Spill as many as you need to. They're never anything to be ashamed of.'

It was a refreshing thing for Clive to hear when he was so used to only ever doing such things in private. 'Even so, I'm not sure this classes as a coffee break if you're here mopping up my tears.'

'Of course it is. I'm sitting down for starters. And between us, I'm sure you're far more interesting company than what I would have had.'

'I doubt that. Not today, anyway.'

'I'm on duty tomorrow. If you need me again.'

'Can it be you? Can I ask for you to be the one that joins me?'

'Yes, of course. I'll make sure of it.'

'Thank you,' Clive said. And for the first time since arriving at the hospital he felt the sense of a human connection. It was as if the world was showing him that there were trails of hope he could cling on to. There were still good people on this earth. There were other people like his Nancy.

Chapter Nine

Keisha

There are very few things that make me more nervous than what Lucy is currently offering.

'We've got time for once. It's not often you get to enjoy my cooking.'

'I'm happy to have Shredded Wheat. Save you the bother.' I can see that my attempts to get out of this are going to be futile.

'I'll just do you an omelette. That's healthy because the eggs don't absorb the fats like other foods.'

'Okay,' I concede. I wonder how long it'll be before I need to check my pulse. There's yet to have been an occasion involving watching Lucy's culinary skills (or lack of) when my nerves haven't deserted me. I already know as she bashes the frying pan on the side that this will be one of those occasions.

'Great. It's such a shame we don't have breakfast together more often.'

'It's probably for the best,' I say, picturing what this scene of harmony that Lucy is imagining would actually be like.

There are four of us in our houseshare. The communal areas are pretty basic and everything in the kitchen and dining area is white: tiles, walls, appliances, table and chairs. We've lived like this for too many years and it's become too comfortable. It's the kind of existence usually reserved for students and young professionals. We're slightly older professionals now, but I don't see the point of living any other way when this is perfectly functional. My only ongoing concern is Lucy in the kitchen, but at least she tries and she always cleans up after herself.

We live with Rob, Lucy's long-term boyfriend. He's the one she's usually cooking for and the reason I don't join them is more down to not wanting to be the perpetual gooseberry. That and the painful nature of watching what unfolds when Lucy cooks.

Rob and Lucy are one of those couples who are made for each other. They met in the first year of their undergraduate course in biology and have been biologically matched ever since. Perhaps my closeness to such a relationship is what has made me reluctantly take up Tess's hundred-date challenge. From the outside I would say they are made for each other. But I have no idea what it is to be on the inside of such a matching.

They both, much to my annoyance, frequently want to set me up with our other housemate, Hiro. Now the problem with that is, Hiro talks to *no one*. He leaves early, gets back late and cooks in his room with a rice cooker, which is the only feature in his bedroom that I lust after. He has an en suite so it's not even like we pass him in the corridor. I know I can be a bit odd, but that doesn't make me an automatic match to someone who is on par with an invisibility cloak.

On the other hand, Hiro does make the perfect housemate. No mess. No fuss. No noise. There's no need to worry about the usual social graces that a houseshare has to endure. Not when he's absent so much of the time.

Lucy cracks the first egg and, without doubt, there are at least three pieces of shell in there. I say nothing as she tries to clear them away using her (thankfully clean) fingers. I've tried explaining the easiest way to gather the shell is using the remaining shell to scoop it up, but when it comes to culinary advice, Lucy likes to do things her way.

When the dish is finally delivered, it looks like a Jackson Pollock gone wrong. I try to appreciate the gesture, even though with every bite I'm expecting to hit the crunchy bits.

'It's nice this, isn't it? Not having to rush into work like usual.'

'I guess it does make a break from routine.' Not that I'm keen on breaking the routine forever. If it hadn't been for case study five escaping from his monitors this wouldn't be necessary.

I don't need to admit any of my concerns to Lucy. That's the good thing about our friendship. She is the yin to my yang. When I have concerns, she helps me relax. Where she is messy, I am neat. Whereas I like to stick with proceedings, she shows me that sometimes chaos is okay. In theory we are so broadly different, we shouldn't get along. But that's not true in any way. Instead we bring to each other a level of functionality that wouldn't exist if we'd never met. We are a broad bean and a pea in the same pod that have defied nature to end up in the same place.

After breakfast, we arrive inside the front foyer of the hospital and it's then that my panic sets in. 'Can we stop for a minute?'

Lucy knows why. She's kind enough not to point out that it's weird or to brush off the need for this hour's check like so many others have in the past.

Sometimes, like today, Lucy stops and does the same. I watch as she also lifts the sleeve of her coat to locate her pulse point.

'Go,' I state, and let the seconds drum by until, 'Stop,' arrives.

'Eighty-two. That's a bit high, even for me. I blame that hill on Dale Road,' Lucy says.

'Seventy-nine. It's definitely the hill. At least the exercise will have done us some good.'

At times like this I always want to add a thank you. But whenever I have Lucy has always told me that I didn't need to thank her, that this is what friends are for. There is comfort in that. It's like a hug on an autumn day when the clouds are matching your mood.

When we arrive on the ward, we both squirt antiseptic hand gel on our palms, knowing the Mecca of germs we will face just by walking along the corridor. It's better to be on the safe side.

Case study number five is on the CCU ward, still in the same bed space. I decide it's going to be easier thinking of him as a case study while I'm here. It's a way of reminding me this is for my PhD study and he is a subject that will help provide me with data. Gathering information is part of my job. It's what I'm here for. Not helping with jars of pickled onions.

Lucy does the talking as we make our way onto the ward. She's far more confident in new environments than I am.

'Ah, and who did you say set up the appointment?'

'It was booked through the consultant, Dr Hutchins,' Lucy says.

It's a different member of staff from the other day. This male nurse is taller, more strikingly handsome, and familiar somehow. He has a floppy fringe of brown hair and his brown eyes are so dark they're almost black, and for a moment I fall into them. I can feel my breathing is shallower, the sensation catching me off guard. I wonder if he knows about my humiliation of practically running away from the ward.

'Ah,' he says again.

'Is there a problem?' I venture to ask.

'There shouldn't be, but I'm not sure if anyone has explained. We're hoping that you won't mind sitting in on his police interview to get some of the information you need. I think some of the questions you need to ask will be covered and we don't want to make Mr Ellington do this twice.'

'This is what we need to know.' I pass over the crib sheet of information and the questions that I need answered.

Diligently, he reads through the papers I'm showing him. 'Some of this will definitely be covered. I just want to let you know that it isn't as shocking as it sounds.'

'What do you mean?' His comment reminds me of the look in Clive's eyes the other day.

'I'm not sure how much I can say. But I just don't want you to think the police are being lax. It's not quite what it seems. I'll find out how much I can say and let you know afterwards.'

'Right,' I say, not understanding at all.

'Do you want to come and take a seat? PC Doyle is waiting already. I'll just go and get Clive.'

By the time we are all stuffed into the small office, I have far more questions than are in the list on my sheet of paper.

Chapter Ten

Clive

This time, Clive had more monitors on than when the police officer had last questioned him. George had very kindly explained that if at any point the interview was stressing Clive, he'd like to know about it, and he felt that he had more chance of knowing that with the extra equipment rather than leaving it to Clive to tell him.

It was true. Clive was feeling too melancholy to admit to anything. This interview had been playing on his mind and he'd not slept properly as a result. Not that sleep was an easily achieved feat in the hospital environment he was stuck in. He was beginning to long for home, but then, when he thought of home, the pain of what had happened cascaded over him.

When he was finally back in the hot seat, he took in the people surrounding him. All of them strangers who only a fortnight ago had never been in his life. He pined for the fatherhood that had never been forthcoming, not for the first time. Wouldn't it have been nice to have a son or daughter by his side right now? Instead, he only had a nephew, who'd moved to Australia some years ago.

He had friends, of course, mostly from the allotments. They'd taken it in turns to pop into the ward. He liked the way they were keeping the distribution of visits orderly, as if they were rotating their crops. But he didn't think it was appropriate for any of them to be here, to hear this.

'Are you okay for us to start off where we got to last time, Mr Ellington?' PC Doyle asked. He had opened his writing pad at the appropriate place and was ready to start taking notes.

'If we must.' Any determination not to be grumpy today had left Clive at approximately 3 a.m.

'If at any point you want to stop you let me know.'

Clive didn't want to do this again, but it was his last and only way of helping Nancy. Maybe that was why he was still alive... To ensure that whoever had done this would be caught. He nodded, encouraging PC Doyle to continue.

'To recap, you returned home from the allotment at approximately ten past three. It was about five minutes later that you realised the back door that leads from the lean-to through to the house was open and this, along with a red stain on the door, alerted you to the fact something was amiss. Is that right?'

Clive nodded again, his throat suddenly dry.

'You said you heard a buzzing noise. Can you give us a few more details from that point?'

It was hard for Clive to do this when it was this precise point that he didn't want to think about.

'I saw something by the breakfast bar. My brain couldn't fathom what was going on. The thought of it being my Nancy lying on the floor didn't even enter my head.' It was hard to explain. It was all a bit jumbled.

'What did you do next?'

'I tried to follow the buzzing sound to see what was causing that.'

'Did you find the cause?'

'It was the freezer. We have a chest freezer in the hallway. We've always needed a big one because of the amount the allotment produces. It means we need the extra freezing space and my produce always sees us through winter.' Clive realised he was waffling. 'The lid was open. It was buzzing because it hadn't been closed properly.'

'And did you close it? Did you notice anything else unusual?'

At the time, Clive had thought one of them might have forgotten. They'd been having moments like that. Occasionally doing things out of sequence or forgetting part of the process: teabags left at the bottom of a mug, windows open that should have been closed, bills not kept as up to date as usual. They were all tiny mistakes that everyone made now and again, but they seemed to be increasing in their frequency. In that moment, he assumed it was another one of those occasions, but he'd been surprised the noise hadn't alerted Nancy to the fact sooner.

'I shut the freezer lid to stop the sound from carrying on. It was stopping me from thinking.'

'Did you notice anything else unusual? Any other sounds?'

'There were no other noises.'

'What did you do after that?'

'I started looking for her. I popped my nose into the lounge. Then into the dining room, then into the kitchen to check there wasn't a note. That's when I found her.'

This was the part that Clive didn't want to go into. It was already choking him up just thinking about it. He glanced around the room and no one was able to look him in the eye other than Keisha, the girl who'd run away when he wanted to dance. He held her gaze and she didn't break away. It was nice to know at least one person was brave enough to hear his report. That she was here for the story, not the clues it gave.

'What did you notice when you found her?'

'The blood.' Clive put his hand to his mouth, not wanting to say more. His first thoughts had been of an innocent accident. That she'd banged her head and knocked herself out.

'What did you notice about the blood? Can you tell me where it was?'

'Do I have to?' Maybe it was time to stop. They said he was allowed to stop whenever he wanted.

'You don't have to. I'm just hoping to find out anything useful.'

'Useful to find out who did it?'

'If we can.'

'The blood seemed to be everywhere. On her clothes. On her hands. Soaked into the carpet tiles. That's when I noticed the cut and called the police.'

'Did you touch your wife or move anything in the surrounding area?'

Keisha the non-dancing girl put a hand to her mouth, echoing his own response. 'They cut her?'

The whole room turned to her and it was a blessed relief to have the attention momentarily away from him.

He held himself then, as if smoothing the skin on his arms would somehow heal the hurt and bring Nancy back. Was it on her arm that she'd been cut? Or was it somewhere else? The image fuzzed in and out of his head like a picture that needed tuning.

'Can you remain quiet as discussed or you'll have to leave.' PC Doyle was quick to scold.

'Yes,' Clive said before Keisha was told off further. 'Nancy had been cut. I knew it was a crime scene so I walked away and called 999.' Clive was talking to the police officer, but didn't take his eyes off Keisha. Her hand hadn't left her mouth. It was easier to observe this woman's reaction than to cast his mind back to the moment he was describing.

'Nothing was moved then?'

'No. I knew she…' Clive took a deep breath. 'I knew my Nancy was gone. There was nothing I could do for her.'

'If you don't mind me asking, what made you realise there was nothing you could do for her?'

'She was white. It's the closest shade to death I've ever seen. And there was one other thing. She was curled up, kind of in a foetal position. Like someone had been trying to hide her. She wouldn't have fallen in that position, someone must have put her like that.'

'Right.' PC Doyle made more notes.

'Is this helpful? Is this going to help you find whoever did it?' Clive wanted to be sure some good was going to come of this.

'I have one more question, Mr Ellington. Can you think of any reason why Nancy's body wasn't there as you've described? Why we haven't found her?'

As soon as PC Doyle said it, Clive knew it was true, and yet he had no explanation at all.

Fragments. All his memories were fragments.

Chapter Eleven

Keisha

Dr Hutchins calls us aside before we leave the ward.

'We are pretty certain what Clive is telling us isn't a true recollection of what happened. When he was brought into hospital it was because he'd collapsed near his allotment. None of the account about his wife is true because he doesn't actually have one. Of course, the police are investigating, ensuring there is no truth to any of it, but nothing is pointing towards any kind of break-in at his house or any mishap elsewhere. We're putting a lot of it down to delirium as a result of a water infection, which isn't uncommon in a patient his age and we're busy locating some of his old notes that have gone AWOL. Despite all of that, he's still a perfect candidate for the study. We just wanted you to be aware that whatever horror movie played in Clive's head, it's not a factual account of what happened. Hence why any police investigations might not be as urgent as Clive might think they should be.'

Lucy and I nod away our concerns. It's confusing to think what we've heard isn't true, but I'm also filled with relief knowing the story isn't anywhere near as bad as we briefly thought.

'What do we do in terms of taking his information? I need to ask what the cause of him becoming unwell was. If he knows why he thinks his heart broke. Is it okay for me to bring it up?'

'That's why it's a bit complicated. As far as he's concerned, that's the cause of him being here. In his mind, losing his wife was the reason he developed broken heart syndrome. To all intents and purposes it was, even if he only dreamed it up. Even though we know it's imagined and we can clarify that fact, take his account of what happened as gospel. Note it down as if it's the truth. We're checking that there isn't any other cause for this other than temporary delirium. And we don't want to shock him further. We're introducing him to the idea it was just a dream reasonably gradually.'

'So we just ask him the questions and let him fill in the blanks?' Lucy says, usefully summarising while I struggle to keep up.

'None of that was true then? The break-in? The blood?' I ask.

Dr Hutchins creases his brow and shrugs. 'Nope. As far as we can tell. We obviously had to take the story seriously, and involved the police to double-check, but it seems it is just a bad nightmare his brain thinks is true. They're clarifying a couple of facts just to make sure it's not a question of it having happened elsewhere, but we're pretty certain it didn't. Not when we know he was found at the allotment and the house was fine, and as far as we know Nancy doesn't exist. At least, not in this lifetime.'

'Astounding,' I say, not quite able to get my head around it.

'How so?' Dr Hutchins asks.

'That he could be so convinced it's true. To the point his mind has broken his heart. That's a case study in itself.' Clive's heart has become weak, not because of the shock of an event in his life, but because of the shock of an event his mind has *created*. This is a first for the study, and for me.

'The human body never fails to surprise,' the doctor points out before he makes his apologies and returns to his other duties.

Lucy dashes to the toilet. My jaw remains slack while I wait for my friend to finish in the loo. She's taking forever. She turned a funny shade of white over the course of the interview and made murmurs about not feeling like having any lunch. Not feeling up to eating is most unlike Lucy.

George, the staff nurse, comes over. 'Clive would like to speak to you before you go.'

I stare at his floppy fringe for a moment too long as I try to process everything that is happening. 'Is that allowed? I mean, with what Dr Hutchins has told us.'

'As long as you let him do the talking. Don't make suggestions of what may or may not have happened, and they don't want anyone to mention that Nancy doesn't exist beyond what has been said today. We're hoping that he'll come to that realisation himself as he gets better. He doesn't need any more shocks.'

'Why does he want to see me?'

'He wants to see if you're okay.'

'Oh.' I should say no, especially after how our first encounter affected me, but there is something pulling me towards this man. Sympathy, probably. 'I don't have more research questions for him at the moment.'

'He'd like to talk to you anyway. Have a cuppa with him by his bedside. He probably wants some company after the interview ordeal. I would sit with him, but I need to get on after the time away from the ward. Let me go get you both a hot drink.'

George heads off before 'no' has the chance to be an option.

I took my pulse when we left the meeting, but I take it a second time now to make sure it's calmer. I check it at the carotid as some kind of sign of respect to Nancy, like a salute, even though she doesn't exist. For a moment, when listening to Clive's story, she was real. The panic of what happened was palpable and I understand why his heart would have given out if it was his belief that such a scene was true. My heart rate is down by over eight beats per minute. I head to see Clive before my adrenaline deserts me completely.

'Hi, I'm Keisha.' I place a plastic visitor chair by his patient chair.

'I know who you are. I have been paying attention.'

'I'm sorry for interrupting.'

'You don't need to be apologising. I'd much rather hear one from the police. What a thing to suggest… They reckon they haven't found a body.'

I take a deeper breath than is my intention. 'They haven't told me anything,' I say, lamely.

'I don't have a home now.'

'What do you mean?'

'I can't go back. I can never go back. I've no idea what I'll do when they want to kick me out of here.'

Being lost for words is a forte of mine, but never more so than in this moment. I can't point out that he's not to worry, that there's no bloodied carpet tiles to be sorted, no traumatic scene to be cleared up.

'Don't worry. You mustn't worry. We'll sort something when it gets to that point,' I say in a panic.

Clive reaches his hand over, his skin thin and papery, showing off mottled purple veins. He takes a hold of my hand and turns my wrist as he pulls me closer, exposing my tattoo. The ink heart that has never been touched by anyone other than myself and the tattoo artist that created it.

'Will you help me? Will you make sure you help me?'

I'm not a fan of physical contact. I'm not one for hugs or pecks on the cheek in greeting. Even shaking hands can be a bit much. I imagine all the things that the human eye can't see. I imagine the germs that are leaping from one person to the other. Normally the thought makes me shudder and draw away, but not today. It's his plea for help that is stopping my usual reaction, along with his crystal-blue gaze holding mine. It's as if he can see me in a way that I've never been seen before. In a way that I'm not even sure I want to be seen.

'I'll help. I'll do whatever I can to help.' I'm not sure why it's so easy to say. Perhaps because it's the right thing.

Clive extends his other hand towards my wrist and only breaks the spell of his gaze to glance at the heart-shaped tattoo. When he reaches out a crooked finger, I know he's going to trace it. I should be screaming. I should be telling him to get the hell off. Instead I am mesmerised. How is it I've become visible when I always try my best to remain hidden?

His finger meets my pulse point and, once again, I stay put. There's a vibration that runs through him to me and it's not something I can explain. I'm not keen on things I can't explain and yet still I don't move.

He uses his digit to trace along what's caught his attention. Not in a heart-shaped loop like I hope. Instead he allows his finger to dance along the faded silvery scar.

The scar my tattoo hides.

The cut in my skin.

The one I survived.

The story I've never told.

Chapter Twelve

Clive

There were fresh tears on Clive's pillow tonight. He was losing Nancy all over again and he was so muddled. What did they mean they hadn't found her? Why had what seemed so clear this morning now danced away like a distant memory? How was it that something that had been concrete in his mind was being questioned by the police?

As he lay there, unable to sleep, time gave him nothing but doubts.

He traced his life back to the allotment. That was his territory, where he spent many an hour working the ground, planting and harvesting as the seasons went by. He had notebooks and he liked to jot down what he'd sown each year.

In one part of his mind he knew that whenever he took produce home, it was Nancy who sat and podded the peas. And yet it was also his hands he was watching in his memory along with the knowledge, buried there, that he'd always been alone.

It was all too impossible to fathom. The reality of knowing he'd come across the body of his wife. While all the memories of their life together were flittering away as if they never existed. It wasn't right, what the police had said. He was sure of it.

In the middle of the night, as he wept, it was impossible to know what to believe.

The only concrete thing he knew was that he had a house and he had an allotment and the knowledge of them both was another reason for the tears to flow, as he couldn't face returning to either of them. But something was niggling away at him. Somehow he knew the allotment would hold the answers the police couldn't find.

Chapter Thirteen

Keisha

For the next three days, I take my pulse thirty-eight times a day. I'm not sure how to get a hold of this newly emerged anxiety.

It's the promise of helping that's done it. Now I've given my word, I know I have to stay true to it. But how do I go about doing that when Clive can't remember his own history?

My angst is amplified by the fact that Lucy, who usually balances me out, has been off sick ever since she went pale at the hospital the other day.

The lab is quiet without her company and, even though my day is running smoother without her, it somehow feels more chaotic. Everything is more of a rush when I'm carrying out the work of two people. Things like being busy with a research participant and then the phone ringing with no one to answer it are rocketing my anxiety levels.

But Lucy has been off sick before. It's not just that causing me to feel this.

For the first time since Lucy has been on sick leave, I head to Tess's café. At least bringing that normality back to my routine might help.

I take my pulse before leaving. I can't help it. And now every time I do, be it at the carotid or my radial, it makes me think about Clive. About the exchange between us.

When I arrive at the café there's a man sitting at my table. Not being able to sit in my usual spot sends me into a spin.

I can't breathe.

It's stupid, I know, but it's enough to make me wonder if I can still carry out the basic functions of putting one foot in front of the other, of drawing breath in and releasing it out.

Tess comes over. 'I'm sorry, it's date number forty. I tried to cancel, but he can't have got the message. He turned up before I had chance to warn you.'

Even though she's talking softly, it's enough to hook the attention of the man sitting there, waiting.

'You're the only date I want today,' I say a little too loudly.

The man gets up from the table and as I see him move towards us in the periphery of my vision I want the ground to swallow me up. I'm not prepared for this.

'I'm sorry. I know the date was cancelled, but I knew it was you. I wanted to check you were okay.'

What he is saying doesn't make sense until I take in who is standing there. It's George. Clive's nurse.

I mumble at him. 'Err. Ei. Um.' The familiarity I sensed when I first met him on the ward comes into focus. He is one of the matches Tess had shown me, with his selfie on the sofa. It's hard to know what to say when my next obvious move is to cry, the events of the last few days becoming a bit too overwhelming.

'I don't mean for this to be a date. Even if that was what was arranged originally. When I realised it was you, I thought it might be unprofessional to still come, but I wanted to talk to you. I know Clive's case is a strange one and he's been telling me you're going to help him. If you're ever worried, I wanted you to know you have someone to call on. Look, here's my number if you ever want to chat about it. We can meet up. Not as a date or anything that scary… Just as friends.'

I take the piece of card, noting that George is taller and broader than I remember. He looks different out of his uniform, casual in a striped polo shirt and jeans. My stomach flutters and I wonder what it's responding to. I remind it that we'll eat soon and allow my brain to catch up to the fact that George is here to talk about case study number five.

'It's just hard to comprehend that Clive believes that happened when none of it is true. Does he have any family?' I'm hoping there is someone.

'None in this country. He has a nephew in Australia, but their contact is rare from what I understand. He's confirmed that Clive is a bachelor and lives alone. His father, Clive's brother, died several years ago.'

I nod, wondering how I'll ever be able to deliver on the promise of help.

'The good news is he seems less muddled. I think he's beginning to realise he was hallucinating. Come and see him soon.'

'I will. For the study,' I add hastily.

George grabs his denim jacket from the back of my usual chair and, when he leaves, I watch as he wanders along the road. He's wearing double denim, a look normally reserved for catalogues, and yet with the woollen lining to his jacket he is pulling it off. For a few seconds I forget myself and unapologetically stare after him wondering if that just happened.

'Sit yourself down,' Tess instructs.

It's what I need to bring myself back to reality.

'Usual?'

'Yes, please,' I say, with positive delight. It's good to have at least one part of the week as it should be.

Once Tess sorts out our food, she comes and joins me. 'What's going on? How come you know that guy?'

I should answer straight away, but I need the comfort of food first. I devour three mouthfuls of Tess's slow-cooker curry before feeling the benefit enough to be able to seek any counsel. 'He's a nurse up at the hospital. He's looking after case study five.'

'Oh, so you *know* him. That's positive. And he gave you his number.' Tess winks. Tess never winks.

'It's not like that. It's about the complicated patient who dances. I've inadvertently offered to help even though I don't know how I can. There won't be any other dates with George when I've come in here on the verge of a panic attack.'

'Why does he think you'd want to talk? What's happened?'

I shovel several more forkfuls of the chicken curry into my mouth, glad that Tess knows me well enough so that I don't have to worry about appearing rude. My ability to communicate well is always severely affected when I'm hungry.

'I'm not sure how much I can say.' Do the rules about confidentiality still apply if the event isn't real? It's not as if the gruesome murder is about to end up in the local newspaper.

'Tell me what you can. I understand if it's the edited version.' Tess takes a sip of drink, giving me her full attention. She's got her well-practised listening face on.

I chew over what I can say. 'As you know, most of the participants for this study have gone through some kind of traumatic event. The shock is what causes the heart to balloon and that's when they become unwell. It's very unusual, but in Clive's case, the trauma is imagined. There's no evidence of the event he's reported. At the moment the hallucination is being put down to delirium as the result of a water infection, which isn't uncommon for his age group. Obviously, what he dreamed up was so realistic it resulted in his heart trauma as well.' I trace my finger over my wrist and brush against my scar, acknowledging its presence. I'm more aware of it since Clive's discovery.

'More of a nightmare if that was the result. Poor chap. Have you been losing sleep? You look tired.'

'I've not been sleeping well. Even though his story isn't true, it kind of got to me. Knowing that in his mind it did happen, I feel sorry for him.' In truth, it has also awoken a part of my past that I don't like to think about. I keep finding myself in fitful dreams that I'd rather not be part of.

'Is that why you haven't been able to pop by like usual? Your messages didn't give much away.'

For the past few days I've been working over lunches and grabbing a quick sandwich to cover Lucy's workload. Today is the first day I've been able to take a proper lunch break.

'Lucy hasn't been well. She was with me when I went to the hospital. At first I thought hearing Clive's story had caused her tummy upset. That or her special method of cooking eggs has given her food poisoning.'

'That's rotten luck. Hopefully nothing you'll catch.'

It's the first time that Lucy has been off work because of an illness rather than an accident. All her previous absences have been as the result of her clumsiness: the time she scalded her palm so badly it needed a nurse to dress it for a fortnight or the time she broke her ankle ice-skating.

'She's been feeling sick. Full-on nausea. Food poisoning would have passed by now. I'm going to get her to go to the GP if she's not feeling better after the weekend. I can't help but think it's because of hearing that story though. It made her sick to the stomach and it's taking her a while to recover.'

'What about you? How's it left you feeling? It's obviously affected you as well.'

'It's hard to explain.' I don't know how to express how hollow the experience has left me feeling – and it's not to do with the story, but the man telling it. Being seen has made me feel exposed, made me remember things that were long forgotten. 'I guess I'm worried for him. He needs help and I'm not sure he has anyone who'll be able to. He doesn't want to go home, but he has nowhere else to go.'

'Can't you talk to that nurse guy? He's given you his number. Maybe you can come up with a plan between you.'

'But I only know about him because of the study. What happens with his hospital discharge is none of my business. I'm only supposed to book in his follow-up appointments.'

'It's your business if you make it your business,' Tess points out.

I shrug. I don't like getting involved in people's affairs. But I feel like I'm being drawn to help Clive. If he has no one else, I can't just walk away.

'Maybe. I'll do what I can, but only if it doesn't affect the project.'

'When will you see case study – scrap that – *Clive* again?'

'He'll have weekly appointments for the first month.' I reel off the information as if I am reading from a textbook, suddenly on steady ground again.

'That's when you'll see him for work. But I'm sure you'll be able to go see him as a visitor. You are allowed to visit in your own time. George seemed to be hinting at the fact that you should.'

'But what about the study? Won't it compromise it?'

'How? If it's just to check he's okay, surely that won't affect any results?'

I can feel my heart pounding, pulsating through my ear drum. I don't need to take a reading to know it's pumping harder than usual.

'It could. It might.' I'm looking for an excuse I can't find.

'Will you forgive yourself if you don't help? If you don't resolve whatever is unsettling you?'

I give in and take my pulse. Tess notices what I'm doing, but says nothing. She knows it's bad when I'm like this, unable to stop myself from taking an ad-hoc reading.

'I don't know. The problem is I don't know why it's left me feeling like this.' I've not experienced this uneasy sensation since my teen years. It's as if, until now, I've navigated life perfectly and now here I am in the midst of an unexpected storm. Nobody has ever taught me how to deal with this turbulence.

'I expect what you're feeling is some kind of empathy. You've heard what he's been through and you're feeling sorry for him. You want to help.'

Tess is good at putting a finger on what I struggle to process. I am lucky to have such understanding friends.

'Empathy is the wrong word.' I hate how sometimes the pedant in me comes along to correct things that don't need correcting. 'Empathy means you can understand what someone is going through. The word you're looking for is sympathy, as in, you feel sorry for what they've been through.'

'Whichever it is, you need to decide what you're going to do about it.'

I pull down my sleeve, knowing that sympathy is all I want to offer. Nobody needs to know about any of the things I am able to empathise with.

'I'll visit him,' I say, hoping that will be help enough.

Chapter Fourteen

Clive

Clive was growing accustomed to being cantankerous. He liked the word. Why would he want to be anything else? Not when he'd spent the last few days struggling to understand what was going on. At a time when he thought he should be busy arranging his wife's funeral, he'd been left with a trail of vacant memories. The gladiolus flowers he thought he'd been growing for his wife, he now recalled dishing out to all the neighbours. The meals for two were replaced by memories of him cooking in bulk and freezing his meals for one. He was beginning to realise there must be some truth in what they were saying. That she didn't exist.

And yet there were those fragments that kept coming back to him:

The red stain on the door.

The open, buzzing freezer.

The knowledge that something was wrong.

Travelling in an ambulance.

The interview with the police.

It was all so muddling. How could some parts be true and others not?

When Keisha arrived it was a complete and utter relief to realise he'd not dreamed her up too. He'd begun to wonder.

'How are you doing?' Keisha asked.

George was on duty and delivered a chair for her, an expression on his face that Clive recognised: smitten.

Clive smiled for the first time in days. 'Rubbish! I mean, physically I'm fine, but this place is driving me batty.' He'd like to go home, if only the images he kept seeing weren't making him feel sick to the stomach. 'I just don't think I can face going home.'

'Have they said you need to yet? Is that the plan?'

'They're on about doing a home visit, but I'm refusing. I don't want to face all of that.'

'It's…' Keisha appeared to be choosing her words carefully. 'Difficult.'

'You're telling me. Can I tell you something that's going to sound stupid?'

'Go on.'

'And you won't tell any of this lot?' Clive let his gaze dart about the place, checking none of the staff were nearby.

Keisha gave a non-committal shrug.

Clive considered for a second. He didn't want to prolong his stay here by letting the staff know he was short of more marbles than he was willing to admit. Although if they did find out, it would prevent him going home like they were threatening. It might be worth the risk.

'I've been asking them lots of questions and they've finally told me their version of things. So if I am a bachelor, like they say, and all of these thoughts of a wife are down to delirium, it doesn't explain some of the other memories that have cropped up. I convinced myself there was a picture of her in my wallet. I even checked to make sure.'

'I take it there wasn't?'

'No, but the memory is there. Like it was real. And remembering her chicken and asparagus pie. I can recall how it tasted. Lots of little memories. I couldn't have come up with all these different fragments in half an hour, could I? I can't have been delirious for long. All these snippets couldn't have turned up that quickly.'

'I don't know…'

'I'm sorry. I don't mean to keep going on. I'm just feeling a bit lost.' The last word sparked something in Clive's memories and he felt compelled to hold Keisha's hand. To bring her closer. To be less lost. To make sure no one else would hear. 'You must help me. You must help me get out of here. We need to find somewhere else for me to live. You must. We must. Promise me we will.'

Without thinking about it, Clive brushed a finger over her scar. The one that she'd tried to hide with permanent ink.

Keisha flinched, only slightly. It was barely perceivable, but it was there. Of course it was.

'I'm not sure what I can do to help.'

He'd not glanced at his own scar for years. But it was important that he told her – that was the good thing about scars – eventually they would fade. Not just from the skin, but from the memory.

He shrugged off his jacket and rolled up the sleeve of his pyjamas to inspect it. To see if it was even recognisable for what it was. It was in the crook of his elbow. A wide, silvery shadow from the past. Over the years, it had faded. In his younger days it had been red and angry; now it was only noticeable in the right lighting. It gleamed like a snail trail on a dewy morning, an echo of something that had passed.

'You see,' he said, brushing his finger over the faint mark. 'We're the same, you and I. We have to help each other. Nobody knows about this. This is my secret. And now it is ours.'

Chapter Fifteen

Keisha

There are a lot of scenarios a first aid course can't prepare you for. It pains me that I'm the nominated first-aider at work, but it's been proven in the past that it should fall to me as the only sensible option. The only problem with the training is they don't teach you how to deal with the way people react. Nor do they school you on how to keep a tab on your own reactions.

In my years at the lab, so far I've only had to attend six first aid incidents at work and, happily, none of those have been emergencies. Considering we mostly focus on the field of cardiology, and most of our subjects have had some kind of cardiac history, this is something of a miracle.

The incidents included a dot of an old lady tripping on a step and banging her knee. She'd not wanted any fuss, but as her graze was bleeding I'd had to insist she at least have a plaster and a hand getting up. Then there'd been the time someone had walked straight into the glass panel without realising it was a wall. It was part of the snazzy rebuild and the design, although chic, was not user-friendly. The gentleman hadn't responded well to the incident, but it was fortunate that the main thing that had been hurt was his pride. I only had to administer an ice pack for that one and it was no surprise to find soon afterwards the graphics that should have been on display had been fixed onto the glass wall. There haven't been any headbutting-glass incidents since.

The other four first aid incidents have all concerned Lucy. To date I've dealt with her burning her hand, cutting her finger, accidentally stabbing her leg with a fork, and a low-grade electric shock.

I'm not sure today's occurrence can be classified as a first aid incident. If you've been ill for several days, but insist on coming to work, does it mean I have to fill out a first aid form?

'Pass me some tissues. Oh God, this is so awful.'

Lucy has been unwell for a week now. Today, she thought that being at home wasn't making her feel any better so she is giving work a try. I really wish she hadn't. Work is turning the nausea into a full-on vomiting session. This is all I need after the week I'm having.

'Why did you come in?'

'You knnnooowwww whhhyyy.' Lucy cries dramatically into the toilet bowl.

'I told you to go to the doctor's.' I sense that perhaps my bedside manner isn't as sympathetic as it should be, but she should definitely be at the GP and not here.

'And say what? That I feel a bit sick?' Lucy cries some more.

'I think you've gone up a level now.' I'm tactful enough not to point out all the illnesses that have 'nausea' and 'sickness' on their list of symptoms as I have done several times during the week in my efforts to get Lucy to see a doctor. If she didn't listen then, it doesn't seem like a good time now to say that she should have.

'You think?'

'Let's sort out getting you home.'

'Howww cann I gettt hommme?' The wail echoes out of the toilet bowl like a banshee is in residence. At least she's gone with the theme of my week. Everyone's worries are about getting home, or not, in Clive's case.

'A taxi?'

'No taxi is going to take a puking woman!'

Ah. I've not really thought this through. And this is one of the eventualities the first aid course hasn't covered… How to transport puking banshees.

'Do you have any ideas?' We always walk to work. Neither of us drive as we both like to be environmentally conscious where possible. The same is true of Lucy's boyfriend, Rob.

Lucy answers by hurling into the toilet once more. The sound is enough to make my stomach turn.

In the end I call Rob. It's not a complete relief when Lucy's boyfriend and his dad come to pick her up. There's the clean-up job that seems to fall to me for starters. There are more study participants due in later this afternoon for the drug trials that are taking place, so there isn't the time to wait for a cleaner to sort it out.

It is the last thing I feel like doing, but at least it temporarily stops me from thinking about Clive and the secrets we now hold. That's how it feels now he's shown me his scar and said as much. There wasn't a chance to discuss the stories that lay behind our marks before he was hauled off by an occupational therapist for a mock home visit in their department. The look of dread on his face is still with me.

As soon as I'm done clearing up, I'll be glad to go to Tess's for lunch and take the time to call George to find out how Clive's occupational therapy visit went.

I go to the cleaning cupboard that is hidden away in the sleep lab. It's a strange room within a room that is rarely in use, apart from by the cleaners to get their equipment. It's otherwise used when studies require monitoring for twenty-four hours. None of the current research requires that level of data. It is basically an unused bedroom.

A thought strikes and I shake my head in dismissal. It's a ridiculous notion and I concentrate on bleaching the bathroom within an inch of its life to help shift the idea.

When I reach the café it is too busy for Tess to sit with me and chat like usual, so instead I use the time to inform the relevant people that Lucy is off work again and to text her boyfriend to ensure she goes to see a medical professional. I emphasise that it isn't normal to be feeling nauseous over a long period and for it to be getting worse rather than better. I really hope they pay some heed. It will feel far too much like parenting if I have to state it any more.

'Everything okay?' Tess asks over the counter as she plays the role of barista at the coffee machine.

'Lucy's gone home sick.' I'm not going to go into detail with so many customers within earshot.

'Again? That's not great for you. Have you called George?' Tess winks as she says it, a gesture that doesn't come naturally to her and makes it look as if she is having an awkward facial spasm. 'We need to make date forty become forty-one as well!'

I shake my head at Tess's eternal optimism. 'I am going to call him, but not for any of the reasons you're hopeful over.'

Once Tess is back to serving customers, I decide it's time to be brave. My first dilemma is whether to call the ward or his mobile. I decide on the latter. Somehow, as he came here to the café for our not-a-date, it feels as if there has been a slight shift from professional to personal, and ringing his mobile is in keeping with that change. I am making a statement to myself as much as George that, yes, I do want to make sure that Clive is going to be okay, that I'm no longer doing this just for the purpose of my study, that I want to make sure he won't be forced to return home when he isn't happy to.

The mobile rings for long enough for me to realise it is probably locked away somewhere on silent as he carries on with his shift.

'Hello, George. It's Keisha here,' I say, when it goes to voicemail. 'I wanted to get an update from you and see if there's anything I can do to help Clive. Give me a ring back. Thanks.'

It's about two minutes after making the call that I realise he doesn't have my number, and even though I know it'll probably show up on his phone log, I message it to him all the same. It's a good job we aren't dating. If we were, this unlocks a new level of uncool.

I wave my goodbye to a busy Tess and manage to pay in between customers without a Spanish inquisition. I'm sad we haven't been able to talk today.

On the walk back to work, and in any unoccupied moment once there, I list some of the reasons Lucy may be unwell. The list encompasses everything from pregnancy to a rare tropical blood disorder. It almost ramps me up to the point of wanting to take my pulse for every new diagnosis I come up with.

Rather than do that, I start to physically write down the potential diagnoses. It's for my benefit. I realise I'm annoyed at Lucy for not taking my advice. If she hasn't seen anyone, or at least got an appointment by the time I return home, I plan to pass her the list to point out why exactly it is so important.

It's when I'm writing down 'urinary tract infection' that my phone rings. It's a relief that I'm not in the middle of carrying out a six-minute walking test, one of the standard markers we use for our studies. I always have to ignore it when that happens and Lucy isn't here.

'Hello,' I say tentatively.

'Is that Keisha?' the voice at the end of the phone asks. I recognise George's voice straight away. I think of his floppy fringe.

'Yes, I hope I didn't disturb you at work. How's Clive?'

'Still refusing to return home.'

'I'm not surprised.' I say it out loud without really meaning to.

'It's an unusual situation. Even the police have said so.'

'What will they do? Surely they can't send him home if he doesn't feel able to return?'

'They're having a multidisciplinary support meeting tomorrow. I'm not really sure what his other options are at the moment. He doesn't have any relatives he can stay with. He's refusing to go into any kind of temporary residential care. The only thing he's willing to consider is selling up and moving elsewhere, but the hospital can't bed-block in the meantime. He'll have to find some place temporarily. It's a shame there aren't any relatives able to house him short-term. Sadly it's not the norm to adopt a patient. If I could have him at mine I probably would, but my parents aren't about to agree to that,' George states.

'I've had similar thoughts. I feel so sorry for him. I wish there was something more I could do, but it doesn't seem possible. I live in a houseshare, and even if I moved to the sofa, it wouldn't be practical.' Hearing myself say it out loud makes me realise how affected I am by Clive. His story. Our shared scars. It is irrational and yet I've made a vow to help. There's an odd sensation rushing over me. The sense of belonging to a secret club that I didn't plan to be a part of.

'When will you next visit him?' George asks.

'I can come tomorrow, after work.' I would go later today, but it's been a long day already and I want to make sure Lucy is okay.

'I'll be on the ward then. I'll fill you in on any developments from the meeting.'

I smile knowing he'll be there, the conversation making me think that perhaps I'm creating more than one connection.

After hanging up, I place the cleaning equipment back in the cupboard ready for the early-morning cleaner, and the same thought I've been trying to shake off strikes me again. This empty room isn't in use. Is there any chance it can be of help, if only for a while?

Chapter Sixteen

Clive

Anyone would think that Clive's ability to make a cup of tea was miraculous. He'd offered to bake the occupational therapist a cake in addition, but the jest hadn't been well received by the young health care professional reviewing him.

Since then he'd been assessed several times over in multiple formats. Short of allowing the doctors to probe orifices he wasn't prepared to have probed, he was passing with flying colours. They'd finally got the balance of medications right and he was no longer on the heart monitors they'd been keeping him on. They were also making certain the hallucination he'd had was just that and ensuring it wasn't something that was going to become a regular thing. He'd not mentioned the additional moments he was recalling. He was holding them close to his chest.

Now they thought his confusion had subsided, and he was once again fully mobile, they kept bandying about a word that was far scarier than anything else he'd faced: home.

He didn't want to go back there. To his surprise, for once, the police were on his side. They'd decided, despite there being no overall evidence of Clive's recollections, they were going to do a full forensic screening of his house. There were details they weren't telling Clive. He could tell. But while his home was a crime scene it gave him a temporary reprieve. It also gave him some hope that he was right. Something had to be amiss if they were prepared to search the place. He was sure of it.

Even when he was given the green light in the future, Clive still planned to refuse to return. He wanted a new home. He owned the property, which made it more complicated than if he'd been a council tenant. It was going to be a slower process. He was lucky. He'd inherited his house after his parents had passed away within five years of each other when he was still in his twenties. A lifetime ago: a period of his life he remembered very little of and which he always referred to as the grieving years if anyone asked.

What it meant was that Clive actually had enough money in the bank to purchase or rent a flat without relying on the sale of his house. Not that there was so much he'd be able to fritter it away by staying in a hotel beforehand. He'd have to find another solution.

The social team looking after him were looking into potential options. As Clive wasn't one for modern technology, he'd taken to getting the daily newspaper from the trolley that came round and perusing the adverts as if they might somehow contain the answer. They may well do, even if renting wasn't the perfect solution. Most of the options seemed preferable to being stuck in a care home.

There had been a few houses where there was a room available, but most of those were student lets. He had no idea what the response would be from the landlord when a seventy-nine-year-old called to make enquiries. He was sure if he explained his circumstances they'd be fairly understanding, but the thought of shared bathrooms and messy kitchens had so far prevented him from making any calls. He'd want an en suite at the very least. That was the thing with becoming cantankerous. He had standards and he was going to stick to them. He doubted a household of students would be concerned with keeping the bathroom floor from being wet or cleaning the shower after use.

He was about to circle another futile possibility with red pen when Keisha arrived. He'd been positive he'd taken things a step too far last time she'd visited and would never see her again. For all his scatty moments, he remembered when he'd shown her his scar.

'Are you okay? You look pale,' Clive said.

'You're the second patient to say that today. My friend Lucy has been admitted to the hospital. She's been sick for over a week and they want to find out why. I'm okay, just very tired. There's been a lot going on this week. How are you?'

'Oh goodness. I hope they sort her out soon. That must be a worry for you.'

Keisha nodded, the mentioned tiredness creeping through.

'As for me, I'm much better. And I want out of this blasted place. They've said I'm well enough to be discharged, if only there was somewhere to be discharged to. If I don't have a wife to go home to, then I want a new home.'

'You do seem a lot sprightlier than when I last saw you.'

'I can prove it by dancing if you like?'

'I'm good, thanks.'

'I'm sorry. About last time. It's not something I usually share.' Clive rubbed the crook of his arm. He was embarrassed that he'd

so openly exposed his old wound, the one from the grieving years.
It wasn't something he was in the habit of doing.

'I guess we're both guilty of that.'

Clive sensed there was something more she wanted to say, but
they were both holding on to their truths.

'Can you believe they're talking about putting me into an old
folks' home? All because they've decided to treat my house as a
crime scene.'

'They have?'

'Something to do with local burglaries and wanting to check
my house hadn't been broken into after all. They put the back door
being open down to my delirium. Now they're wondering if there's
more to it. I know they're saying it didn't happen, but to me it really
did. It's very hard when what you thought was true doesn't match
up with reality. And between us, all this talk of burglaries doesn't
sit right with me. I know something is up. You mark my word.'

'I don't think…' Keisha trailed off, her sentence hanging. 'I'm
not sure what to think.'

'Nobody is, other than not believing me. But I'm *not* crackers and
I certainly don't want to be shoved into a care home as a solution.
I know I've been poorly, but I'm not due at that juncture yet. They
wouldn't even be putting me there because I need care, just because
they don't have any other answers. This is where having children
would have been handy. I've never been in need of someone loaning
me a sofa bed more.'

'Are there any other options?'

'I've started looking at some myself.' Lifting the paper, Clive
waved towards the circles he'd penned around the ads. 'But it's

thin pickings. I'm not sure any student houses want an old man staying with them.'

'Not all of them are the same. I'm still in one even though I'm way past the point of being a student. I'd offer you Lucy's bedroom, but she shares with her boyfriend, so I think he'd have something to say if you started sleeping in their double bed.'

Clive laughed at the thought. 'It's kind of you, but I'll find something. I'm just not sure what. Anyway, you've not come here to worry about my predicaments. You must be here for your study. What do you need to record first? Blood pressure?' He lifted an arm like he did so regularly for the nursing staff.

'Nope. Not today. My manager gave me a day off after everything that's happened with Lucy. I'll get you booked in as soon as I'm back. Hopefully you'll be able to come to the cardiac lab at the university next time.'

'That must be hard work without Lucy there. How's she doing?'

Keisha's expression went through a rotation of tiny grimaces, the question catching her off guard. She was pushing away tears. Clive could tell. It reminded him of Nancy when she was doing her utmost not to cry. He shook his head, recalling also the many evenings he'd sat watching television alone; that memory wasn't possible. And yet it was there. The wife that was his and yet wasn't.

'She's going to be off work for a while.'

Clive took a moment to recover. 'I do hope she's better soon. A youngster like her isn't due any kind of illness to land her in hospital. Here, have some fruit.' He offered the basket his allotment friends had sent.

Keisha opted for a satsuma and Clive nodded approval at her choice. It would occupy her hands for longer than any of the other fruits and therefore it would occupy her mind.

'They're not all grown at the allotments of course. They've obviously been to the local greengrocer as well. They're a good sort my allotment crew.' That was one place he did want to get back to. He wasn't able to escape the feeling it was important somehow.

Keisha peeled it slowly, pulling off the white fibres that hadn't come off with the rind.

'It's nice that they've done this for you, and thank you for sharing. I feel like I need the vitamin C. I haven't been carrying out the same amount of self-care as I normally do.'

'Fruit and veg are very important. It's why I have my allotment. I've always liked the idea of home-grown. Good for the environment and I know mine is organic when it's all cared for by me. It's why your study fascinates me. I like the idea that this beetroot-juice regime is somehow good for me.' He'd had another dose first thing this morning.

'Hopefully we manage to prove that, although it'll take a while.' Keisha chewed and stared into the middle distance as she popped in segment after juicy citrus-filled segment. She seemed far away and Clive decided to join in the contemplative silence by eating one as well. There was a great deal of delight to be found in knowing Keisha had returned and was here as a visitor. The moments that passed could have been awkward, but it was one of those contented kind of silences.

'What if there was another option?' Keisha said.

'For fruit and veg?'

'For somewhere for you to live… If it was temporary.'

'Do you know somewhere?'

'I might do. Only strictly speaking I'm not sure it would be allowed.'

'Does it involve sharing a bathroom?'

'No, you'd have your own.'

'Does it involve sharing a kitchen?'

'Only with me.'

Maybe Clive's delirium hadn't lifted because he was feeling mightily confused once again. 'What's the catch?'

'No one would be allowed to know. We'd have to say you were living with me at my house for the time being.'

'I still don't get it.'

'You can walk now, can't you?'

'Certainly. I've been spending half my days walking along these boring old corridors.'

'We don't need anyone overhearing. Come for a walk with me and I'll explain.'

Without even hearing what the plan was, Clive knew he would say yes.

There was something about Keisha that made him feel she was the one that was here to save him. It was a strange stance to take when he'd spent the last couple of weeks surrounded by medics. His life was in their hands, surely? But he'd much rather trust Keisha. There were certain things that required heart and he trusted hers implicitly.

Chapter Seventeen

Keisha

The idea is simple. It pops into my head so satisfactorily that I can't ignore it. Before I'm able to talk myself out of it (which I will try to several times over later this evening) I'm telling Clive.

And it isn't only Clive, it's George as well. With a health care professional approving my suggestion, it somehow makes it acceptable.

The plan is simply this: Clive will be discharged to live with me. Only he won't be living *with* me. He'll be living at the laboratory.

When the thought pops into my head I see it as a solution to two problems at once. It solves Clive's need for accommodation and it'll give me company if Lucy is going to be off. None of my anxieties attach themselves to the idea straight away. That will come later.

'What's at the laboratory? Where will I sleep?' Clive asks after I've shared my genius idea.

'Well, that's the great part. There's a bedroom there. My department houses a sleep laboratory. It's for when we need to monitor cardiac patients overnight, but none of the current studies call for it so at the moment it's unused.'

We're at the coffee shop at the front of the hospital. It might not be a top-secret location, but the hubbub around us means that no one will overhear our conversation. George is here, joining us on his break.

'Won't the other university staff notice?' George asks. He sips his black coffee.

'It's an internal room within the lab I work in. Only Lucy and I go in there. Our line manager is based here at the hospital. He does our six-monthly reviews and lets us get on with it most of the time. Even the cleaners arrive later in the day if there's a sleep study in the diary.'

I'm not sure why exactly, but I'm glad to think I might be able to help Clive. The enthusiasm in my voice is surprising.

'So they wouldn't know I was there? Wouldn't there be security going through the campus or something?'

'There would be normally. But whenever there is a sleep study going on we let them know so they're aware someone is in the building.'

'Won't that alert your boss, though?' George is fiddling with a sugar sachet, his coffee clearly not sweet enough as he adds a second.

'I'll just block out the online diary with sleep studies so security won't bother us. They don't communicate that kind of thing with my boss. They'd have no reason to question it.'

'What about in the daytime? You'll have people coming in and out, won't you? Will I have to hide in a room all day?' Clive asks.

'This was where I was hoping the plan would work to my advantage as well. With Lucy off sick there's lots of additional tasks that need doing. I was wondering if you'd be happy to do a few things to help out.'

'Like what?' Clive asks, not unkindly, but as if curiosity has well and truly caught him.

'Answering the telephone. Getting hot drinks and biscuits for the study participants. Making sure the equipment is wiped down. Nothing onerous, but all things that take time and I'd struggle to keep up with as well as collecting all the data. Lucy and I usually run a pretty tight ship. If you don't feel like you can, I'll be looking to get an undergraduate to volunteer to help.' It is a lot to ask, I realise as I say it, especially as he is well into retirement now, but I also discover I'd much rather it was Clive than anyone else. I feel a duty towards him and this will help us both. 'Obviously you don't have to, but I figured in the daytime we could just say you're a volunteer and that won't be questioned if you're carrying out the odd task or two.'

'Sounds delightful to me.' Clive picks up one of the marshmallows that came with his hot chocolate and grins.

'How long would you be able to have him there for? What will you do when Lucy returns?' George asks, adding a third stick of sugar to his coffee. His concerns are endearing. His sweet tooth, not so much.

I realise I've not thought very far ahead. Clive has a problem and this might be a solution and that is as far as I've run with it.

'I guess we could get away with it for two to three weeks. As for Lucy, I'm only going to tell her if absolutely necessary. They still need to diagnose her and start to get her better before they even think about discharging her. From what she told me today it'll be about a month before she's back at work.'

'A month, poor thing,' George says into his coffee. 'So that gives us about three weeks to sort out something more permanent for Clive. Is that doable?'

'If the back-up plan involves a retirement home, we're no longer friends I'm afraid, George.' Clive smiles as he says it.

'George has got a point. We need to sort out something long-term… If it isn't your home, what's the plan?' Since this idea came along, I've not thought about my pulse once. Until now, that is. I force myself to ignore the desire.

'I have enough savings to rent or buy a little retirement flat somewhere near the allotments. There are those new places that they've just finished along the way. Perhaps I can see about getting one of those reserved?'

'We'll have to get the ball rolling as soon as possible. It's not ideal, but it's workable. But I never heard any of this. Not at all.'

George winks in my direction and it sends a shock through me that is both alarming and thrilling. It causes my stomach to flip like it has before and I'm not able to blame it on food so easily this time.

'Do you think it'll be okay?' Now the doubts are creeping in. It's a simple idea until I start to think about all the variables.

Clive and George both smile and nod in response.

It's only when I'm on my way home that I start to list all the things that may potentially go wrong.

My boss could find out and I'll lose my job.

There might be a fire alarm and Clive will be discovered.

Or it might be a real fire and he won't be found at all.

He might not turn out to be the kind gentleman I think he is and instead he'll start streaking naked around the campus.

He might be like Lucy and I'll have to frequently get the first aid bag out.

There are so many things that may go wrong that by the time I'm home I do the only thing I'm able to… I curl up under my duvet and place my fingers on my pulse point, falling asleep to the gentle rhythm of my heart.

Part Two

The Right Ventricle

The right lower chamber of the heart that pumps deoxygenated
blood to the lungs.
In other words, it's where we start to revive…

Chapter Eighteen

Clive

Getting to the university facility had been quite the experience. Clive had been officially discharged to Keisha's address, which had involved being deposited there by the ambulance service. They'd kindly made sure he got in okay and carried his bags in for him.

It made Clive feel a bit bad that it was all a ruse. Keisha wouldn't be sleeping on her couch like they'd claimed. He wouldn't be using her bedroom as they'd said.

Instead they had a cup of tea and a satsuma each and waited for George to finish his shift to then take them on the second part of the journey.

Now, for the second time that day, Clive had been deposited. This time George and Keisha had fussed over him and made sure his belongings were safely inside and he had everything he needed. Keisha had supplied him with sandwiches and everything else he would need for a makeshift picnic that evening in his temporary residence.

It was late in the day by the time they'd left. He sent them off saying they'd done plenty for him already. Keisha had given him instructions on all the appliances in the small kitchen. He hadn't wanted to be rude to the youngster about knowing how to boil a kettle given how often he'd done it in his lifetime. They were doing their best to make sure he was okay.

And he was okay. Mostly.

Now he was alone, there was a new eeriness to the place. He had a certain sense of being somewhere that he shouldn't be.

Keisha had said he was fine to have the light on in the small kitchen alcove and the bedroom itself, but once it was dark they were keeping the main room's lights off so as not to attract the attention of anyone unnecessarily. Of course with the cover of Clive being here for a sleep study, it should be fine, but that excuse would only work for him once. The security guards might start to ask questions if they found the same subject wandering around night after night. Instead he had a small torch that he was to use if he wanted to head to the kitchen once it had gone dark.

Right now he was standing in the lab between the bedroom and the kitchen. He kept the torch off, as if he was a burglar on the prowl not wanting to be caught, and for a while he simply appreciated the absence of sound. After his spell at the hospital, where night was as noisy as day, he'd forgotten what it was to experience true quiet.

In the dark, with only green fire-exit signs illuminating the space, it looked like any public building. It could have been a GP's surgery or a school or a gym. If he didn't know where he was it would have been hard to identify from the objects alone. There were chairs and desks and a single bar that ran along a wall. Next to an exercise bike there was a wide space with mats on the floor and then five trollies filled with medical equipment. There were gym balls along one side and everything was neatly stacked away as if it had been put to bed for the night.

There were only two windows to the outside world in the laboratory. One near the main desk and the other was at the opposite end. The bedroom that was temporarily his also had a window, but the curtains were pulled across in there and would be for the foreseeable future. He didn't need any students going by (they were on the ground floor) and spying his belongings. His large suitcase containing his worldly goods that the police had gathered for him might be a dead giveaway to the fact he wasn't just going to be there overnight.

One of things that he hadn't been able to enjoy at the hospital was his usual nightcap of a hot cocoa. It was hardly a vice, but he loved a hot chocolate, and if he ever had trouble sleeping he liked to top it up with a tot of whisky.

He didn't have whisky here. When Keisha and George had asked him to make a shopping list for things he'd like here, he'd not added anything as indulgent as that. But he had added cocoa and the simple process of being able to boil a kettle by himself was luxury itself. He'd not enjoyed the occupational therapist overseeing things as if he were a complete idiot.

As he watched the kettle's red light glow, indicating it was boiling, his thoughts ran to what had led him here. Whenever he thought back to it, he saw the spread of blood across the carpet tiles. The heartache it had caused him in that moment. Those images were still so acutely real it seemed impossible that it hadn't been true. He didn't believe it wasn't and that was part of why he couldn't face going back.

He decided to do a circuit of the room in a bid to forget about those things. To shake away the sense of losing a love that he wasn't able to fathom. Everything appeared different in the dark. It was bizarre to be in a place that normally only mice frequented at this time of day; any rustle of a piece of paper had to be put down to creatures of the night.

After returning to the kitchen alcove, Clive managed to find everything he needed to make hot chocolate. He took his drink to the bedroom by torchlight and closed himself in for the night.

It was strange to be in a small cocoon, but it was also welcome. It was for a short period and weren't cocoons the kind of place it was possible to be reborn from?

There wasn't much in the space. There was a single bed along with a side table and lamp. The bedding was a grade up from hospital blankets and everything was beige. The carpet, the walls, the duvet cover. It was aiming to be homely while missing the point of what homely was.

There were other details that the average hotel wouldn't feature. There was a camera for starters. If was off, Keisha had reassured him, and was only there for studies. There was also a TV monitor that wasn't for the purpose of watching telly. Again it was for observations for particular studies. And thankfully he wasn't here as a subject to be studied overnight. He wasn't going to miss trying to sleep with probes attached to him.

As Clive allowed his drink to cool, he unpacked some of his things from his suitcase into the three drawers of the small bedside table. In the top drawer his personal items: his allotment journal, the joke book he liked to flick through of an evening if he was feeling blue and a few clean handkerchiefs. In the other drawers he squeezed in what clothing would fit. The rest he kept in the suitcase as there was nowhere else to house them. The police had selected an array of items and it was pleasing that they'd chosen many of his favourites (his brightest shirt, a loved tartan bow tie and his woolly slippers amongst them) based on what he'd said he needed.

It would take some getting used to and, even though it wasn't perfect (because nothing ever would be again, he remembered), it was perfectly adequate for him right now.

Thankfully there was a bathroom, and in there Clive unpacked his wash bag and got into his pyjamas, ready for bed. He was glad there was a shower he would be able to use. If Keisha wanted him helping about the place, he didn't fancy smelling all the time.

While Clive settled under the covers with his joke book and hot chocolate, he decided if it wasn't homely, it was at least practical and would be much like staying in a hotel. At least the creamy, sweet hot cocoa provided some comfort.

'Ahhh…' he said out loud as he took a gulp of the smooth, milky drink and listened intensely to the absence of bed number four screeching for attention. He would have had more of the same if he'd have been placed in a rest home. He was lucky to find himself in this rather unique situation, brought about by the new friends he'd found. It was nice to discover there were good people out there in his time of need. He just wished it hadn't been because he'd lost Nancy. Because whatever had happened, she was certainly gone.

He didn't like reminding himself of this fact at this part of the day, but it's where his thoughts always ended up.

When he finally switched off the side lamp and tucked himself under the covers, he knew he was safe here. In his sleep cocoon, no one would find him. There were just his thoughts to trouble him. There was no escaping he wasn't at the end of the road yet. In fact, he knew as his head hit the pillow that he was far from it. There was something bothering him. In amongst the mishmash of false memories, he knew there had to be *something* that was real. It *was* Nancy. He was almost certain of it. But how could that be? Not when the police had said different.

In this foreign place none of it made sense. There was nothing concrete for him to rest his memories on. Maybe if he was somewhere more familiar a more accurate account would come back to him. Even though the thought scared him, he'd like to visit his allotment to see if being there would help. That might shift a clearer picture into his consciousness. He needed something to.

Because however impossible it was, he wasn't able to shake the feeling that a crime had been committed.

Chapter Nineteen

Keisha

Other than myself, there are only three people who know about Clive's temporary living arrangements. Clive, obviously, George and Tess.

It's safer not to tell anyone else. The more people who know, the more likely it will be for news of this temporary plan to leak out. But I trust Tess. Other than Lucy, she is the person I confide in the most. The thought of visiting her every lunchtime while harbouring an elderly gentleman at the laboratories without telling her seems like an impossibility. Because of that, and the fact I'm ready for work far earlier than my usual time, I pop to Tess's Treats. For once, I feel in need of the added sparkle it brings.

'Do you really think that's the best way forward?' Tess asks.

'It just seemed like *a way* forward. Clive doesn't have many options.' The maths is simple, but now it seems complex. 'Besides, he's there.'

'Already?'

'Already.'

Tess's reaction doesn't inspire the confidence I'm hoping for. Especially after a sleepless night of worry.

'Invite him to come to the café for breakfast every morning. A man can't live off microwave products alone.' I'm pretty certain there's many a student diet that will disprove that theory. I'd go as far as to bet a clinical trial can prove as much, but I'm not going to say that. Not when Tess is being kind on Clive's behalf. 'It'll work far better for a cover story if he arrives from here rather than popping out of a cupboard each day. What will the cleaning crew say if he does that?'

Tess's point is a valid one.

On her suggestion, I phone him at the laboratory to invite him for his first meal at the café so they can meet.

The café is busy this morning. Recently Tess has been throwing herself into all sorts of different ideas to try to attract new customers to make the footfall more consistent. They seem to be working. There's a new scheme she has briefly mentioned, loyalty cards and inviting various groups to use the café as a meeting place.

Rather than sitting and waiting, I go behind the counter to lend a hand. I'm discovering more and more that being busy helps reduce the number of readings I take.

'A black coffee and I'll pay for a pay-it-forward please.'

I jot down the order. 'What's a pay-it-forward?'

'It's the new scheme I've been trialling. I've made the cost of coffee slightly less and given customers the chance to pay it forward. It means they pay for another coffee for someone else in need. If someone else comes along, they can ask for a pay-it-forward coffee. I'm doing the same for breakfasts. So when Clive visits he can have some meals on the house. It's working great and it's nice to know some people are being helped along the way.' While Tess speaks she manages to negotiate the coffee machine and ensures the orders go through to the breakfast chef in the kitchen.

'That's amazing. And talking of Clive, he should really be here by now.' I take two more orders and realise that Tess is fine without my help. Seeing her waltz behind the counter is a bit like watching a *Dancing on Ice* audition, only if I were the partner, we'd end up getting zero points for our scores.

I manoeuvre out of the way and return to my usual table to stare at the door intensely, willing Clive to appear.

'He may have taken a wrong turn somewhere?' Tess offers.

'He said he would be able to find his way here without any problems. I would have met him and shown him the way if I thought he might get lost.' I should have gone back to escort him here.

In the night, I made a long list of potential problems I might face with Clive staying at the sleep lab. All of them are hypothetical, of course, but they all have scope, including:

- An elephant (on the scale of a dinosaur) might stampede over campus, taking the sleep lab down with them.
- An audit might occur without any prior notification of it happening.
- Another discovery of an unexploded WW2 bomb resulting in an emergency evacuation in the middle of the night.
- A swarm of flying ants might take over the university grounds.

The list of possibilities is extensive and growing, but as I sit here waiting I realise the list is all wrong. What I haven't really given enough thought to is Clive himself. He is the biggest variable in amongst this whole thing. The university has its pattern of behaviour: doors that are closed at particular times, security patrols that occur at certain hours, authorised staff only allowed in defined areas. Those aren't the things I should be worrying about. It's Clive. Clive with the heart condition. Clive with the recent history of hallucinations. Clive who might fall. Clive who might become confused again.

Not so long ago he was found collapsed at his allotment believing unimaginable things. Had I really thought him able to navigate his way successfully out of an unfamiliar building to a place he's never been before? It was a very illogical thing to presume and yet because he had stated it would be no problem, I simply took his word for it.

It is in this moment I realise that perhaps this whole plan is more than just allowing this man somewhere to sleep for a while. For the period that he is staying in the lab, I am his custodian.

'I'd better see if I can go and find him,' I say, no longer able to nurse my anxieties in the bottom of a coffee cup.

'Let me know when you do. If he's gone missing, I can shut up shop. I'm sure some of the customers wouldn't mind looking round the local streets if needed. Especially if it's because he's only gone and got lost.'

I head outside into the brisk wind, the grey clusters of clouds readying themselves to bring a storm. My heart hammers, bouncing on my sternum as if it's a trampoline and I can feel the heat in my cheeks as my body responds to the notion that Clive isn't where he should be. The weather doesn't help my concern, seeing as it isn't far off turning. A true British spring in the making.

'You alright, Keish? You look like you've been running,' a voice says as soon as I've left the café.

It's Clive, sitting on the only chair not in view from inside the café. He's smoking a cigarette.

It's the first time in my life that I've ever wanted to strangle someone. Not least because of his casual shortening of my name, making it sound like 'quiche'.

'It's Keisha,' I point out. 'And surely you shouldn't be smoking?' I waft away any lingering trails of smoke that the wind pushes back.

'Old habits die hard, I'm afraid. One of the students offered me one and I couldn't resist. Nancy always hated me smoking, but I'm from a generation that didn't realise there was much wrong with it at the time. And if there was ever a time I've needed a fag, well, the last few weeks have certainly been it. I figured one swift cigarette wasn't going to hurt and if it did, I'm not sure I'd mind so much.'

'Nancy?' I say, scared to repeat the name. It lingers in the air along with the trails of smoke.

Clive holds the cigarette vertically in front of his face, almost crossing his eyes a little, it's so close. It's as if he's forgotten what it is and he's having to examine it closer. In a rush he stubs it out, half-smoked, as if he recognises it's poison.

'Disgusting things. Haven't had one for fifty years. I'm not sure what came over me.'

'Did you want some breakfast?' I say in an attempt to get us back to what we should be doing.

'I'm okay for breakfast, but a coffee wouldn't go amiss.'

I think we'll both benefit from one. I shake my head before going back inside, trying not to dwell on what's just happened.

We're inside the warmth of Tess's café as quick as possible and I notice there is a slight shuffle to Clive's gait as if his left foot isn't entirely willing to follow the right. It makes me wonder about his health and whether he'd be willing to tell me, a relative stranger, about how he is doing. I'm getting the impression that if there were any problems he wouldn't be quick to report them. Or even notice them.

An idea occurs to me. I'm only supposed to take Clive's vitals once a week for the trial, but I can increase it to daily to try to keep an eye on things. It will be a minor white lie to make sure he's okay.

'This is Tess,' I say, when we reach the front of the queue.

'Hello, Clive. I'm so glad you've made it.' Tess skips round the counter to give Clive a quick hug. 'Any time you need breakfast or a coffee, you just pop by.'

'Ah, so you must be the lady who knows about our arrangement.' Clive nudges her with his elbow in a completely unsubtle way.

I glance around wondering what anyone in hearing distance would make of the statement.

'Indeed,' Tess replies. 'I'm Keisha's friend, confidant and match-maker as well as the best café owner she knows.'

'Matchmaker you say?' Clive raises an eyebrow. 'Keisha never said.'

'She's having a short break. She'll be back on the mission soon.'

'Really? Well do let me know if I can be of any help. And I love this café. Perfect amount of décor.' Clive gives the surroundings sweeping looks of admiration.

I wonder what assistance Clive thinks he can provide on the dating front. I can't imagine he'd know anyone to send me on a blind date with.

After Tess provides us both with takeaway coffees, we head back to the university campus, rushing as much as we can to get there before the storm clouds break. It isn't the route I regularly take, but I figure Clive needs to know the simplest path from A to B. We wander past a row of shops and takeaways and I figure this way has the advantage of more landmarks and people around to ask directions.

'I'm sure you're aware of this, but there's no smoking anywhere in the research building.' I blame Lucy for the way I approach health and safety at work. She needs everything explained to her as plainly as possible. I tend to apply it with everyone.

'Don't you be worrying about that. I haven't smoked for over fifty years. I'm certainly not about to take up smoking again any time soon.'

'But you just…' I don't complete my sentence, catching the blank look on Clive's face. 'When did you last have a cigarette then?'

'I've not even had a cheeky puff since the sixties. Not even the good stuff.' Clive smiles as he says it, proud of the achievement.

This truly confirms it. Clive is a ticking time bomb and I've brought him right into the centre of my world. The heavens start to open as if they know something is wrong.

What I'm witnessing is a glitch. A tiny slippage in his memory, and it makes me wonder… How many other moments does he have like this? How big can those slips be?

As we run in from the rain, I realise, if I wasn't worrying before, now is the time to start. If the picture in Clive's mind isn't clear, maybe I need to find out what really happened to help make it clearer.

Chapter Twenty

Clive

It had been a considerable time since Clive had worked for anyone, and in all his seventy-nine years, he'd never had a desk job.

After serving in the army, he'd become a postman. He'd enjoyed the exercise it had required and much preferred putting hours into walking and getting to know the community around him to working in an office. It was what made the world work, he'd mused... The fact that no two people were made the same, and he relished the opportunity to mix with everyone.

When he'd retired, he'd found the allotment occupied him enough to fill his time.

Despite having never held an office job, he was quite capable of answering a phone. It made him chuckle that Keisha had little prompts printed out and Blu-Tacked to various places around the laboratory. Fortunately they hadn't been placed there for his benefit, so he was saved that insult. But she did like to refer to them just in case he didn't understand.

The one on the telephone was more of a checklist than one simple instruction.

- State Good Morning/Afternoon depending on the time of day.
- State where they've called: Southampton University Cardiology Research Department.
- State who's speaking, for example, Good Afternoon, Southampton University Cardiology Department, John speaking.
- Ask how you can help.

It was quite the list.

Clive's morning task was to answer the phone. It was simple enough if not a tad boring. More than once he was tempted to introduce himself as John, just to see if Keisha noticed. He had a feeling it wouldn't take much to send her over the edge, so he thought better of it. She was likely to send him back to the hospital with signs of confusion. She'd looked ready to do that earlier when he'd said he'd not smoked for years. The truth be told he hadn't known what had come over him. He was denying it at the same time as recalling the few puffs he'd had not long before. Muddled sometimes didn't come close enough to describing how his memory was working these days.

Rather than stress out Keisha for his own amusement, Clive took himself on mini jaunts around the lab to read the other labels. The place looked different in the daylight. More functional. Less lonely.

The small kitchenette was the most fertile area for instructions. Not only did it hold the usual warnings about hot water and 'please switch off after use' labels, there were also several that Keisha had obviously added to help her absent colleague. They included:

- Please wash up mugs after use and return to the cupboard.
- Please unplug the kettle at the end of the day.

The fridge was a positive Mecca for the signs and was obviously a source of some anguish between workmates.

- Please remove any leftover lunch items in a timely manner.
- Milk to be taken home on Friday.
- Any out-of-date food will be removed and disposed of.
- Only eat your own food supplies. Please don't take what doesn't belong to you.

It made Clive chuckle. It would seem this fridge had seen quite a bit of action.

The most worrying label in the kitchen was the one that stated: *ABSOLUTELY NO metals in the microwave.*

'Everything okay?' Keisha asked, poking her head round into the alcove as she took a break from her computer screen that was full of numbers.

'Just stretching my legs between phone calls. Would you like a drink while I'm up?' He might as well make himself useful. He wasn't exactly rushed off his feet.

'A tea would be great. Do you need any help?'

'It's okay. I can handle making a cuppa. Now, tell me, are all these labels here because these things actually happened?'

Keisha returned to her chair and leaned back a little. 'Every. Single. One.' She punctuated the words and rolled her eyes to the ceiling as if she'd been awaiting counsel on the matter for a very long time.

'Even metal in the microwave?'

'Yep. Admittedly it was a soup sachet that had some metal as part of the lining, but it would have only taken a few seconds to read the instructions properly to realise it needed pouring into a bowl. Lucy's savvy enough, she's just always in a rush.'

'I hope it didn't cause too much damage.'

'Fortunately the noise it made meant we reacted quickly and got it out before the sparks actually set anything alight.'

'That was lucky. Do the labels help?' Clive gestured to another one he'd just spotted above the light switch stating it needed to be switched off when leaving at the end of the day.

'They help me. It means I can point out I have already told her if she ends up doing it again. Don't get me wrong, we get on really well. We're just complete opposites.'

'Are they any closer to knowing why she's unwell?'

Keisha shakes her head sadly. 'Soon, hopefully. I miss her being about. We live together as well so I'm feeling her absence everywhere. It's nice having you here, though. It helps.'

Clive knew that feeling all too well. The absence of Nancy was complete. And yet how could that be?

'I know what you mean. Even if I only dreamed I had a wife, I still miss her. I can't imagine living and working with someone and then them not being there. At least you know it's only temporary.'

'I'm sorry. I keep forgetting that, in a way, you've suffered your own loss. I guess we're both adjusting to a different set of circumstances.'

Rather embarrassingly, the thought of never seeing Nancy again brought a tear along and it was sliding unapologetically down his cheek.

'Ignore me,' he said, wiping the evidence away.

'Have you remembered anything else from when you went into hospital?'

'Nothing. I'm lucky to be in an environment that doesn't remind me of what has happened. You must be aware of Lucy not being here all the time.' Clive took a fresh hankie from his jacket pocket to wipe away any remaining tears.

'She'll be back. I'm sure I'll be writing up new instructions for her before I know it. Did you sleep okay? I know it's only for a while, but I want you to be comfortable.'

'Really well, thank you.' Clive had had a much better sleep than he'd expected. The relative silence had been like music to his ears, and after weeks of broken dreams, it was the deepest snooze he'd had in a long while.

'Is there anything else you need here?'

The place, even though it wasn't a home, was pretty well equipped with everything he was going to be needing for the next week or three.

'I don't think so. I can top up food from the local shops by the looks of things. Although I'm going to need help with securing my new place, as you know, and if it isn't too much bother, I'd really like to check on my allotment. I've researched the bus routes and it's not straightforward. I'm hoping you might know someone who would be able to give me a lift.'

The kettle finished boiling and Clive poured water into the prepped mugs. He already knew how Keisha took her tea and sensed he wasn't the only one who needed a little looking after. At least this was one way he was able to do that for her.

'Tess will be busy with work and George is the only other person I know who drives. I don't have many friends and the ones that I do have are like me and still live like students. I'll have to get in touch with him.'

'Could you? I'd really like to start making some solid plans. I don't want to be here bothering you any longer than necessary.'

'It's no bother.'

'All the same. None of us want to be carrying on with this secrecy any longer than absolutely necessary. I'd like to make sure we secure a flat as soon as we can. And I'd like to visit the allotment. Check everything's been okay in my absence.' Wanting to visit the allotment was becoming increasingly important to him. He was sure he might find some answers there as to why he'd become so confused.

His first sleep here may have been a good one, but he knew now the exhaustion had passed he would spend too many night-time hours awake. The occasional insomnia he suffered was sure to come along with so much on his mind. The night would give him far too much time to try to make sense of everything. That was why he needed to go to the allotment. He was hoping it would help him work out what it was he'd forgotten.

Chapter Twenty-One

Keisha

As someone not particularly at ease with change, having Clive around is turning out to be surprisingly okay. Despite my concern about his memory blip, he hasn't done it since, which I'm hoping is a good thing. I'm trying to convince myself it was a one-off and not something to be concerned over. I wish I knew more about what really happened, but other than asking Clive, I'm not really sure how to find out anything. The more time I'm spending with him, the more I realise I'm only familiar with the made-up version of events.

I tend to worry at night when he's alone, but in the daytime, working together, we seem to be getting along. I won't voice this out loud, but he's even proving to be more helpful than Lucy usually is. At least with ensuring things are running smoothly.

When he takes phone calls, he makes notes and actions them where he can. When he makes tea, I don't need to redo them because the tea bag has been stewing for a full ten minutes. When he cleans something, it doesn't need to be redone because at least thirty-three per cent of the item remains unclean.

It's going swimmingly for the first few days, until this afternoon. That's when it starts to go wrong.

In the synchronised way the days are going, we are ready for the first of three subjects who are coming for follow-up reviews. Each one will be in for a full hour, but the session should be over in half. We allow the extra time so there's no rushing. We don't force them to drink their tea quickly so we're ready for the next client.

Roy is in for his final assessment. He's the only client in who is part of my PhD study looking at the effects of beetroot juice – the same study Clive's part of. I don't know why I'm only just twigging on to this fact as Roy enters the building.

Having been okay with Clive's presence, I'm struck by an overwhelming sense of dread that this meeting of two people might screw up the whole project. Like atoms colliding, but not in a good way.

'Roy, can you wait here for a minute?' I offer him the chair at the desk. 'I just need to sort a couple of things. I'll be with you shortly.'

'No problem,' Roy says before taking up the seat.

I'm not sure how delaying things is going to help. Clive is already busying himself with preparing a tray of tea and biscuits. I panic myself into indecision. Will it really matter if they meet? Would it in any way affect the outcome of the study? Will this act of kindness result in the failure of my PhD? It's certainly not the done thing to introduce the subjects.

As I don't have answers to these questions, I hesitate on my journey between the desk and the kitchen. I'm not sure whether to dispense of Clive for this appointment to ensure the purity of the study, and I'm not even sure how I'd explain it or what I would do. The fire exit has an alarm and chucking him out that way will get me in lots of trouble, and garner attention we don't want, and it's already too late for that without ushering Roy out.

There is no way of preventing their meeting. Apart from the fact that Clive is in the little kitchen alcove, they're already in the same room. There isn't even a wall between them. The only thing that is between them is me.

'Everything okay?' Clive asks.

My fingers are on my neck. One. Two. Three. Four.

I've done it without realising.

Five. Six. Seven.

I'm not even doing it properly. I've not checked where the second hand of the wall clock is to know when I need to stop counting.

Eight. Nine. Ten.

And what do you do when you don't know how to stop? When there is no end to the habits you've created for yourself?

Clive walks over. And that means there is nothing stopping this meeting.

My feet are rooted to the spot. My pulse is thumping harder than it ever has before. And the more beats I feel – Eleven. Twelve. Thirteen. – the more I realise that rather than gathering them to take a reading, I'm letting them slip away without being used. I'm taking my pulse, not to garner a figure, but purely for the comfort of feeling the rhythm.

I should stop. I need to stop. But the panic won't allow me to let go.

It's Clive that makes me. Without much warning, as my breathing gets shallower and my heart beats harder, he takes my arm and gently eases it away from my neck.

Fourteen. Fourteen isn't there. My fingers are off the carotid enough that I'm not able to feel the whoosh of blood through the artery. I have no way of knowing whether it has been and gone or not. The sensation is startling, as if a great gush of wind is pushing itself into my lungs and is running out again as quick as it arrives.

Fourteen isn't there and yet it must have been. I am upright and breathing and that is a pretty clear indicator that everything is continuing as it should.

Fifteen isn't there either. I'm still standing, I remind myself.

'What are you worried about?' Clive asks, his crystal-clear eyes seeing right through to the place that is hidden. The place I don't want anyone to see. The place no one else knows about.

'I'm not sure you should meet Roy.'

'Why?'

I'm not sure how to voice it in a way that makes sense. 'You shouldn't be in the same room together,' I say, like that's a reasonable explanation.

'What will happen if we are? Am I about to set his pacemaker off or something?' I hear the jest in Clive's voice. It makes me relax a fraction, my arm a further half inch from my neck.

'You're in the same study. It might upset the results.' Some clarity finds its way to my mind. There are no lightning bolts about to thunder down on the laboratory. There are four walls, a floor and a ceiling that aren't going to crumble because they've met. The project will not be null and void because case study one and five are in the same place. I flop my arm down by my side. 'Roy is part of the takotsubo study. I was concerned about two participants meeting.'

It's Lucy that I miss in this moment. She would have pre-empted this. For all her klutz, she can also be the most methodical person I know when it comes to schedules. Seeing shapes and patterns and how they'd react way before it gets to breaking point. She would have pointed out this minor anomaly and fixed it before it became a problem.

'Far too many broken hearts for one laboratory, huh?' Clive says.

I nod. Far, far too many. And it makes me conscious once more of how this man, who is virtually a stranger, sees me in a way I never even admit to myself. Of how he sees through me and seems to understand… I am the one that is broken.

Chapter Twenty-Two

Clive

It had taken a couple of days, but Clive was getting used to the routine of being in the lab. Once he was dressed, he drank his beetroot juice, then walked to Tess's Treats for a light breakfast of poached eggs and toast before heading back ready for the day to begin. The participants usually partook in several measures for each particular study. There were their vitals to be taken, a six-metre walking test, a cardiopulmonary exercise test and the Minnesota Living with Heart Failure Questionnaire to fill out. Even though some of the projects were studying different treatments, a lot of the measures used were the same. He was familiar with them all now. 'They are quantifiable,' Keisha said of the tests. Whatever quantifiable meant.

Admittedly, Clive's favourite part of the day was making the hot drinks. He'd been left in charge of purchasing the biscuits and was making subtle upgrades from Lucy's previous selection of plain digestives and rich teas.

Since Keisha had faltered over her pulse-taking the other day, Clive had been waiting for a moment to ask about it without startling her. It was while they were having their tea break without any study participants present that he decided it was the right time. He offered her a chocolate chip cookie beforehand to soften the blow.

'When did it start?' Big questions were always hard to ask. He wasn't sure he was going about it in the best way.

'What?' Keisha responded with a jump, as if she'd spotted a spider and was ready to bat it away.

'Taking your pulse. I've seen you noting it down. I wondered if you remember when you started taking it?'

Keisha's skin turned pale. Every part of her was visibly tense, most noticeably her forearm, already prepped for action.

'It's just something I like to do for routine.'

'Do you ever consider not doing it?'

'It's not hurting anyone,' she said defensively.

'I never said it was. I'm just trying to understand *why*. And I'm pretty certain there is a why.'

Keisha regarded Clive in a way he had never been looked at before, a piercing glare calling for deference.

'Why does it matter?'

'I think to understand a person you need to understand their quirks. Some are just more obvious than others.'

'So what are yours?' Keisha selected a cookie, not ready to give up her secrets yet.

There were several that Clive had, but which would he choose to share?

'In my entire life I've never purchased a new item of clothing. I'm the original upcycler, me! I've always purchased clothes second-hand and I've saved myself a fortune and a lot of waste in the process.'

Clive thought about his favourite item of clothing. 'I have a sewing machine at home, and over the years I've become very adept at making alterations. I only wish I was able to make another jacket like my patchwork one.' He was wearing a lighter pale-blue jacket at the moment, the patchwork one too thick to wear in the lab and in need of a trip to the dry cleaner's after its stint in hospital.

Keisha looked at him in that strange, thoughtful way. His example probably wasn't quirky enough. It wasn't exactly a serious revelation, not one to help unlock the truth of her pulse-taking routine.

'Are your pants second-hand too?' she asked, her face creasing with the question.

'Ah, you've got me. Pants, socks and vests are my only exception and only ever Marks and Spencer. But anything other than the base-layer clothing has been second-hand.'

'And when did that start? What made you decide to always buy clothes to recondition?'

'I think it stems from the era I was born in. We were coming out of a war where resources had been limited. It meant we always made the best of what we had. If clothes were beyond repair then they would find another purpose. They'd become tea towels or rags or furniture covers. They should put rations in place again at some point. There are a lot of skills to be gained from not having everything you desire at your fingertips.'

She finally looked satisfied. 'I take my pulse because I find it reassuring. It's something I often desire to have at my fingertips.' Keisha clutched her wrist to her body. 'I know you're trying to be helpful, but you need to understand it's not a problem to solve. I know it's unusual, but there's nothing wrong with that. There are all sorts of things going on in the world that need fixing. Me taking my pulse isn't one of them.'

Clive nodded, helping himself to a second cookie at the same time. 'My apologies. I was just being curious. I figured there was more to it.'

He knew there was, but he also knew that was a wall that wasn't about to move with just a gentle nudge.

Later, once Keisha had left, Clive had another night of trying to amuse himself. The expected insomnia had set in. After his first stint of decent sleep, he'd not had a great one since. All this space and time to think wasn't a good thing.

After Keisha went home, the evenings stretched out in a long and never-ending fashion. He'd taken it upon himself to carry out an activity each night to try to fill the time. Sadly, the resources for such attempts were limited, and he was restricted to the areas where he wouldn't end up attracting the attention of the security staff. One evening he'd given all the mugs a proper rinse with bleach to get rid of all the tea stains. On another he'd taken it upon himself to deep clean all the gym equipment. When he found the label maker he had great fun making up motivational notices to counter all the instructions about the place.

Clive would freely admit that Keisha not noticing these changes was disappointing. He thought she'd be very quick to pick up on any differences. But apparently *Smile, it costs nothing* branded on the fridge wasn't slogan enough to get her attention, not even the hoped-for smile.

Now on his fifth night, Clive was running out of things to do. Organising the desk drawers seemed like a good idea and, because he wasn't in someone's home, it didn't feel like prying. He wasn't doing it in the hope of learning more about Keisha. Not when all he was moving about were staplers, hole punches and sharpeners.

It wasn't even a mess, to be fair, but once he'd started Clive decided the inside was gathering dust and it would do the drawer some good to have a clean. It made him feel useful. He guessed it was the kind of task Keisha wouldn't normally find time for, and while he was living in limbo it gave him something to do.

It was when he removed the organiser tray that he found them… Keys.

He'd been of the understanding that the only spare set to the lab were with Lucy and Keisha hadn't wanted to ask for them. The idea had been that while he was here, of an evening, Clive would remain inside. If there had been any kind of emergency he would have been able to leave via the fire exit. There was less chance of them being caught that way.

'I wonder,' he said, enjoying the echo of his voice in the large space. There were five keys attached to some science-fair keyrings. They seemed similar to the Chubb-style ones he'd seen used on the door and as he slid the metal into the lock, it turned with ease.

Freedom.

It was strange. He wasn't an inmate, not even close, but he'd been getting cabin fever, he realised, when the relief of being able to go out presented itself.

Pulling the door closed, and keeping in the shadows, Clive took an appreciative deep breath. The coldness of the evening's spring air was a welcome break from the stuffiness of being inside a room that didn't lend itself to occupancy for any length of time.

Discreetly, he slipped back in to get his jacket and to double-check that he was able to open and close the door once outside. When he was happy that it was possible, he slipped off to explore his surroundings. He knew there was a theatre on campus and figured that some of the people out and about were wandering along to see a show. The storms that had rolled in during the week had passed and it was a calm spring evening, ripe to enjoy.

Clive headed towards the theatre, following a handy signpost. Perhaps he would get the chance to enjoy a performance or two while he was here. It had been some time since he'd been to see a show, but it had always been something he'd enjoyed in the past.

His forehead furrowed at the thought. His past had become a jumble in recent weeks. Some memories he had to question: Did he used to enjoy the theatre alone or with someone? Alone, he realised. He enjoyed shows with dancing most.

The space was large and while the theatre was on the left, there was a box office and bar to the right. A bright light seemed to indicate a show was in progress.

A lady glanced up at him from the front-of-house desk. 'Are you okay, sir?' she asked quietly.

He went over. 'I've just moved nearby.' That wasn't a lie, at least. 'Do you have a programme I can take a look at?'

There was one on the desk right in front of his nose. She politely passed him a copy.

'Excellent, thank you.' Clive was delighted by the prospect of attending a show. It would beat disinfecting gym balls. 'Is the bar open?' That prospect was even more inviting.

'Yes. It's closed on Mondays and Tuesdays. But it's open from 7 p.m. until 11 p.m. for the rest of the week.'

'Marvellous. I'll check it out now while I look at this if that's okay?'

'Of course,' she said with a smile.

Clive wasn't entirely sure why he was checking. But he'd always thought of theatre bars as being for theatre-going people. It was there for before and after the show.

As he'd been given permission, Clive entered the bar. It was somewhere between a pub and a coffee shop. It was artier than any of the joints he'd ever frequented, with large windows offering a view of outside. A good place for people watching, he considered, before ordering a pint of pale ale called Stag that had a small chalkboard attached to its pump, advertising it as the offer of the week. He took his ale and chose a seat to one side where he was able to watch all the comings and goings of the campus and the theatre.

Even though it was nearly nine in the evening, there was a reasonable amount of footfall on the paths outside. He wasn't sure where the student accommodation was on the campus, but he'd take a bet at it being at one end of the path he was observing. That route went towards the shops and all the nearby takeaway outlets and he was sure that was where most of them were headed. Someone returned with a full carrier bag of a bargain bucket of chicken, and confirmed the thought.

He was also aware there was a gym on the campus. He'd seen it on one of the signs and a few students were carrying what looked to Clive to be gym bags. The thought of joining a gym appealed to Clive. He laughed to himself and dismissed the idea as he supped his pint. It had a pleasant malty undertone and was very palatable. He might stretch to a second given that it was on offer. There was certainly entertainment to be had here, even if he wasn't watching a show.

It was just as he was getting more comfortable, taking off his jacket, that the play broke for its interval. A considerable number of people poured into the bar. There must have been at least fifty of them and Clive noticed that along the bar were several prepared orders. Customers were presenting pieces of paper and the barman would supply them with a pre-prepared tray of drink. It was a nifty system.

The bar was a buzz of noise, of brief conversations and halfway reviews. And then an announcement called them back to their seats and they filtered out again. The contrast of noise and ensuing quiet reminded Clive of the difference between being in hospital and staying in the lab.

The keys were on the table and he caressed them, appreciating the freedom they'd given him. It reminded him he wanted to return to the allotment as soon as possible. A shadow of a memory was still playing on his mind.

He paid more attention to the keyrings this time. There was one with symbols from the periodic table that he'd forgotten the meaning of many years before. The other worn keyring had a sleeve over a plastic square displaying a couple of dates. They seemed to be birth and death dates, the sum between them only giving the person forty-seven short years. He pushed out the plastic square to see it more closely. An image on it made his heart flicker as if it was playing the crescendo of a tune. It was a young Keisha with a black man who was undoubtedly her dad. It was a photo-booth snap of Keisha on her father's knee.

It would seem, without meaning to, Clive may have stumbled across Keisha's *why*.

Chapter Twenty-Three

Keisha

The evening has grown dark by the time I arrive at the hospital. George is waiting for me at the main entrance, true to his offer of helping me find Lucy's ward. He looks so incredibly cool, leaning against the wall, a black hoody draped over his uniform. I wish I still had my lab coat on rather than the crumpled T-shirt and cardigan that I'm left with now. I try not to worry about not having made an effort.

'Hey,' he says.

'Thanks for this.'

'So, Lucy is your colleague, right?'

I nod, struggling to find words with my anxiety rocketing. I'm not sure if meeting George has made it worse. I gulp to moisten my throat.

'She's also my best friend. We live together. It's a houseshare. You said you live with your parents, didn't you?' My nerves are making me ramble.

'Yes. Rebuilding my funds after travelling for a few years and working abroad. The NHS is quite deluxe after volunteering in Namibia, but sadly no one takes good will as a deposit.'

'Wow.' I can't imagine what that must have been like – I don't even own a passport.

'Did you know there's a name for fear of hospitals?'

'Is there?' I ask. It comes out as a squeak.

'Nosocomephobia or something like that. Have you never liked places like this?'

I wonder what the name for a fear of everything is. That might be closer to the mark.

'I struggle with the size of this one,' I say, not ready to own up. 'It's so vast, especially when you're not sure where you're going.'

As we enter the hospital the rush of people makes me glad I have a guide.

'That's understandable and I'm glad to be of help. I'm just sorry I'm not off duty until Tuesday. You know, to help Clive view the flats.'

There's a blush to his cheeks which I've never witnessed before and, on spotting it, my tummy flutters.

'Can I ask you a question?' I glance around at the people passing in the corridors, wondering if this is the right time to bring it up. Identifying we won't be overheard, I go for it. 'Can you tell me about what really happened when Clive came into hospital?'

George glances around as we walk before answering. 'It was called in by a member of the public. He'd collapsed while pushing his wheelbarrow on the way back from the allotment. He was disorientated and unwell when the paramedics picked him up and he went on to have his cardiac event on the way to hospital. He gave his version of events when he came round from that and the police were contacted. Clive's back door was unlocked, but there was no body like he described.'

'Right,' I say, not quite sure what to make of it all. 'I just, I don't know. I guess I feel like there's more to it.'

'I know what you mean. I'll see if I can find out anything. They're still looking into it from what I understand.'

'Thank you. You've been so helpful. I want to understand more about what happened, but I really don't know where to find any answers. I'll be glad to get you-know-who set up somewhere. And he's desperate to get a look at his allotments.' The more I talk, the more I settle.

'I'll get the flat viewing booked in for Tuesday when I'm off. We need to find out what Clive wants to do with his home. If he can't go back there, does he want us to go and sort his things? Or we could arrange for a house clearance.' George's brown eyes remind me of the perfect shade of mahogany furniture. For a moment, I'm lost in them.

'I'll ask him. Hopefully he'll want to keep some things. It seems such a shame that a false memory is making him want to get rid of the real ones. He's had a whole life in that house.'

The maudlin thought stays with me until we reach the ward and George briefly touches my shoulder. 'We'll catch up again soon and give me a call if you need to for, you know, anything.'

George lingers, as if he wants to say more, but doesn't. I find myself wanting to know more about him. About where he travelled and why he chose to volunteer.

'Thank you for everything.' It's all I can manage, even though I don't want him to go yet. I watch as he leaves.

When I see Lucy, she looks pale. Not at all her usual sprightly self. I give her a rare hug, which takes her by surprise.

'Will you sneak me out of here?' Lucy asks.

I guffaw without meaning to. I've done enough sneaking around lately.

'What? What's going on? I know something is. Tell me.'

Lucy knows me far too well and before I think too much on the matter, I tell her *everything*.

'You know what you need to do, don't you?' Lucy says, once she is up to date.

'What?' My voice feels hoarse from whispering so much.

'Investigate. If you're going to be clearing his house, you'll have access to all his things. It might give you some clue as to why he keeps talking about his imaginary wife.'

'But the police have already done that. They've ruled it out.'

'It won't hurt to look though. I can always help once I'm better.'

'Just don't say anything. To anyone. I don't want any of us getting in trouble. And the only investigating you need to worry about is the doctors finding out why you're still poorly.'

When I leave, I say a little prayer that at least that investigation is solved soon. I need my Lucy back.

The following day I find that, after a full working week, I like having Clive around quite a bit.

Clive greets study participants when they arrive, offering them tea or coffee. Most will take him up on the offer and, as he arranges that, I introduce myself and go through the details of what they'll be doing this visit. Most often it is a series of tests with some heart monitoring. For the majority of the subjects, they are joining us for the third or fourth time and they are familiar with the drill, but because of the fact that it is a research project, I have to ensure their consent and give them an accurate overview of what they'll have to do. It can be, for want of a better word, boring, but the studies won't pass an ethics board without such considerations.

Just when the participant looks about ready to pass out with the formalities, Clive comes along and revives them with his hosting skills. In the week that he's been here the standard of the tea has risen astronomically. Gone are the mugs originally given away as freebies by medical companies that were chipped and way past their best. Instead we have a beautiful set of vintage bone china. The cups are delicate with floral patterns.

'Tea should be served properly. I have standards if you want me to do this job,' Clive says to me with a smile.

It makes me smile too, this extra level of care and thought. One that I never really consider when my only interest is in the figures, the data I collect.

Every day when Clive returns from his lunch break, he seems to have found another piece of treasure to add to the finesse of his duties.

'Where have you managed to find all these things?' I ask when he produces some vintage sugar tongs.

'This is from a charity shop. You'd be amazed at some of the wonders you can find.'

'I didn't realise there was a charity shop near here.'

I studied for my degree at the university and my work has been here ever since. It always strikes me as surprising when I learn something new about the area. It goes to show I spend far too much time inside.

'It's down a side street. Awful signage. You wouldn't know it was there unless you're nosey like me. It's where I've found nearly all of these treasures, although not the biscuits. They're from the Polish store.'

The biscuits are the other thing that have undergone a massive improvement. Lucy has always been in charge of those stocks and, because we are on a tight budget, she usually sticks to plain rich teas and digestives. I think about last night's visit. Of how pale she looked. In the next day or two they hope to do an endoscopy – passing a small camera down to look at her stomach – and I cross my fingers that'll be the end of her hospital stay. Despite Clive's good company, it doesn't make up for her not being here.

When I put Clive in charge of getting supplies, I'd explained very clearly to him that we only have an allocation of three pounds per week for refreshments. That small amount was tricky to budget every month. But he has been coming back with an amazing array of biscuits.

Now, every day, they are displayed on a plate complete with a doily. They are so tempting that I'm even opting to try some of the new ones on offer. There are caramel wafers and some white-chocolate-covered bourbons. Today, I take one of each.

All he needs now is a tea trolley to deliver it on, but in the meantime he has a polka-dot tray with handles to make transport from kitchen to desk easier 'and with a flourish' as Clive likes to say.

I'm beginning to enjoy the element of fun bordering on eccentricity that Clive brings with him. I don't try to second guess what he will produce next, but it comes with the guarantee of bringing a smile. If not to me, then to the clients that are here. He is managing to engage our study participants on a level I've never really witnessed before. Once they are done with their refreshments, we commence the tests and the subjects are always jollier than they've been on previous occasions.

I often wonder if such enjoyment and laughter make a difference. If the resting heart rate will be higher because of these fleeting moments. Whether the week that Clive has been here will make a difference to the outcome of my studies.

'Everything ready?' Clive asks from the other end of the test walkway. It's taped out to an exact length. Of his own accord, Clive has redone the tatty markings for me to ensure they're the precise distance they should be.

The stopwatch is in my hand and I realise I'm staring at it without taking action. 'Yes, ready. Are you set to go, Mrs Baldwin?' The lady is in the chair under instruction to move only when I say 'go'.

I look to Clive, who smiles in that endlessly cheering way of his and I find myself smiling back. It makes me realise that Mrs Baldwin celebrating eating a pink wafer biscuit, which she hasn't done in years, and how delightful it is to be receiving the gold-star treatment isn't going to alter her results. The altering result is mine. I am no longer anxious about the stores being stocked up or everything being ready like it should be. I no longer have concerns about what fungus is growing in the fridge this week. There is no worry over trying to analyse Post-it notes with illegible messages.

Everything is as it should be.

And for the first time in a long time, there has been a change.

It isn't a noticeable difference at first. A beat or two, nothing significant. But by the fifth day of working with Clive by my side, my resting heart rate is five beats less a minute.

And there is something more than that... Something that by my standards is bewildering. I missed a time slot.

At the end of the previous day there were fewer recordings in my notebook than there have ever been. It must have been the gingersnap biscuits distracting me. Clive was beyond belief that I'd never tried one before. He insisted I should and my senses were blindsided by the melt-in-the-mouth snack, so much so that I had two.

Two biscuits and no half-hourly pulse check. It is a whole new world.

'Go,' I say to poor Mrs Baldwin, who has been waiting patiently, wondering if her reflex skills are part of the test.

I concentrate on her as she walks up and down, Clive carefully taking note of the number of times she has done so. We have come to a happy harmony. Each with our own eccentricities and methodical ways. Today he has worn a favoured pale-blue jacket along with a bow tie the likes of which I've only ever seen in *Mary Poppins*. Even his attire makes me smile.

I've been wanting to ask him questions about his past. About whether he has ever been in love with anyone other than his fictional wife. Whether perhaps when he was younger he was engaged. But I want to avoid putting any thoughts in his head, like Dr Hutchins has said. I'm left waiting in the hope he'll bring those things up.

When Mrs Baldwin has left with some extra pink wafers in a tissue, Clive asks if we can discuss the plan to visit some retirement flats over our lunch break.

'Ah.' It is rare that I am ever busy over my lunch, apart from catching up with Tess when I can. 'I'm actually doing something.'

'Are you?' The note of surprise in Clive's voice is unmissable. 'I mean, of course you are. Naturally. Why wouldn't you be?'

'I know I'm a creature of habit.' I smile at him, knowing he can fit the same description. 'But as it happens, I have a date.'

Clive raises an eyebrow. 'Really? Well, that is something that can't be missed.'

'It's my forty-first,' I say, realising I should have kept it to myself.

'Forty-first date? Is that not clocking up into something of a relationship? You've not mentioned the lucky man, or woman, before.'

'Not my forty-first date with the same person. It's a first date. I'm not sure I'm very good at dating, to be honest, hence all the firsts. Tess believes that there is someone out there for all of us. She's the one that's been encouraging me to do it.' I'm not sure why I'm telling Clive this.

'If Tess believes there's someone out there for all of us, what do you believe?'

I ponder this for a moment. I believe in physiology. I believe that only certain things are guaranteed, right up until they aren't: the drawing in of a breath, the electrical impulse of a heart, and the ability of the cerebellum to let us know if we're upright. They are the things that I believe a human body is capable of. But these interactions with their unknown quantities, they are what I don't understand.

'I like to believe that somehow the human body would know if it had met *the one*. That in some way, shape or form it would react and let you know. I guess it wouldn't surprise you to know that I always take my pulse when a date arrives. I've always expected it to give a little jump.' I stop talking, realising my hand is over my pulse point, almost as if I was hoping that there will be some trace of what that feeling is.

'It's not always like that you know. It's not always love at first sight.'

'It was for you, wasn't it?' I seize the chance to take a glimpse into Clive's world. The story of him and Nancy meeting sounded like true love. When he first mentioned their tea dance it struck me as being a kind of Cupid's arrow scenario, where the heart misses a beat or gives off a sign. I shake my head, forgetting myself. Nancy isn't real. That story hadn't been real.

'Oh yes. It truly can be like that. I knew the moment Nancy spoke to me. But I'm not sure that it's the heart that reacts first. It's your pupils dilating or your cheeks flushing. The heart comes later. Now, where are you going for this date today?'

I stare at Clive for a long minute, the mention of Nancy lingering between us in the air. It feels like static electricity, as if a ghost is moving by us. He mentions her so often even I'm not sure what to believe. Maybe Lucy is right. Maybe I should look into whether there is more to his story. I shake the sensation away and jumpstart myself into answering the question.

'The café. Tess has been arranging them. She thinks I should be able to find love within a hundred dates. I'm really not so sure.'

'Can I be a fly on the wall? I can sit at another table and see if your cheeks flush. If your heart rate isn't indicating anything, maybe you need someone else to keep an eye on the signs.'

My initial instinct is to say no. Especially when I've already said no to Lucy, knowing she'd never be discreet. I find the whole palaver strange enough already without adding to the stress, but then I reflect on the fact Clive seems to be having a positive effect on my heart rate. His presence might make me calmer.

'Is it for the purpose of helping with my research?'

'If research is what we're calling it, then yes.'

I nod. 'Then I guess that will be okay. Just don't be surprised if I disappear.'

Because before we even get there, it's almost a guarantee that I will.

Chapter Twenty-Four

Clive

Unlike Keisha, Clive wasn't experienced in working out which seat was the best one to take up for his purpose. Rather foolishly, he'd sat nearby, but facing the wrong way. It meant he was able to listen in, but not see what was occurring.

He'd seen the gentleman come in before he took his seat. He had a striking beard and he wore a chequered shirt with the sleeves rolled up. As far as Clive knew, the term to describe him would be 'hipster'. He'd chosen a nice aftershave, Clive was able to note from his poorly chosen back-to-them position.

The conversation started off badly when the hipster insulted the café's décor: 'This place is a tad blinding with all this unicorn stuff, don't you think?'

'I find it cheering,' Keisha had replied. She might not be peppered in glitter herself, but Tess was one of her best friends. She'd stick by her to the end. She was that kind of girl.

Within a few minutes the conversation had stilled to nothingness. Things didn't seem to be going to plan, least of all for Clive, who wasn't able to see what was going on without arousing suspicion. He would really need to take up a better seat next time.

A phone rang behind him.

'Really? What now?' came the gentleman's voice. 'I'll come straight away.'

Clive managed to crane his neck somewhat at this point.

'Sorry. Another time, maybe,' Hipster said, before hurriedly making his way out.

'Well, that was swift. What was his rush?' Clive asked, joining the rather ashen-faced Keisha.

'His ex-girlfriend has just gone into labour!'

With the date over in the blink of an eye, and with good reason (or awful, depending how he looked at it), Clive hadn't witnessed enough interaction to give any kind of feedback, other than to say that that particular date was stricken and the fault was not Keisha's.

With date number forty-one declared a dud, Keisha then told Clive over lunch about the agreement she'd made with George, who would help Clive view the flats. George was on shift over the weekend, but apparently that worked out well because they only held viewings on weekdays. Clive knew he wouldn't be able to wait that long. His urgency wasn't in being shown round a new flat, but in wanting to visit his old allotment. He decided, there and then, that as it was Friday, he was going to go on his adventure that evening.

The rest of the day dragged, knowing what plans lay ahead. While Keisha had been at the library to get a medical journal, Clive printed out street maps for the route he would need to take.

When Keisha finished for the day, she asked her usual questions, checking he'd be okay. 'I'll come and check you're fine at around eleven tomorrow. We can go to Tess's café for lunch.'

'Will being here at the weekend be more problematic? Are people more likely to notice any comings or goings?'

'We've held sleep studies over the weekends before when it was the only time people were able to attend. It won't be that different on campus, I just won't be about as much.'

Clive didn't want to say that he wouldn't be about as much that evening either. He decided to keep his set of keys quiet for the moment, not wanting Keisha to dissuade him from his adventure to the allotment. He also didn't want her to know he'd had a bigger glimpse into her world than he should have had.

He waited all of ten minutes after Keisha had left before setting off. He wanted to do as much of the trip in daylight as possible.

The walk to the east side of the city was a fair trek, passing along some dual carriageways that demonstrated how big the city of Southampton was. Fortunately they were roads that, despite their vastness and rumbling rush-hour traffic, still provided room for pedestrians and cyclists so he wasn't putting himself in any jeopardy as he journeyed along the couple of miles. The views consisted mainly of grey concrete, with many of the houses hidden, set back away from the road. It didn't make for the most picturesque tour ever, but he'd opted for the quickest route. The bad views ended when he reached the River Itchen. It was one of those spots where it was possible to see every part of the city: the new and the old. Warehouses that had seen better days next to flashy, new-build apartment blocks. Church spires and riverside pubs were all within his sightline. It seemed the bridge itself must be at least half a mile long and Clive decided to pause and get a drink and a snack from his bag before crossing the river.

It was nice to feel the spring breeze against his skin, the weather much kinder than it had been in recent days. The storms had cleared the way for these brighter, fresher evenings.

It was a good spot to indulge in the doughnut he'd purchased for the occasion to keep up his energy. He was sure that was what all the young runners were doing these days: eating high-energy snacks to keep them going. Those probably weren't as sugary, but he was an old man recovering from a heart condition. If this was the treat that ended him, he'd take it as somewhat of a triumph.

The river water was murky and the boats bobbing about were dappled in sunshine as the evening drew in, the clouds scattered across the sky. It was going to be one of the nicest Aprils for some time, according to the weather reports. However nice it was to be having an evening stroll, he reminded himself it would be more of a hike by the end. Especially as he would have to do the return journey.

Leaving half the doughnut for later, Clive pressed on. The next part of the journey would be the hardest with a hill to tackle. Out of breath and a sweaty mess, Clive reached the road he needed to turn into and took a moment with his handkerchief to compose himself. By the time he'd get there it would be past the normal opening hours, but thankfully Clive had long been a holder of one of the keys for the main gate. It was one of the possessions he'd had on him when he'd been admitted to hospital. He'd get a reputation as a key collector if he wasn't careful.

There was still a fractional amount of light in the sky and the street lamps were yet to come on. As he got closer, Clive summoned his last ounces of energy. He wanted to be in his allotment – his place of sanctuary – as soon as he could. If it was possible for a heart to belong somewhere, his definitely belonged amongst the peas and the carrots and his heart pumped a little harder the nearer he got. He almost broke into a jog when it was in sight. He needed to be there. He needed the answers he hoped it would give.

There was no one about and he managed to unlock the front gate with ease. He opted to lock it again once he was on the other side, not wanting any opportune thieves to come along and take advantage.

Clive's patch was the first on the right so he was there in an instant. Glancing out over his plot in the half light, he searched for some kind of memory. Perhaps the bit of ground where he fell? But there was no disturbed soil giving an indication in amongst the untended onions and asparagus. Instead it was as it had been, only more overgrown, the polytunnels he'd made still in place.

Something had been calling him here. He didn't have any recollection of collapsing, but he'd hoped that being here would remind him of what had happened. Of what had caused him to imagine a whole life with Nancy. He also hoped it would eradicate the version of events that kept replaying in his head. Ever since he'd been in hospital, this place had been calling him back.

Reaching his shed, a static sensation ran up Clive's arm when he placed the key in the shed's lock. It was excitement, he realised. It shot up and down his arm so quickly it made a shiver run along his spine and made him look round to see if anyone else was there.

There was no one. He was alone. He let the sensation that someone had walked over his grave wash over him, then entered his shed.

It was nice to get reacquainted with his striped canvas deck chair. He needed the rest. He had overestimated his fitness levels. The good thing about being in his chair again was that it was as cosy as a second skin. As soon as he settled himself down he felt bereft without his usual flask of tea to enjoy. It was another reminder that he wasn't here under his usual set of circumstances. At least he had his bottle of water. He took a sip, but it wasn't the same. Nothing felt the same any more. It was strange to feel that something was missing and know that mostly it was his memories. How was he supposed to rebuild the jigsaw if he didn't know what pieces belonged?

At least the musty smell of his shed gave a comfort he'd not experienced at the hospital. It meant he was able to think a fraction clearer and that was why he was here. In the hope of finding some clarity.

It was dark now in the shed and no doubt the lingering light outside was vanishing. There was a torch here ready for him. Once he got a hold of the light, he inspected the corners of his old shed. At least this space was like an old friend. It was full of cobwebs and trinkets and tools and it was in desperate need of decluttering, but he was often too busy on the plot to worry about the mess in here.

In amongst his things, he had numerous recycled pill pots that he used to house little things like nails and screws, stacked up in cabinets. There were old tea towels strewn about that were now used as oil rags or cloths for cleaning mud off his tools. There were three pairs of wellies. There was all sorts of paraphernalia that he kept here, rather than at the house, to save Nancy accusing him of hoarding.

There she was again. As if he had a home with a wife. Everyone was telling him she didn't exist. And yet she kept popping up in the cavern of his thoughts.

He glanced at the items again and tried to recall why he kept them here, aside from Nancy. It was because he liked to keep the house respectable. Still, the notion of Nancy lingered, giving him a headache he didn't need. Not when he had miles to trek back to his current abode.

A note by his empty thermos flask caught his eye. It was a page taken from his allotment journal. He couldn't recall having torn it out and yet he must have done. The writing was in his hand after all. He glanced at what had been so important it warranted vandalising his beloved book. In capital letters, he'd scrawled *NEW ALLOTMENT HOLDER*, going over the writing several times so it was bold. The information had clearly been important but it didn't make sense. And yet it seemed significant. Glancing at the page one more time, checking there was no other information, Clive folded it and popped it away. He'd have to look in his journal to see if there was anything else there that would throw more light on the obscure message. There were new allotment holders all the time, many people only lasting a season before deciding it wasn't for them.

Mulling over why he'd written the note, Clive closed his eyes and allowed himself to rest. It was nice to be in a cosy spot of his own, to sit and breathe for a while, taking in the familiar wood-stain scent of this space. He had spent far too many weeks inhabiting other people's spaces.

He'd not had a proper check of how the allotment was faring. It was too dark outside to see anything without using the torch and he didn't want to highlight the fact he was here any more than he'd already done. One of the neighbours (there was a whole row of houses that faced the green space) would probably report him for thieving vegetables. It was a sad fact that it wasn't an uncommon occurrence and his being the first space, it was often the one to be ransacked. He'd never forget the year some cheeky blighter had stolen all but one of his pumpkins just before Halloween.

'It's no good. This chair is far too comfy.' It sounded like a line from 'Goldilocks and the Three Bears', but it was an attempt to wake himself up. The last thing he needed was to fall asleep. What he needed to do was remember.

This place reminded him of lots of things: of the seeds he would normally be planning to plant now it was spring, of the crops that he should be harvesting but had been neglected and were going to seed, of the decluttering he needed to do but never got round to – but none of that was what he was looking for. What had happened here? And why did he write that note? Was it even significant?

Realising if he stayed still for too long his legs might seize up and he'd never make the return journey, Clive decided to have the remains of his doughnut and some more water in the hope it would prepare him. He couldn't help being annoyed at the wasted journey, with no memories whipping themselves up to help him. However nice it was to enjoy some time in his own space, he hadn't got what he'd come for. If only he knew what that was.

Everything was as it should be. Everything in his shed was as he remembered. Apart from the name 'Nancy' lingering in his thoughts and an odd, unhelpful note, there was nothing concrete.

Clive decided it was time to go. Being here was only causing him more confusion.

It was dim outside, with only a couple of nearby street lights casting fractured shards of illumination across the plot. It was hard to tell if anything was any different. There were no arrows pointing in the direction of what would unlock what he was unable to remember.

Setting off for the return journey, Clive was feeling decidedly worn out. He was beginning to question whether he was losing his marbles. He'd tried not to let on about these fleeting thoughts about Nancy, but the more they cropped up, the more he worried. The diagnosis of temporary delirium was beginning to look more and more unlikely. Because to him she was real.

It was a low point, knowing there were no answers at his allotment like he'd hoped.

Chapter Twenty-Five

Keisha

For all of my looking after Clive, I realise I've been neglecting myself. This is particularly evident as I peer down at my evening meal and wonder when I last had such paltry offerings. My noodles are gelatinous and aren't tempting in the slightest. Sitting on the sofa, I stare at the wall feeling somewhat broken. I know I need to work at getting everything back to normal. But that seems impossible with Lucy still unwell and with no plans in place for Clive.

'How are things?' I ask Rob when he returns. I'm still in my staring position.

Rob is like a shadow in the house now. He's become much like Hiro, our resident hermit, who comes and goes without a trace. Every day Rob returns with a bag full of any washing he needs to do for Lucy and a pre-packaged sandwich. He's given up on cooking, returning only to the house to sleep. What with making sure Clive is okay, I've not seen him for a few days.

'They're planning to do a scope tomorrow. Once that is done, hopefully she'll be one step closer to discharge. She's still on a liquid diet to try and calm any inflammation down.'

'That sounds more like good news.' Guilt pricks at me and my instinct makes me reach two fingers to my radial pulse. I've been too busy and tired to consider another visit to Lucy. I'll be so happy when she's able to return home. Seeing Rob's exhaustion reminds me that we're all under pressure.

'Do you want a takeaway?' I ask, after moving my uneaten noodles around my plate now that they're in a solid lump.

Rob plonks down onto the kitchen sofa as if the question has pushed him in that direction. 'You never eat takeaway. In all the time I've known you, you've never ordered one.'

'I think the time has finally come. It's about time I surprised myself by indulging. Anything will be more appetising than this.'

I don't like being wasteful. I think of Clive, and how he never buys any new clothes. But even I'm able to admit when something is inedible.

We agree on Chinese food and opt for the dishes that offer the most vegetable content. It's a forty-five-minute wait and even though my tummy is grumbling, we both get on with the life admin that we need to tend to. Rob puts on a load of washing and I plonk my uneaten meal in the bin and clean my plate, running a cloth over the kitchen surfaces for good measure.

When the doorbell goes my stomach rumbles in a low wail and I'm not sure if it is in relief or a call to the wild so everyone will know my belly needs to be first in the queue.

Much to my stomach's disappointment, there are no complimentary prawn crackers awaiting me on the other side of the door. Instead, I recognise PC Doyle, along with a colleague, on the doorstep.

'Evening, sorry to call so late, but we've been trying for the last two days and no one's answered.'

I sense the floor falling out from under me.

'I'm so sorry. Is there something I can help you with?'

Please go away, I echo in my head. I'd never wish an emergency on anyone, but if something relatively urgent draws them away right now, it will be a marvellous turn of events.

'We were wanting to talk to Mr Ellington. We understood he was staying with you. It's with regards to his property.'

'He's not here,' I say, short on anything more to tell them.

'Can you tell us where he is?'

No, no, I can't.

The knowledge that I have the police at the house and I can't come out with the truth is enough to make me want to run away. 'He's out,' I say.

It's not a lie.

'Is everything okay?' Rob joins me at the door after clocking I'm not having a discussion with a delivery driver.

'Do you know where Mr Ellington has gone out to?' PC Doyle sounds impatient.

'Who?' Rob asks.

'He said he was meeting a friend at the pub. I don't know which one. Can I take a message?' I say it quickly, hoping that the rush of words will camouflage my housemate's questioning expression.

'We need to speak with Mr Ellington directly. Can you ask him to call me when he's back?' PC Doyle looks over my shoulder to Rob. 'I don't suppose you know which pub Mr Ellington went to?'

Rob's expression is blank as he looks to me for answers. 'Nope. Not a clue.'

'Hmmmm…' the police officer muses. 'We're on duty all evening. I want to hear from him before I go off shift, understand?' He passes me a card.

It's at that moment that a terrified-looking delivery driver arrives. Judging by his age he's one of the university students and his expression says he's never been this close to what might be trouble before. 'Chinese order,' he says, weakly.

'I'll make sure he gets in touch as soon as he's back.' I try to sound confident and cross my fingers, hoping Rob doesn't say anything that will give the game away.

The police leave, but not without throwing a narrowing of the eyes in my direction. It sinks in that this is the closest I've been to trouble as well.

Once the delivery driver scarpers and I close the door, Rob rips open the prawn crackers and offers me one before also helping himself.

'What was that all about?'

I dish up our order of sweet and sour chicken with vegetable noodles and despite everything that is going on, my stomach continues to rumble.

Lucy obviously hasn't told him anything, like I requested. 'They're just trying to get hold of someone.'

'Yeah, but who? And why have they come here trying to find him? Unless we have a new housemate I don't know about?'

'He's not a housemate. They just think he lives here.' We both settle at the table, eager to eat.

'Why? What's been going on?' Concern pushes through Rob's features, an extra crease appearing on his brow.

I hesitate for a while, not least because I'm chewing the biggest piece of chicken. It's my first taste of takeaway in years and it's divine. The last one must have been nearly a decade ago, when we first moved into this house.

'No, nothing like that. It's just someone I've been trying to help out.'

'They're not taking advantage of you, are they? There are some nasty people out there. If you're saying this is his address it could be a fraud thing. He could be taking out credit cards and other stuff. Do you know where he is?'

'I know exactly where he is.'

'Who is he? Are you going to elaborate?'

I don't want to. I don't want to haul anyone extra into this temporary plan. 'He's nearby. I'll give him a call after we've finished eating and get him to contact the police.'

'And nearby is where exactly? Come on, Keisha. I've been spending every bit of my spare time up at the hospital. If there's something interesting going on, you have to tell me. It's not like we've ever had police turning up at the door and if they turn up again, don't you want me to back you up?'

'I haven't done anything wrong. At least nothing that would get me in trouble with the police, but work might have something to say about it. That's why I've only told a few people.'

'Have you told Lucy? Because I'm pretty sure her hospital admission will work as an alibi, if it comes to that. Are you going to tell me?'

I finally relent. If Lucy knows there's no harm in telling Rob as well.

'One of the study participants didn't have anywhere to be discharged to from the hospital. He's an elderly man, and has no one. I felt sorry for him. I came up with the idea, that as it was only short-term, he would be able to stay at the sleep lab at work. It's not in use. It seemed wasteful that there was a bed that was vacant when he needed one. In the daytime he's been helping out while Lucy is away.'

Rob chews on some of his food while taking in the information. 'Okay. None of that seems terribly unreasonable, so what's with the secrecy? Why do the police think he's here?'

'Work doesn't know. I knew it was something they wouldn't authorise. They'd make mutterings about health and safety and insurance and dismiss it before even considering it. So I said he was staying here temporarily so we had an address to discharge him to.'

'What made you consider it? It doesn't sound like the kind of idea you normally come up with.'

'I felt sorry for him.' It was more than that though. 'He's had a hard time of it. He thought something terrible had happened at his house and didn't feel able to return there. I guess I felt connected to him somehow and knowing what he's been through recently I knew someone had to help, so why not me?'

'Because you might get in trouble at work? Or with the police?'

'I'd already made the offer before I started to think about the possible consequences. I'd not really thought that far ahead before the suggestion was out there and being taken up. It's been fine so far and it's not for long. I thought it was going without a hitch. That was before I knew the police had been trying to get a hold of him.'

'Why do they want to speak to him?'

This part is complicated and I'm not even going to try and explain fully. 'There was potentially a break-in at his house. He doesn't want to return home because of what happened.'

'You'd best get your stowaway to ring them before they start looking for him more thoroughly.'

With the events of the evening, I've not been keeping an eye on the time. It's getting late. 'You're right. He might be in bed already and they didn't sound like they wanted to wait.'

Abandoning my plate of half-eaten food, I retrieve my mobile phone. Clive doesn't have one of his own, but as he is becoming an expert at answering the laboratory phone, hopefully he'll have the good sense to continue doing so out of hours.

The other end of the line rings until the answerphone kicks in.

'No answer,' I tell Rob. 'I'll try again.' If he was asleep, it might take two or three tries to get his attention. After the fourth go, I'm no longer sure a simple phone call will be the solution. 'He's not picking up.'

'Maybe he's worried that answering the phone will give away the fact that he's there. Is there any other way you can contact him?'

'No.' My voice is shrill. I'm not sure why I hadn't thought about how we'd get in contact with each other if there was a problem. 'What if he's had a fall?'

'There are lots of reasons I can think of that would explain him not answering. There are lots of reasons that don't involve being injured. I'm sure he's fine. He probably can't hear the phone if he's tucked away in that room.'

'Whether he's okay or not, it doesn't change the fact I need to get hold of him. Otherwise we'll have the police here again asking why he isn't back yet.'

'These are the kind of occasions when a car would be handy because we could do with getting there quicker than your half-hour morning hike. Do you have anyone who can get us over there to check he's okay?'

I think of George, but knowing his shift pattern for the week I know he's not free. I decide, as it's evening, Tess is the best person to ask. The café will be closed at this time of day.

Fortunately Tess isn't in bed already and is more than happy to help when I explain why. She's taken a shine to Clive. He's been in a few times for a breakfast of poached eggs and she's been telling me about it on my lunches. Most of our discussions revolve around Clive these days, and it's no surprise that I'm calling about him.

'I'll be there as soon as I can.'

While we wait we turn off all the house lights. If the house is dark, and PC Doyle returns, hopefully he'll think we're sleeping and leave us to it. I don't want to have to lie to the police twice in one day.

I just have to hope when we get there, Clive is okay.

My fingers don't move from my pulse point as we travel in Tess's car. It has been a quarter of an hour and I'm beginning to lose sensation in my arm. It is past the point of pins and needles; there's a fizzy numbness along my arm. Still, I can't take my fingers away from my neck. A sixth sense is shouting at me that something is wrong.

I know the sensible thing to do would be to stop taking my pulse, especially when I'm not counting like I should be. What help is it right now to know my heart is beating? I know I'm worried. I know something is wrong. But I can't seem to stop myself.

I try to count how many cars we pass to ease my anxiety and I'm thankful that neither Tess nor Rob are paying any attention to me. Tess is concentrating on driving and Rob is having a doze, his exhaustion obvious.

It doesn't help that I'm doing my usual thing of listing all the possible eventualities in my head. It is part of my job as his temporary guardian to make sure he is safe. Suddenly it doesn't seem as straightforward as simply providing him with a room. Maybe it is a death trap. Maybe all the safety labels in the world aren't enough to help a man who's lost his way.

Pickled onions. The resounding memory of my first meeting with Clive, the tangy taste, springs into my head. His allotment. If he's wandering off, will that be the place he goes to? He certainly mentions it often enough.

For the first time, and without thought, my hand springs away from my neck as I endeavour to message George. I need to keep him in the loop and if Clive isn't at the lab we might need his help. At least if that is the case, I know where to look first.

Chapter Twenty-Six

Clive

'Keisha,' Clive whispered under his breath. He wasn't sure why he kept saying her name. He was plodding along the pavement like a tortoise – all the energy having drained out of him about half a mile away from campus.

'Keisha,' Clive said again. It was a source of encouragement, he realised. Part of him wanted to give up, curl himself under a bush for the evening and not worry about when he'd be found. But he didn't want to be the defeated man who'd lost his mind as well as his wife. He was going to state the name of the friend he'd found, not the wife he'd lost. Clive attempted to say it louder, but it was barely a croak.

He wasn't sure why he'd been so stubborn about visiting the allotment. His snack and drink were long gone. A fat lot of good the doughnut had done him. He should have taken a whole bag of them.

It was a blessed relief when he reached the parade of shops near to the university. Even though a drink would be welcome, he didn't stop for fear he'd never start again. Once he was back, he planned to crawl into bed and remain there for as long as possible. He might even find he was able to sleep after his long jaunt.

When Clive turned into the lane that marked the start of the campus, his mind was slow to react when he spotted the lights in the laboratory were on. He'd not been so stupid to leave them on like that, had he?

Letting himself in, Clive jumped when there was a complete stranger sitting at the desk. He held a hand to his chest. His heart rate needed to settle and quick. He didn't want his heart to weaken again.

'Everything okay?' Clive asked, as if it was normal to be entering a private laboratory coming up to midnight.

'You must be Clive.' The young gentleman stood and held out a hand for Clive to shake.

Friend and not foe then. 'Indeed. And you are?'

'I'm Rob. Lucy's boyfriend. I've learned tonight that apparently we live together.'

'Is everything okay?' Clive repeated. He'd not expected any visitors and certainly not at this time of night. His thoughts flickered to Lucy and how unwell she'd been.

'Have you spoken to Keisha yet?'

'No.' Hearing her name was making him strangely emotional after repeating it so many times on his way here. Keisha meant he'd made it home.

'She's been trying to get hold of you.'

'Why has she been trying to get hold of me?'

Right at that moment, Keisha made her entrance and told him herself.

'You need to contact the police.'

Chapter Twenty-Seven

Keisha

I want to quit. I want to quit spreadsheets and numbers that mean nothing by themselves. I want to quit work so I can spend all day at Lucy's bedside until they make her better. I want to curl up in a ball and wait until everything has perspective again. I've got myself into this mess and I can't see my way out of it.

I've never been in the laboratory in the middle of the night. There's a bleakness to this place when there's no daylight in the room. The colourful gym balls and exercise bike are all grey inanimate objects at this hour of day.

Clive is currently on the phone and Rob and I are hiding in the kitchenette trying to be quiet, while listening intently. When we got here and there was no sign of him, panic set in. He hasn't told me he's able to come and go as he pleases. Not that there is anything wrong with that, but it would have been nice to know. If I'd have known I would have supplied him with a cheap pay-as-you-go mobile phone so that in an emergency, such as this, I would have been able to get in touch with him. Instead, at the time, we decided I should scour the campus and Tess should drive to the allotment in the car. Rob stayed put in case he came back. As luck had it, Clive turned up twenty minutes later.

He looks decidedly dishevelled on his return, his jacket is off, a spider's web is attached to what there is of his grey hair and there is a flush to his cheeks that's so bright he may well have a fever. His excuse that he's back from popping to the shop doesn't sit right with me and now it's making me question everything.

'Right, yes, okay, I'll see you then,' Clive responds on the phone.

It's impossible to hear the other end of the conversation. I'm curious to know what's being said, even though, strictly speaking, it's none of my business. But then again, at some point it's become my business, I realise. I care for Clive.

'Uh-huh. Will do,' Clive says.

I open the fridge door to pop my head in there briefly to cool myself down. There are a few items in here to keep Clive going, along with his beetroot juice with their uniform labels on the bottles, and behind them, what I recognise to be a jar of pickled onions. I've no idea when he snuck that in here. After a minute, the plastic-pig fridge magnet that Lucy installed to stop her munchie sessions starts oinking at me. It takes all my strength not to finish it off for good by 'accidentally' letting it fall to the ground.

I think I ran around the campus in record time before seeing Clive's figure in the window of the lab. Not having the chance to reduce my sweatiness isn't helping my mood. I want to be mad at him, but right now exhaustion is winning. It's probably fortunate for both Clive and the pig.

'What did they say?' I ask once Clive is off the phone.

'They want to speak to me on Monday afternoon. Nothing to worry about, they said. You don't need to look so concerned. I'm not in trouble.'

'Where are you going to meet them? Do they want you to go to the station?'

'Ah. They said they'd come and see me at home. I guess they didn't mean here,' Clive says, with a chuckle. 'I didn't really think about that when I agreed.'

'What time did they say they'd arrive?'

'About two o'clock.'

'Okay,' I say, even though it's not really okay. 'Will you need someone with you? I'm not sure I can get the time off with such short notice.'

'I'll be okay by myself. I can just get a taxi over to yours, save inconveniencing anyone. I've been doing enough of that as it is.'

'Are you sure?' I reply, knowing that I'm very unsure myself, but too tired to come up with any other plan of action.

'It'll be fine.'

I wish my tiredness would allow me that kind of strength of conviction.

Tess arrives back from the allotment and insists on giving Rob and I a lift back home. Not wanting to keep any of us up any longer than necessary, we ensure Clive is okay (I take a quick set of observations to make sure his flushed cheeks aren't an indicator of anything else) before we head off.

'Is everything okay?' Tess gestures to the blood pressure cuff as she asks.

I should nod. I want to issue out some kind of reassurance that he's okay, but is he really? His heart rate is fine, as is his BP, but are those indicators really telling me everything I need to know? Because something tells me knowing his heart rate is in the correct parameters isn't telling me the whole story, and nor is Clive.

Chapter Twenty-Eight

Clive

When all was quiet (it was surprising how busy the university campus was turning out to be in the middle of the night), Clive retrieved his allotment journal from the bedside drawer he'd placed it in. Perhaps what he'd found was a half-note. What didn't make sense in isolation might when he found the rest of what he'd written.

It was a brown moleskin notebook and it was well-thumbed. Clive took pride in the things he'd documented inside its pages. It was not something he'd ever choose to deface unless it was very important. He'd invested time and effort into its contents.

He leafed through the journal page by page. He'd had it for at least ten years and it contained all the information about his allotment for every season. He knew what varieties of potato had done best (Maris Piper), what organic remedies he'd tried when there had been a particularly bad infestation of blackfly and in which row he'd planted which seeds each year.

Since he'd been in hospital, even though it had been with him, he'd not opened the journal. He'd not really felt like it. There didn't seem much point when he wasn't in the throes of planning what to do next. It would have only depressed him. Even now it made him sad that he wasn't down there every day sowing seeds that would come to fruition over the coming weeks.

Clive cheered himself up with a sip of hot chocolate. It was the first he'd had with a tot of whisky after he'd toured the alcohol section in the Polish store and quickly worked out that whisky translated as whisky and they had some miniatures on sale. They were perfect for the job.

It was easy to find the torn page. It was like a scar in the middle of the book, reminding him of the scar in the crook of his elbow.

He shook his head at another non-memory.

Placing his mug down, he gave the journal his full attention, creasing it wide open so he was able to see. Other than the tear where the paper had been removed, there was nothing else. No other notes or indicators as to why he'd ripped out a page. The only mark was on the next piece of parchment where it was possible to see where he'd pressed so hard the words had made an impression.

Clive got the note from his bag to check it matched up and if it was definitely his writing. It was, but he was no closer to knowing what *new allotment holder* meant or why it had resulted in him defacing his precious book.

It really wasn't the answer he'd been after. All that effort and it was something else he couldn't remember or understand. The only upside was the combination of exercise and a midnight whisky meant he slept for the first time in what felt like forever, like he didn't have a care in the world.

During the night, he dreamed of Nancy.

Chapter Twenty-Nine

Keisha

In the morning, with only fits and starts of sleep to go on, I decide to write myself a list. I start scribbling it while enjoying my morning bowl of rice.

Lists are my go-to when life isn't going to plan and I'm not sure how I've been flailing through the past week without one. I like to write down goals rather than tasks. Writing a list of tasks, such as 'sort the laundry' and 'don't forget to make sure Lucy's red thong isn't caught in the washing machine again', won't give me the same satisfaction as writing down goals.

- Complete my PhD and find out if beetroot juice will help cure broken hearts.
- Get through Tess's 100 dates.

It is far easier to write those than the real underlying hope:

- Find someone to love my broken heart.

Suddenly, I find I'm crying. It doesn't feel satisfying writing them down after all. Instead, they feel too big. Too absolutely huge for me to tackle. I feel overwhelmed.

The thing is, not many people appreciate my passion for my PhD study. But my desire to look into broken heart syndrome stems back as far as I can remember. I feel like this is the mystery I'm supposed to solve – my life's ambition. Nobody fully understands how takotsubo cardiomyopathy occurs. The sudden ballooning of one of the vessels is a little understood condition and while there are some drugs that can help heal a person if they survive, there is nothing available to prevent it from happening in the first place. There is no algorithm to indicate who will suffer from it and who will not. I've spent my life in a laboratory in an attempt to save at least one person. To make sure at least one heart doesn't end up shattered. I am determined to make up for the life I was unable to save.

I often have to remind myself, on the days I am plugging endless figures into a spreadsheet, that this will one day help someone. I might not be there when it happens or oversee the event, but I could, one day, change the path of someone's life. This could all be worth it.

Clearing away my tears, I realise my mistake. Perhaps I should try breaking down the goals into smaller steps.

I know what I need to do first before anything else.

• Find new accommodation for Clive.

The anxiety about housing Clive has become too much, especially knowing he's been out wandering. Something about it doesn't sit right and I know I'm going to have to speak with him about it so I can put my finger on what's wrong.

The next step is easy to come up with.

- Get Lucy back to full health.

Another tear slips out at that thought. I am missing my friend dearly. I would normally be talking these kinds of concerns through with her. Having her back at work and home will get more than fifty per cent of my world back to where it should be.

Clive has been a great help, I have to give him his due. But, equally, labelling the telephone with 'People will hear your smile!' isn't quite the same as liaising with cardiology consultants in different counties. There are skills I won't be able to teach him in a fortnight.

Writing these things down makes my chest ease a little. It's hard to admit that in the face of attempting to do the right thing it has ended up feeling like the wrong thing.

Alongside those goals, I add some mini ones.

- Call George.
- Find out how long the waiting list is for the flats Clive wants to move into.

I scribble a bullet point on the page, struggling to know what to write after it. I was going to add *Liaise with Clive about his police interview*, or should it be *Liaise with the police*?

Whatever they wanted to speak to him about, it seemed important. There is still a question mark over what has happened to him and why he keeps mentioning the wife that never existed. The more time I spend with Clive the more I want to know, but the less I am able to find out anything. Hopefully the police are one step closer to really knowing what is going on. Because what hope do I have of finding out anything else when my avenues of enquiry are only producing dead ends?

Chapter Thirty

Clive

Clive was getting used to occupying unfamiliar spaces. He decided the first thing he should do in Keisha's home was get acquainted with the layout of the place. It would look odd if a police officer arrived and asked to use the toilet facilities and he wasn't able to point them in the right direction.

Because it was a house with tenants, it felt far more like prying. Whereas back at the lab, the rooms were owned by the university, here, they were people's personal spaces. Fortunately he didn't need to go into the bedrooms other than sticking his head round the door to check which one was supposed to be his.

There was a narrow corridor with one room to the left that had a sign saying: *Hiro. Keep Out*. Keisha had already said not to go in there. They never knew whether their housemate was in or out and he didn't like it if he was disturbed, apparently. Clive was hoping he wasn't home. It would be hard to explain why he'd turned up and the police had followed shortly afterwards.

The corridor opened out to the living area. It was neat and basic, a kitchen area against one wall, a dining table and lounge area with a sofa and TV. The floor had white tiles, as did the kitchen wall, almost as if the landlord had got them on special offer. The walls were also white and the sofa had a white blanket thrown over it. There were no pictures hanging up and it was almost clinical in appearance.

It made Clive think about his home for the first time in a while. His living room was far more homely than this and had a lot more colour. It was dated, admittedly, but Clive liked the brown-and-orange swirling carpet that he wouldn't be able to get anywhere these days. There was nothing here filling the space, but in his he had old boxes, shelves full of trinkets and ornaments. He had two upright chairs and a sofa all in green. They kind of clashed with the carpet, but that's why he liked them. His home was as colourful as he was, he thought as he admired the Hawaiian shirt he'd opted for today. He'd hoped the bright red-and-orange flowers would cheer him up after his failed trip to the allotment. So far he hadn't worked out why he'd written the note and his shirt hadn't brought the cheer he was hoping for. As far as he could tell he was still in Keisha's bad books and all he had to show for it was a stupid bit of paper that made no sense.

He thought on it some more as he wandered round the house, heading up the stairs to the other bedrooms. It seemed important and yet *new allotment owner* also meant nothing to him. It certainly didn't relate to why he'd lost Nancy. He considered telling Keisha, but then it would mean admitting what he'd been up to. Although he was beginning to think he should just come clean with her.

A knock at the door brought his short tour of the house to an end.

Clive took his time getting downstairs. Even though he'd put on a cheery smile when talking about it to Keisha, he was dreading encountering the police. Surely this should be over already if he'd only ever dreamed up the crime in his imagination.

'Ah, Mr Ellington, at last. It's been quite the task to try and get a hold of you,' said the officer, once Clive had opened the door.

'Sorry about that.' Clive showed PC Doyle and his colleague PC Yeung through to the living space. 'Can I get you both a drink?'

'We're fine, thank you. How come you haven't been here when we've called round?'

Clive breathed a sigh of relief at them declining his offer. For all his familiarising he'd not thought to check where they kept the mugs. That would have given his cover away immediately.

'I've been looking into new housing possibilities. This is all very nice, but it's a bit bland. I need somewhere to call home again.'

'I have some good news for you, in that case.'

'You do?'

Not being entirely truthful with the police was making him feel somewhat of a criminal. Staying at the university wasn't the world's biggest crime, but it could be classed as trespassing if he were to be found out. For some reason, he felt sure he was in trouble. He'd not expected them to declare they had good news.

'Yes, the forensic tests haven't come up with anything. Your house is all yours again. We wanted to be certain, but you're free to move back in whenever you wish.'

'Really? They didn't show anything?' There had been a part of Clive expecting the police to find something.

'Nothing.'

'But…' Clive's mind went back to what he thought had happened. It had seemed so real.

'I know what played out in your head was very upsetting. It was an unusual case for us and, because of your altered state of mind, we didn't want to dismiss the possibility. We wanted to make sure we hadn't missed anything.'

'But you have, haven't you?'

'What would that be?' The two colleagues glanced at each other, a look of pity in both their expressions for the eccentric gentleman in his bright shirt.

'Nancy.' The name left his mouth like a heavy stone dropping in the ocean.

'Nancy wasn't there. Nancy was never there.'

'If that's true, why does it feel like she was?' He knew something was amiss, but arguing with the police didn't seem like the smartest move, even in his new life as a semi-criminal, however much he was beginning to believe he was right and they were wrong.

'Like I've said, we've looked into everything. We've investigated more than we originally planned just to make sure. We've even checked the records and you've never been married. I don't want to upset you by dwelling on the fact, but as the doctors have said, those events and the memories of Nancy were clearly brought about by delirium.'

It seemed impossible that Nancy was made up. Even though this had already been stated to Clive, he realised the police involvement had given him hope. Not that he'd ever want to come home and find his wife dead. No one would want that. What he'd hoped was real was that feeling, that companionship and life together. He kept seeing it in fragments. The moments when he'd returned home to his wonderful wife who'd made a casserole with vegetables from the allotment. Then he'd see the same moment once more, only this time he was alone, washing and chopping the veg himself. Two versions of his life kept playing in his head and he was at pains to tell the difference.

'The important thing that we wanted to let you know is that you can move home.'

Clive shook his head. Even if they were trying to convince him that his life with Nancy wasn't real, somehow it didn't feel like it was a home any more without her there. It made no sense at all, but there was a blood-stained carpet in his head and it was enough to block any rational thought.

'I'm going to continue looking for somewhere else to live. Thanks all the same.'

He didn't want to sound ungrateful, but his despondent tone gave him away. He was back to being Mr Cantankerous. It had been on the cards ever since his trip out.

'If you ever need anything, you have my card,' said PC Doyle.

Clive nodded sadly, the false memories stirring up far too many emotions. 'If you hear they've created a memory erasure, you let me know.' He attempted a smile, but it fell beside that stone in the ocean.

Chapter Thirty-One

Keisha

'You look wretched,' Tess says when I arrive at the café the following Tuesday. I didn't make it in yesterday after spending my time making sure Clive got to the house okay for his police interview and then worrying the entire time he was there.

'Sleep's been evading me. It's been a strange couple of days, as you know.'

'Do you know how the meeting went?'

I take up my usual seat and Tess delights me when she immediately produces a vegetarian lasagne for us both and joins me.

'Clive said it was only to let him know that he was able to move back to his house.'

'Couldn't they have told him that over the phone?'

I shrug. 'I guess, given how his hallucination affected him, they didn't want to risk telling him while he was alone in case he went on to have another cardiac event. It must have been a nod to their care in the community.'

'Do you really think that was all there was to it? Is Clive telling you everything?'

'I'm not sure any more. He hasn't told me anything more about Friday evening. But saying that, I don't have any other reason to doubt him. I think the only thing that isn't telling Clive everything is his memory. There's more to it, I'm sure... Lucy keeps telling me whenever we video chat I should try and investigate, but there's nothing to look into.'

'How is Lucy?'

'Feeling better now they've done the endoscopy. They'll give her the results soon, but she already said her appetite is improving.'

'That's good.'

'It is.' My own stomach feels better too, as if a knot of tension has undone itself. 'George is going to pop by soon. Maybe he can tell us what he thinks. He's taking Clive to view the retirement flats this afternoon so hopefully he won't be hiding in the sleep lab much longer.'

'George, eh?' There's a twinkle in Tess's eye.

I shake my head to discourage any thoughts in that direction. 'He's supporting getting Clive new accommodation, that's all.'

Tess dips some garlic bread into her lasagne sauce. 'It's such a shame that Clive can't move back to his house when there is nothing wrong with it. Even the police reassuring him hasn't been enough, I take it?'

I shake my head as I help myself to a piece of bread too. I don't normally indulge, but I feel like an extra bit of carb loading isn't going to go amiss with the week I'm having.

'It does seem a shame. When I first heard his account of what happened, it was really shocking. Even when I think about it now and the images it conjured up in my head, it sends a shiver down my spine. That's hearing it as a third party. I can't imagine what it would have been like to believe those things had happened. I knew that was why I had to help him. I understood completely why he wouldn't want to go back there.'

Mentioning the shiver means a real one finds its way through my autonomic nervous system and sends goose bumps along my arms. Images from my past try to bubble to the top of my consciousness. It's the thought of blood that does it, the pooled, unpumping kind that has formed a puddle in a place it shouldn't be.

'You know, I've been thinking… My lodger Iness, the foreign student, leaves at the end of this week and the next foreign student has been cancelled. The university isn't able to arrange a replacement immediately so the spare room upstairs will be free for a couple of weeks.'

'Really?'

'Yes. If he can't move into his new accommodation straight away, I'd be more than happy to help him while I'm between students.'

The café door pings to indicate new custom and it's George joining us. I'm glad to see him, even though I am still eating and would rather not have him witness me chomping away. That fluttering feeling creeps into my abdomen again. Strange when I'm not unwell, I note.

'Love begins at forty, I'm telling you!' Tess says before getting up to sort out a further portion of lunch for George.

I'm momentarily confused, and it takes me a minute to realise she's referring to his date number that wasn't really a date.

When the usual niceties are over and Tess finishes replenishing and supplying food and drink, we are quick to settle to the matter in hand: Clive.

'The police didn't find anything then?' George says, tucking into his grub like a man that is rarely offered such good fare.

'Not according to Clive. They were just letting him know he's free to go back to his house,' I confirm.

George nods as he finishes a mouthful. 'The police went through all his medical notes, you know. Dr Hutchins said the old notes are still missing. You have to swear that neither of you breathe a word to anyone. I'll get in trouble at work if anyone finds out I've told you.'

I'm not the only person taking risks in order to help Clive.

'My lips are sealed,' I say and Tess mutters her complete agreement.

'The paramedic's notes say he was found not far from the allotment, most likely on his way home. He was very unwell at the time and fairly incoherent and all he kept saying was he knew what had happened. The police wanted to check that what he reported couldn't have happened elsewhere. They didn't seem worried about the old notes being missing.'

'Are the police sure Nancy isn't real?' I ask for added clarification.

'Nobody who knows Clive knows anything about her. They've gone through what they've investigated with me and I'm afraid she is a figment of his imagination.' George takes a gulp of his Diet Coke. 'They've been really thorough, as you know. They checked and there's no record of Clive having ever been married. As far as they're aware, Nancy never existed and she certainly hasn't been recently murdered at Clive's property.'

Tess flops back. 'What a horrid nightmare to have.'

'It's not made up,' I say. 'It's as real to Clive as if it actually happened. That's why he fears returning home so badly.'

'It's a horrible thing for his imagination to present him with. Like I said, the police have been very good and taken those concerns seriously, but it's not unearthed anything.'

'Poor Clive,' I say.

'Now we just need to work out what he wants to do with the house. I'll talk to him about it this afternoon when I visit the flats with him. If he gives the okay, between us we can get it on the market.'

'Saying goodbye to the memory that never was,' Tess says, wistfully.

Chapter Thirty-Two

Clive

Like every morning these days, Clive started it with his beetroot juice. At first the earthy taste hadn't been to his liking. He much preferred to start the morning with a hot cup of English breakfast tea, but now he was a couple of weeks in, he was getting used to the rustic taste. Although, to be fair, it might be the fact he knocked it back like it was tequila that was helping. As always, he jotted down the details for Keisha. They were pretty much the same details on repeat: the batch number, the amount, the time of day. But she'd need this record for her study. The juice set him up for the day at least and he was feeling a lot more optimistic than he had been recently by the time George arrived to take him for a viewing.

'This is very kind of you. Especially on your day off,' Clive said.

'It's no problem. I'm only sorry I wasn't able to do it sooner.'

George held the car door open for Clive to get in and again for him to get out once they'd arrived at the flats. The new complex was a stone's throw from the allotments. They'd been built on the old grounds of a private school that had sold off some of the land.

Clive was going to enjoy getting a peek inside the flat complex. He'd watched it go up as he dug up carrots and potatoes on the other side of the road. At least it wouldn't leave him far away from where he wanted to be. Although he wasn't really sure where that was any more. He felt as if his anchor had been cut off and now he was in the midst of grabbling to find something to cling on to.

'I think we need to head to the show flat. The estate agent said he'd meet us there and then take us round. What are your first impressions?' asked George.

'It's an upgrade from my current living quarters.' Clive smiled, but it fell short of reaching his eyes.

'Has it been hard staying there?' George asked, as they made their way to a central building that had red flags advertising new homes for sale.

'Quite the contrary. It's been a delight. I think I'm going to rather miss it.'

'Is the lab turning out to be more entertaining than the allotment?'

'In its own way, yes. My tea-making abilities have never been so appreciated.'

'I'm sure they'd still engage your services as a tea-maker if you offer.'

'Do you think they would?'

'You'll never know unless you ask.'

Clive hadn't considered the possibility of staying on. The thought gave him the real smile he'd been after. They entered the sales room, but there was no one there waiting to greet them.

'Do you think you'll miss your old house?' said George.

Clive replied with a blank expression, his smile fading. 'I don't think I will. My memories of my home life are rather muddled since, well, you know. My overriding recollection is of something that didn't happen there. I don't feel the pull of anything wanting me back, only the last memory pushing me away.'

'Do you not even want to visit? See if that brings back any happy memories?'

'I have to admit, I'm afraid that it'll make that scene play in my head even more fiercely. Look, don't ever say this to anyone else will you? Especially not Keisha.' Clive glanced round to make sure no one else was about to join them.

'Cross my heart.'

'What happened made me want to end my life. I was so utterly convinced Nancy had been killed.' Even saying her name caused his heart to fluctuate. 'I wanted to go and meet my maker as well. Life didn't seem worth continuing with. I wanted to go and be with her. Daft as it may sound, I'm not sure what hurt more… Seeing my wife dead or being told I didn't have a wife at all. The love I felt for her was so real. Even now I find it hard to accept that it only ever existed because of a having a high temperature.' Everything about her had seemed so certain, until he'd been told it wasn't.

'Wow. When you put it like that I think I understand. Whatever memories that house holds, it's not worth the possibility of your heart breaking all over again, right?'

'Precisely. Given how poorly it's coped recently it might finish this old bugger off.'

'And we don't want that.'

Clive nodded. 'I'm glad to say, I agree. We don't want that. If love exists like the one I imagined, it's worth staying on the planet a bit longer. Keisha and you have shown me that maybe life isn't all that bad… You two have helped me from the kindness of your own hearts.'

'Let's hope it does exist.'

'It will for one of us at least. I'm well past it, but you're not.' Clive gave George a mischievous grin, recalling the way the lad always got misty-eyed over Keisha.

'If you don't mind me asking, what do you want us to do about the house?'

Clive paused in thought, rubbing his chin for a moment. 'Selling it seems like the wisest thing to do.'

'What about your things? Won't you want them for your new place?'

'Some, perhaps.'

'Do you know what you'd like to keep?'

'My chair. The dining table. My kettle and toaster.'

'We'll write a list. I can make sure anything you want to keep gets delivered here.'

They were talking as if they'd viewed the flat already. Just then a tall, suited chap came in as if the wind were carrying him.

'Sorry about the delay.' He shook both their hands, neglecting the formality of introductions. 'Shall we go and have a look? Preference was for ground floor, correct?'

'I thought that would be sensible. What do you think, Clive?'

'That does seem sensible. Save some energy for the allotment.'

'You're lucky, we have one left. Let me show you.'

The gentleman rushed them as if there were only five spare minutes in his day to give them the tour. It seemed an odd way to go about trying to sell a place.

'Communal access, but only one entrance on the ground floor so the corridor is almost an extension of the flat.' He rattled off facts about the place so quickly that Clive was through the kitchen, lounge and bedroom, and being shown the walk-in shower before actually comprehending any of the features.

'I hope you're keeping up with this,' he whispered to George.

'Just about.'

By the time they were at the end of their whistle-stop tour, Clive found he was verging on being breathless. The space was small, but it was enough to wear a man his age out when being motored around it.

'So, what are your thoughts? You'll have to decide today if you do want it. There are others wanting the ground-floor apartment. It's a prized position for retirement flats in my experience.'

'I need to check out one very important thing.'

'What's that, sir?'

'I need to see how long it'll take me to walk to my allotment. Young George and I will go for a stroll and check to see if the distance is agreeable.'

'And if it is?'

'You'll have your sale. Now if you could wait here patiently like a good boy.' Clive didn't mind talking to someone like that when they'd not even bothered to give him their name. George stifled a grin like an excellent co-conspirator as they made their way out.

'What do you think of the place?' George asked, when they were beyond the manicured forecourt and on the path.

'Not enough colour for my liking, but that can be added.' The one-bedroom flat had reminded him of Keisha's shared house. All very practical, everything where it should be, but lacking any injection of personality. He wondered what charity-shop trinkets he would be able to find to brighten up the place.

'Is it near enough to the allotment? I don't think we'll find anywhere closer.'

'I know it's close enough, but I wasn't about to sign anything that quickly. I don't like salespeople who are like that. Too pushy for their own good. I'm lucky in that I inherited the house I live in. I've never had to pay a mortgage so I have enough saved to buy the flat, but people like that never make me feel encouraged to hand money over.'

'Ah, so you're making him wait.'

'Of course. Plus it's an excellent chance for you to see my pride and joy. See how it's faring with me being away. You don't mind, do you? If I'm keeping you, please say.' Perhaps seeing it in daylight would bring back the memories that had been missing the other night.

'No, you're good. I've got as long as it takes.'

When they reached the T-junction, Clive hesitated. It was a glimpse into his old life. If he chose to wander down the side road rather than over to the allotment, he'd be heading back to his house. He glanced across, recalling the many times he'd strolled along here with his wheelbarrow. Empty when he ventured out, full when he returned home. Had there really never been anyone to receive him at the other end?

'Are you sure you don't want to at least see it before making any big decisions? You don't have to go in,' George asked, seeing his hesitation.

The upset of knowing Nancy wouldn't be there caught Clive unawares. There was a swell in his throat so big that he yanked a hankie out of his pocket in preparation.

'I'm sorry,' he said, wiping his tears away one by one.

'You don't need to be sorry. I think I have my answer. I asked to be certain.'

'Maybe one day I'll be able to walk by without getting upset. But if I can't even glance up the avenue without it happening, it's not going to be any time soon.'

Clive finished wiping his face and placed his handkerchief neatly in his jacket pocket. 'Come and see my pride and joy.'

The allotment was definitely more scraggly than usual, but not as bad as he'd imagined it would be. He had a feeling some of his allotment pals who knew he'd been poorly had been doing a bit of tinkering to keep it tidy at the very least.

'It's impressive,' George said, taking in the strip of land and admiring the rest of the plots.

Clive spotted Frank was busy weeding on his, two rows up. He'd know about any new owners. 'Go and admire my polytunnels. Made them myself. I'm just going to say a quick hello to Frank.'

It was nice to see a familiar face.

'Alright, Clive. You're looking well. How's it going? You going to be back soon?'

Clive spent a moment filling in Frank on his health, letting him know he was moving somewhere smaller and then he'd be back.

'Can I ask you something, Frank? Did I ever talk to you about someone called Nancy?'

If she was real, he surely would have talked about her to his friends.

Frank, who was leaning on his shovel, shook his head. 'You've never mentioned anyone called Nancy.'

'Oh.' Clive wasn't sure why it was a surprise. 'Do any of the new allotment holders go by that name?'

Perhaps that was the link. Maybe he'd met someone by that name, fallen instantly in love, and found himself in a delirious state over the whole thing.

'No. Both new owners are chaps. Haven't had a chance to introduce myself yet, but I haven't seen them here with any family or anything. Why?'

'Oh, nothing.' It was nothing. Not the answer he'd hoped for.

'You okay?' George asked once Clive had returned.

He wished he knew.

The allotment, at least, was neutral ground. Here the mishmash of memories was less noticeable. This was his shed. His tools. His hobby.

Here he didn't have to miss his wife. He just had to try his hardest not to dwell on the fact she wasn't waiting for him at home.

Chapter Thirty-Three

Keisha

I have lots of questions building up. I want to ask Clive about his past. I want to ask where he went last Friday. I want to ask how the flat viewing went. But I keep freezing. Every time I go to ask, I end up with my fingers hovering over my pulse point instead. I'm really not keen on any kind of confrontation and it feels like this might be one. How do I ask him to tell me the truth when sometimes he doesn't seem to know himself? Instead, as so often happens, my awkwardness is crippling my ability to act naturally.

We're in the middle of a six-minute walk test when the phone rings. We've got Mrs Baldwin in for her weekly check. There's a flush to her cheeks and I'm not sure if it's because of the exertion or Clive's company. I'm timing proceedings and Mrs Baldwin is wandering into her fourth minute. Clive is busy noting down how many laps she is managing. Both need to be accurate so we let the ringing continue. The answerphone takes a message and it is only once Mrs Baldwin has gone, with a couple of extra pink wafers in a tissue again thanks to Clive, that I get the chance to check who the call was from.

When I discover it's Rob, I ring him back straight away.

'Is everything okay?' Whenever he calls my heart flitters like a bird in a cage. Lucy's illness has been a mystery and I can't help it when my brain jumps two phases ahead and imagines the worst possible outcome.

'Lucy's going to be discharged in a couple of days.'

'She is? That's amazing.' A mix of shock and delight floods me. 'Is she well enough to come home?'

'They found the problem. They think she'll recover quickly with a course of antibiotics.'

'What was the problem?' After weeks of being poorly, I'd lost hope of it being a simple fix.

'Once the inflammation had subdued enough, they found a piece of egg shell embedded in the lining of Lucy's stomach. The doctors said the probability of it happening were extremely remote, but it was a large piece that had lodged away from the stomach's natural enzymes so it had caused the widespread irritation that caused her to be so unwell.'

I gawp and blink in Clive's direction, not quite able to believe it. For the weeks that Lucy has been unwell, I'd been hypothesising all sorts of diagnoses, all of which were either long-term or incurable. 'So, they've removed the shell and she should just get better?' What are the chances?

'That's what they're thinking. She already has her appetite back. She wants me to buy her a sandwich, although, funnily enough she's requested that it shouldn't be egg and cress. But she needs to progress with food gradually. The dietician said binge eating after a period like this will make her feel ill so they're giving her a menu to follow over the next couple of weeks.'

'She'd better stick to it.' I laugh in wonder and disbelief. 'And don't let her cook. You know the meal she had before she got sick was an omelette.'

There is a buzz of adrenaline running though my veins. I can't quite believe it. I jump out of the chair when I come off the phone, all thoughts of my previous questions leaving me.

'That sounds like a happy noise,' Clive says from the kitchen area where he's cleaning the cups and plates.

'It is,' I say. *It is.* 'Lucy is better.' *Lucy is going to be okay.* I quickly relay the details.

'So you reckon her cooking skills caused this?' Clive asks with a laugh.

I nod. I won't ever be so impolite as to point it out to her, but it seems that way. 'I remember distinctly that the last meal we had was eggs. It was the morning we came to see you. For the first few days I assumed she had food poisoning, salmonella or something. But I couldn't work out why it wasn't both of us.'

'I think I might understand the labels now,' Clive says, a small smile stretching across his face.

'Believe me, I do them for her own good. Not just because I'm a tad on the neurotic side.' I also smile.

Lucy is better.

Clive is going to move in with Tess.

Things are moving on even though I'm standing still.

But my jubilation is met with sadness as I realise there won't be biscuits served on doilies once Clive has gone.

Chapter Thirty-Four

Clive

On the occasions when Clive managed to join Keisha for lunch, he enjoyed it immensely. Not that they were sitting at the same table. That would be after date number forty-two was complete.

There was corned beef hash on the specials menu and it had been many years since Clive had enjoyed that particular home comfort. It was an easy choice when Tess asked for his order and she offered him a wink, knowing they were all in cahoots.

'She knows you're here then?' Tess said in a whisper.

'With full permission.' Clive nodded in confirmation.

He wasn't au fait with dating. The modern culture of using the internet or phone apps to find love was not something he was familiar with, so it was as much for his entertainment as anything.

Not that entertainment was the right way to think of it. He wasn't here to laugh or make unfavourable comments. He was here to observe, as if taking part in a study on human behaviour. He was pretty sure that was the way Keisha looked at it.

Clive thought about his love life, but those memories weren't there. There were only fragments. Those moments would be whipped away as soon as they arrived. It was odd. His delirious episode did mean he knew what it felt like to be in love. But Keisha wanted to know whether the pulse rose or if the heart contracted when it fell in love. And much like the research project he was part of, in the same way that a heart wasn't usually monitored when it broke, the same was true of when it fell in love. It was unlikely there would be anyone present at the time to check the heart rate and blood pressure and good job, quite frankly. It would rather ruin the special moment.

Clive had settled on a pink shirt today, to blend in with Tess's pastel shades. He'd not gone as far as adding sequins to really fit in with the décor. He doubted Keisha would regard that as camouflage.

He stopped daydreaming when the café door rang and for a second he didn't know where to settle his gaze. He didn't want to stare; that would be too obvious. At least he'd picked a better vantage point this time.

The man who had walked in was tall and gangly and his Adam's apple was too pronounced, as if he hadn't quite grown into his features. He may well have been one of the local students popping in for his lunch.

Clive glanced over to Keisha, her fingers lightly placed on her wrist in a way that made what she was up to unobvious. There was no flush to her cheeks, if anything she was paler than usual.

The lanky guy, or date forty-two as he would become known, bought his coffee and went and sat with Keisha. He looked like a nervous interview candidate, already aware he was unqualified for the job.

Clive wasn't close enough to hear what was being said (maybe he'd strike third time lucky with his stakeout spot), but they were talking and that seemed like a good sign. He wished he was able to lip read, but he was already conscious of staring more than he should. He was doing his best to be inconspicuous.

One thing he had noticed was that Keisha wasn't smiling. Whatever was being said hadn't even made her curl her lip, and there was a complete lack of any laughter. Those were things that struck Clive as essential in a relationship. Those were the things that made the heart love a little harder. Those moments that made it easier to appreciate a person more each day.

A shiver ran through him as if someone had jumped on his grave. The complete sense of having loved pushing though his core. It was a shame that they weren't able to do a lie detector of the heart. For now he had to accept it for what it was. He knew how to love even if he had nowhere to place it.

Keisha got up. She said something to the man and nipped to the toilets. She didn't look at Clive so there was no exchange of glances to know how it was going.

Clive looked to Tess instead. She would know if this was a good or a bad thing.

From his vantage point, Clive noticed that rather than heading for the toilet at the back, Keisha ducked sideways to the kitchen.

A moment or two later, Tess joined him at his table, delivering his corned beef hash at the same time. 'This is the interesting bit,' she said.

'How so?' Clive asked, tucking in.

'Seeing how long it is until they notice.'

'What? That she's gone?' His hushed tone came out rather more theatrically than intended.

Date forty-two was busy looking at his phone.

'Yes, and how they react can be fun as well.'

'Like what?'

'It's varied greatly so far. From nonchalance to full-out fury.'

'What are your bets today?'

Tess glanced over. 'Quarter of an hour to notice and disbelief. And yours?'

'Five and fury.' Clive raised a bushy eyebrow.

'We'll see who's closest.' Tess left the table and busied herself with clearing another before heading back to the other side of the counter ready to observe.

Clive had to feel sorry for the chap. Dating in the modern age must be hard enough without this. Although he knew Keisha wouldn't leave without reason. To ensure the bet with Tess was a fair one, and possibly because he'd spent too much time with Keisha recently, he decided to accurately time how long it was before this chap left. As luck would have it, he actually had a stopwatch in his pocket from the lab. He started it, realising he would have to add a minute for accuracy.

Clive returned to his corned beef hash as the seconds soon moved on to minutes. The dish was delicious and was melting in his mouth. Tess was a spectacular cook. This recipe would be particularly good if he ever had a glut of potatoes that needed using up.

The thought gave him an idea. Perhaps, if Tess was open to the suggestion, he could provide the café with anything surplus to his needs. That way dishes like this would be locally sourced. It was nice to think about doing something productive as he watched the seconds and minutes click by. Over the past few weeks – or perhaps it had been years – he'd been in a hiatus, and it was astonishing to think this young group of strangers had helped him so willingly. It would be nice to somehow thank them for all their kindnesses.

It was a clear ten minutes before date forty-two even glanced up from his phone.

Clive couldn't help feeling sad about the younger generation. They were always on the go. Always switched on. Never fully present. Not able to notice when a date had vanished into thin air.

Date forty-two peered at his phone again, tapping something into the small screen as if that was more important than checking the woman he was here to see was okay.

If it wasn't for the fact he knew Keisha had taken a different exit, Clive would be going to check himself. At least by sitting here and observing this non-reaction he knew that Keisha wasn't missing out. This man was certainly not a gentleman of the kind of standing he'd want for his young friend.

Tess was leaning against the back counter with her arms crossed and when Clive glanced her way, she did the biggest eye roll he'd ever witnessed. It took all his restraint not to laugh out loud.

It would seem the muffled noise he emitted was enough to wake date forty-two. He peered around and for the first time paid attention to the fact his date was no longer there.

Then he slinked out of the café like it was all par for the course.

'Well I never,' Clive said once the door closed. 'Is that really how it plays out these days?'

Tess came over, bringing a hot chocolate for him. He always had a hot chocolate instead of having any kind of dessert.

'Honestly, I know Keisha walking out is rude, but why don't they check? I've known women to take more than ten minutes in the loo. You'd think they'd at least ask if she was okay. In all the other dates, only three of them have asked me to check if she's okay!'

'Really? Those statistics are terrible and we know how Keisha likes a statistic. Wherever you're getting these men from, I'm sure they can't be representing the national average.'

'I'm really hoping not.'

'Am I right in thinking you normally set up these dates for Keisha on her behalf via a phone application?'

Tess nods. 'But I can't be held responsible for the lack of quality out there.'

'Not at all, dear. I just wondered if it's really the best way to go around selecting appropriate candidates.'

'The majority of my friends use the internet or dating apps. Although they probably don't tend to get their friend to do it on their behalf. I know it's not exactly creative, but it's the best way to go about it given that Keisha's reluctant about the whole thing.'

'But isn't it a little, I don't know… Boring and impersonal?' Clive was trying to form an idea, but like so many things of late it was ever so slightly out of his grasp.

'The thing is, there are all sorts of ways to try and meet new people. But they all tend to focus on being social, and it's not that Keisha isn't capable of being social, but she very much knows what she likes and prefers to stick to what she's happy with. It took me quite a while to get her to agree to do this.'

'It seems such a shame they don't have the youth groups and tea dances like we used to.'

'I doubt you'd get Keisha to dance, whatever the circumstances.'

'That's true. I did try once. She didn't take it well.'

Tess laughed, her smile as bright as the glitter in her café. 'At the moment it's the best idea I have. If you can think of anything better, you let me know. But remember she's comfortable doing it here. She likes the fact she can buy her own drink and not argue over who pays the bill. She likes the fact that there's an exit if she ever needs one, which she nearly always does. She likes the lines to be defined on her terms.'

'Have you ever tried the newspapers?'

'What, like the lonely heart ads? Do they still do them?'

'Well, how about inviting all the lonely hearts here at once?'

'For Keisha to date? I'm not sure that'll work out if they're all over fifty.'

'No, of course not. We'd have to work out the exact details, but you've got the seating. Wouldn't it be possible to do one of those speed-dating evenings? And if we get Keisha to agree, you might be able to strike more than one number off your chart at once. If she believes that you can work out if your heart belongs to someone the moment you meet them, and she prefers to run away if there is no glimmer of cardiac response, then three minutes would be the perfect length of date, surely?'

'You have a point.' Tess gazed up as if trying to peer at her own thoughts. 'I wish I'd thought of it. I'm just not sure how soon I'd be able to arrange something like that.'

'I can help. If you're having me to stay here then I'll need something to keep me amused. We can see if we can make some money for the café as well as find love for Keisha.'

'That would be amazing. Are you happy to come and stay here? It's going to be nice having your company for a while.'

'More than happy. The sleep lab has been great, but it was only ever for a while. Your offer of your spare room is very generous and perfect for while I secure the new flat.'

The bell of the door rang again, signalling Keisha's return. As she joined them both they had to hope the rest of their lunchtime conversation lasted longer than the date had.

Part Three

The Left Atrium

The left atrium receives oxygenated blood from the lungs.
In other words, it's the point at which we start to recover…

Chapter Thirty-Five

Keisha

In all the years I've worked as a research associate for Southampton University, I've never taken a day off sick. That is until now.

It seems wrong somehow, given that I don't have a cold and I'm not in hospital like Lucy is. But this is a mental-health day. This is a day because it has all got too much and because this morning I woke up with my fingers plugged to my neck, smothered by the thickness of my anxiety. Clive has become Tess's temporary tenant. Lucy will be back home tomorrow. I have this window of twenty-four hours without responsibility, but the walls are pushing in on me, not allowing my fingers to let go of my neck.

It must have started in my sleep, when I was dreaming. It seems taking my pulse happens so instinctively now that it can occur when I'm not awake. In my dream, my heartbeat was absent. I went to take a reading, like I so frequently do, only this time there was no reward of tracing my heart rhythm. There was nothing. For the first time in my life, I felt what it is like to be flatlining.

The dream brought with it so many difficult memories and when I jolted myself awake, there was nothing I was able to do to stop myself from checking. I needed to feel that rhythm to take myself away from a time and a place where there'd been none.

Even though I am able to make myself tea and toast with one hand, I'm not capable of leaving the house today. So I take my breakfast back to bed and slide under my duvet to create a cocoon. Normally the thought of getting crumbs on the covers is enough to drive me away from this scene, but today it is a comfort. In the end, it takes me four hours to peel my fingers from my neck.

When I was dreaming, every thought and feeling was piercing me like tiny ice shards crawling into my nervous system. For some reason this reminds me of Clive's scar, the one not unlike mine. It's two inches wide, a slash as opposed to a cut, and the more I know about Clive, the more I realise that scar holds a secret.

I glance at my own mark. No one knows what secrets this scar masks or the tragedies it led to. Those secrets stayed in London, stuck firmly in my past. I didn't let them follow me down here. I hold the lock and key to the story and I don't utter a word of it to anyone. With my tattoo, I've gone as far as to try to hide its very existence.

So is the same true of Clive's scar? Or does he hold the lock, and is he just waiting for someone to come along with the key?

My fingers hover over my carotid again, eager to do the next check even though it isn't time.

'Nobody knows about this,' he'd said. '*This is my secret. And now it is ours.*'

The more I wonder... Is the key supposed to be me? Am I supposed to find out what happened to leave his heart broken? Not in the way I thought with my PhD study, but in finding out what happened to Clive?

What I want is for life to get back to normal. I'm hoping Lucy being home will be the first step towards that. Then work can go back to the consistent tick-box process that it usually is even if that does mean the return of boring biscuits. And any future contacts with study participants will be scheduled appointments, with no added risks of forming friendships and being compelled to care.

Despite trying to cast my thoughts elsewhere, I keep coming back to the dream. I don't know how to block out the sensation of not feeling a pulse. The memory of my father is closer to the surface than it has ever been. It's floating there and pointing out with no uncertainty that it was my fault. That I was unable to save his broken heart.

My coping mechanism has always been to trace my pulse. It may be totally irrational, especially given that I can't stop, but I find it's the only reassurance that helps. It's stupid, I know, because if my heart was in trouble, the likelihood of being able to take my own pulse is minimal.

But what once was serving to check that I was still alive is now beginning to prevent me from living.

Today, I should be at work. I should be seeing Tess and making sure Clive settles in. I should be preparing for Lucy coming home.

Instead I'm stuck. I function only to make tea and toast, to use the loo and take my pulse. I'm only able to stop checking my heart rate for two minutes at a time. I know, because I've taken count.

Each of those one-hundred-and-twenty-second periods are longer than any pop song I've ever listened to on the radio. They seem longer than a five-minute wait for the bus. They seem longer than the length of time it took for the paramedics to arrive all those years ago. It seems infinitely longer than so many things and yet, of course, it isn't.

It takes two minutes to wash my hands. Two minutes to butter my bread. Two minutes to change into fresh pyjamas. You can achieve a lot in two minutes.

By midday, I know I need to get a handle on things. Everything within my logical mind knows that *nothing bad is going to happen.* If I take my hand away and give that small patch of skin an hour or so just to breathe, everything will be fine. No harm will come to me. My heart will not stop. Life will carry on. But how can I be sure? How can any of us be sure?

In the end, I use the rational side of my brain to wean myself. Two minutes become three and three become four. It takes me just over an hour to achieve a ten-minute gap. Realising I'll be here for far too long at this pace, I brave increasing it by two minutes at a time so I can reach my usual half-hour break.

When I finally get there, in my exhaustion I feel elation and defeat all at once. If this is what it has come down to, why am I even trying to function? Letting the anxiety win seems like such a pleasing possibility. Because why does it matter?

The thought makes my scar pulse without me having to feel for it. I promise myself to never go there again. Even if it means taking my pulse constantly, I am never going back to a place where that seems like the best option.

Chapter Thirty-Six

Clive

Arriving at Keisha's house, Clive thought it was nice to know that he wouldn't be waiting on the police this time round.

'Get your shoes on,' he insisted, when she opened the front door.

'I'm not dressed to go out.' There was a paleness to Keisha's skin and her neck had the start of a blossoming bruise, right on the point of her carotid.

Clive didn't need the science degree requisite to work in the cardiology lab to figure out why.

'Get changed then. I'm afraid I've sent the taxi away now and I don't know anyone else around here so you're going to have to let me in until you're ready to come out.' Clive knew that a little tough love would be needed; a built-in instinct had told him so. One he was unable to explain. He had a bag of unusual gifts with him to help soften the blow. He'd put them in place while Keisha got ready.

Thankfully, she let Clive in, but her reluctance was apparent in her hesitation.

'I know life can be a bit much at times. I thought you might like a walk. Only round the block or something. Not far.'

Keisha wasn't able to hold his gaze. Her eyes darted about, unable to settle on anything for any length of time.

'I can go if you don't feel up to it. I just thought it might help.'

'Yes, I'd like to. I just need to go and get ready.' She was still in her dressing gown and it was likely that she had been all day.

'I'll make myself at home. Take as long as you need.'

Clive really did take the opportunity to make himself at home. First out of the bag was a colourful fruit bowl that he placed near the microwave on the kitchen side. Next was a cheap oil painting he'd picked up. It was a portrait of a woman staring out her window and at the view beyond. She appeared to be at the start of something: the glorious day awaiting her just outside. When he'd been here before, he'd noticed the landlord hadn't bothered to remove any of the previous fixtures and fittings. There was a nail ready and waiting for him to hang the painting from. Last, he produced a pretty rose-coloured glass vase from his bag along with the pink flowers he'd got to match. After he'd unwrapped them from their newspaper protection and completed his flower arranging, he'd admired his efforts. His charity-shop finds lifted the place from the white box it was currently decorated as. He hoped it would provide the same lift for Keisha, and for Lucy on her return.

Keisha reappeared in a pair of jeans and a slogan T-shirt that had some algebra on there that Clive wasn't able to make head nor tail of. But still, it was nice to see her out of the lab coat she normally lived in.

'I hope you don't mind. I brought a few things to brighten the place up. I thought it might be nice for Lucy when she returns. And for you.'

'They're lovely. Thank you.'

'Let's go and get some fresh air, shall we?'

'Thank you,' Keisha said meekly. It didn't sound like her voice, it was so caught up in her throat.

For some time they got by in companionable silence. There was a chill in the air as if the day was willing to give up and wanted to go to sleep already. Clive knew how that felt.

There was silence as they tried to find a rhythm to match each other: Keisha's pace was much slower than usual and Clive upped his to what he could comfortably manage.

'Are you looking forward to having Lucy home?' Clive realised it was a bit of a silly question, but he wanted to start the conversation rolling somehow.

'More than anything. It's not been the same without her about.'

'And I don't expect I've been a particularly good replacement,' Clive said, meaning to be jovial, but missing the mark.

'You've been great. Unexpected, yes, but still great.'

'I've not been so great. I need to tell you something,' he said, the guilt getting to him.

'What is it?'

'Last Friday when I was out late. I hadn't popped to the shops. I'd been for a visit to the allotments.' Having to confess was an embarrassment to Clive. He wasn't someone who lied. Not even little white lies, but he'd felt so certain he was doing it with good reason.

'They're miles away! No wonder you looked flushed. What made you go there?'

It was a relief that Keisha didn't sound angry. 'Ever since I was admitted to hospital, I thought I might find some kind of answer back there. Something that would make it all make sense. I was desperate to go and see if that was the case.'

'And was it?'

'No, not at all. It was bitterly disappointing. All I found was a note I'd written that doesn't make any sense. No jolts to the memory to help me figure it out.'

'What did the note say?'

'It just said "new allotment holder". But I checked with a friend and none of them are called Nancy. I don't even recall writing it to know what I was on about.'

'Do you think it's important?'

Clive shrugged. 'If it was, I guess it would make more sense. Anyway, I just wanted to say sorry for not being more open. I thought you'd tell me not to and it seemed like it was important even if it turned out it wasn't.'

'It's okay. I'm glad you've told me.'

'Now that's over with, there was something else I wanted to talk about. I know I'm not staying at the sleep lab now, but I'm more than happy to help out and still be your volunteer. If you'll have me, that is.'

'Would you?' Keisha sounded surprised.

'Yes. I probably wouldn't be able to do it every day, but I'm sure I could make a couple of afternoons a week.'

There was almost a smile drifting onto Keisha's lips. 'That would be amazing. I'd miss you if you stopped. We'll have to go through the official channels and get you registered as a volunteer. Lucy will be off for at least another couple of days and will appreciate the help while she's getting back to full strength. I'm looking forward to you two meeting properly – I think you'll get on.'

'I'm looking forward to getting to know her too. I feel like I know her already.' It was strange to get to know someone mostly through labels.

'Is everything okay at Tess's flat? Have you settled in?' The conversation, and possibly Clive's apology, was beginning to open Keisha up, he was glad to notice.

'I'm still living out of my suitcase, but I'm beginning to get used to that. It's more homely there of course, especially with Tess's wonderful cooking.' Clive patted his tummy, knowing that it was already becoming more rotund. 'I'm going to need more than this walk to keep myself in shape. I'll be glad to get the allotment back up and running. I wish it wasn't so far away and easier to get to. That's been my main form of exercise for years. I need to get back to it.'

'Are you sure you want us to handle everything regarding your house?'

Clive nodded the most certain nod of his life. 'I feel very lucky that I've met such kind people willing to help. I know it's a lot to ask, but if you are happy to, I'd really appreciate it. I've come to the conclusion that going back there will only make me ill.'

'George is the one you have to thank mainly. He's been getting it organised. We thought we'd box everything up for you. Put it into temporary storage if necessary. That way you can go through everything and decide what stays and what goes.'

'I'll be very much obliged if you are happy to do that. I can pay you for your time. It's not a burden that is yours to take and I know you're only doing it because you're good people.'

'None of us want any money. We want to make sure you're happy and settled and we understand why that can't happen in that house.'

They reached a corner and turned. Many of the houses were of multiple occupancy so there were more cars than buildings and at every pavement they had to navigate dodgy parking.

'Thank you for being so understanding. Is there anything else you want to talk about?' Clive sensed there was something on Keisha's mind.

There was a long pause as their feet crunched on broken twigs that a recent April shower had torn down.

'Can I ask you a personal question?'

Clive had been in receipt of lots of personal questions recently. Being under the care of the hospital and the scrutiny of the police had seen to that.

'You can.'

'I've been wondering… You showed me you had a scar. What caused it?'

'I used to be a lion tamer,' Clive was quick with his run-of-the-mill reply. 'One of them got me one day.'

The response didn't evoke the laughter it usually received.

'What really caused it?'

'I wish I knew.' Clive placed his hand on his elbow. The scar wasn't visible with his coat on, but even blindfolded, he reckoned he would be able to accurately trace the wound.

'Do you really not know?'

'It was a random chainsaw attack.' Clive said it with a smile in the hope it'd make Keisha grin, but his usual humour wasn't going to work. He clearly needed to dust off his pocketbook of jokes. 'I honestly don't know,' he said with a shrug.

Keisha glanced away, paying more interest to where her feet were landing. There was a small crack like a starburst in the pavement, where a weed was pushing through. A gum wrapper, complete with chewed gum, discarded on the ground. An unlucky scratch card abandoned in a puddle.

'Something happened to me,' Clive said, 'but I'm not sure what. My memories from what happened never came back. I was attacked, as far as I know, but it was such a long time ago. Sometimes I trace that line and feel a connection as if I can go back to find out what went on. But I'm only ever filling in the blanks. So when people ask, I guess. But I figure you knew that already.'

'So you really have no idea? Did you tell the doctors about it?'

Clive shook his head. 'No. It happened a lifetime ago and it doesn't ever give me any bother. It's an old arm injury that I can't vouch for. I don't see any point in telling people about it.'

'I just wanted to know if you really didn't remember or if it was a cover story.' Keisha's gaze caught Clive in that way she had of really looking into him. Through him, even. 'Sorry to ask. I wanted to be sure.'

'And are you?'

'Yes, I think I am.'

Clive wished he was. He didn't feel sure about anything. For years he'd been putting one foot in front of the other, leaving his past behind him. It seemed to be where it belonged, and the truth was he didn't know what had happened. Not now and not then. Because if you say you're a lion tamer enough times, don't you begin to believe it in the end?

Chapter Thirty-Seven

Keisha

I feel anxiety prickle against my skin. It is never far from the surface and here it finds its way through because the place I'm going to is new. I thought that knowing that the house belongs to Clive would make it easier. A home from home. He's my friend, therefore his place should be friendly.

But as I walk to it, I know it isn't true. I'm somehow channelling the anxiety Clive has for this place. I'm expecting to see blood splatters on every surface of the kitchen even though I know there are none.

I try to think about later instead. About when Lucy will be home. I've made her a banner ready for when she returns from the hospital, but I'm making myself scarce. A small effort to avoid being Rob and Lucy's gooseberry.

Those happy thoughts get me to Clive's house without a panic attack taking hold. I'm glad. I don't want that to be the predicament I'm in every time I meet up with George. He'll start to see my weird more clearly if I do.

George is in the throes of preparing multiple brown boxes for us to fill. I find myself looking forward to helping our friend by spending the day getting his place clear.

The house has a small, perfect lawn in the front garden. There are borders filled with plants ready to bloom again come the summer. Clive clearly looks after it well.

George is blocking the porch with his attempts to assemble brown boxes.

'I managed to get these from Freecycle. Someone had moved recently and had a load of them to dispose of. Perfect for what we need.'

'Clive would approve.' I smile as I think about his love of upcycling. He is the original eco-warrior and it's doubtful he even realises how on trend he is.

'I've just been putting them up so far and distributing them throughout the house. I haven't made a start yet. Be warned, there's a lot to do. A lot more than I imagined. This might not be enough boxes.' George pushes another box and forms it into a square, taking it inside and making space for me to enter.

'Where do you want me to start?' As I look around, I realise that Clive is somewhat of a hoarder. There are pictures and shelves full of trinkets in the hallway. A mirror shaped like a shell and small jewellery boxes made of real shells. Another shelf holds a collection of owls: ceramic, wooden and plastic. My mouth is ajar taking in the number of items.

'Wherever you like. The choice is yours. If we pack up a room each by the end of the day, it'll be a miracle.'

George passes me the box he's holding and returns to his mission of putting them all together so that he'll be able to close the front door once again. My stomach flutters and for the first time I admit it's in response to him being close.

'We should keep an eye out for anything that tells us more about Clive's story,' I say to divert myself from my realisation.

'I'm not sure Clive's charity-shop collection is going to tell us much I'm afraid.' His fingers brush mine as I take the box from him and it's too late to take my pulse.

I shake the thought away. My stomach playing up doesn't mean anything. What I need to do is focus.

'There does seem to be a lot here. I'll go and get started.' I take my box to the end of the hallway, where there are two doors to go through. The first leads to the lounge, which seems like a good place to start. But I don't go in there straight away. Instead, I find myself drawn to the kitchen.

It's the same as Clive's description of the scene that never was. There is a door in the middle that leads to the lean-to. It's the doorway that tallies with Clive's depiction of the red mark.

Only there is no red mark, just the remnants of powder left by forensics where they've been dusting for fingerprints. We'll have to make sure it's clean before an estate agent takes any photos.

The breakfast bar is as I imagined and as I move into the kitchen area, I can't help but stare at the carpet tiles. I'm not sure what I'm expecting to see. Especially when I know the answer is nothing.

I realise I don't want to pack up the kitchen. Part of me thinks I'll start treating it like a crime-scene investigation, trying to locate the things the police have missed. Already I'm looking at it like a place where something awful has happened rather than as a home. Lucy's suggestion that I should investigate rings in my head, along with my own sense that there is more to this. But what will there be to find? I consider this as I trail a finger through the remnants of grey powder that are clinging on to the glass panel of the door. Surely nothing when the house has been subjected to such scrutiny?

It's a silly thought process so I clean off my finger and move to the front room to get cracking with what's in there. George is right, it will be quite the task. Every surface is covered with ornaments. An over-sized snow globe of Blackpool tower sits in the centre of one sideboard. There is a bookshelf with books cramming every nook and a display case full of more trinkets.

'See what I mean,' George says when he finds me gawping. 'It's quite the stash. I didn't want to be in charge of deciding what stays and what goes so I thought boxing it up will be simpler. That was before I saw how much there would be to pack away.'

'We're not going to get Clive down here to make the decisions though. He'll be able to decide for himself if we box it all.'

'I'll start making enquiries about storage units for when we'll need one. He certainly won't fit all of this into his flat. I have a feeling we're going to need more newspaper to wrap things.'

Looking around, I'm not entirely sure how he's fit it all into this house. This number of knick-knacks shouldn't squeeze into the space and yet he's managed it.

'We will,' I agree.

'Let's see how far we get today. I'm going to make a start on his bedroom upstairs. I figure he might want any remaining clothes and he might prefer that I sort that.'

'Thanks,' I say to George as he goes on his quest.

I make a start on the ornaments on the mantelpiece first. As I gather them, I wonder if any of them hold memories. If the owl made out of pebbles was something he made himself out of rocks he discovered on a favourite beach, perhaps. Somewhere Clive might have travelled down to on the summer bus.

Or has the thin silver vase ever held special flowers? Some carnations for his mother? Or something he's grown at his allotment? Every piece I put away tells a story, but it's hard to tell if those stories belong to Clive or the people that once owned them. Is the snow globe with 'Oxford' written across the front an indication that he'd visited there? Had he perhaps studied there? Or was it merely a bargain he's added to his collection from the charity shop?

After the first few, I start to pack them more systematically. If I ponder on each object I'll be here forever more. The good thing is I'm not making decisions over whether they should stay or go. And because none of the items belong to me, nor do I have to reminisce about any memories I rake up by holding each piece once more.

Instead, for each sheet of newspaper, I grab an object, wipe off any dust with an old rag cloth I found and wrap it up, placing it neatly into the waiting box. It's as if I'm stacking up a puzzle of memories without knowing what the overall picture should end up looking like.

As I dwell on these thoughts, there are creaks coming from above that remind me George is upstairs doing the same. Clive's wardrobe will also be a collection of clothes sourced from charity shops. Did Clive choose them because they reflected the things he likes, or was it to provide a medley of colour from other people's lives? Maybe that's what you do if you aren't certain of who you are. Some people hide behind lab coats. Others take parts of other lives and make them their own.

The mantelpiece alone takes a long time. Next I decide to go through the display cabinet. It's full of similar items and a large collection of spoons, some of them in need of a clean, others sparkling and more recent additions to the collection. They all have little shields or pictures, with many of them naming the places they are from. An old-fashioned equivalent of a Facebook check-in.

I try not to slow myself down by dwelling, but with some items I can't help it. I wish Clive was here to ask, but I'm also glad he's not or he'd see the fingerprint dust covering so many surfaces.

'How are you getting on?' George asks after we've both been at it for a couple of hours.

'There's just so much. This cabinet is so tightly packed.' I'm less than halfway through the display cabinet, which hides far more than meets the eye. 'What about the clothes?'

'I can safely say that Clive has a hat for every occasion and enough belts to last a month. I've filled a suitcase so he has some more clothes with him, but I've had to start using the boxes as well.'

'I'm guessing there's a lot more up there besides the clothes.'

'Oh, yes. If you thought this bookcase was impressive then you didn't account for upstairs.'

'Are there really that many?'

'Yep. And I haven't dared to look in the back bedroom yet.'

'I guess when you've lived somewhere for a long time you don't realise how much stuff is stacking up.'

'How long has Clive lived here?'

I shrug. 'I never asked exactly how long. For quite a while, I'm assuming.'

'It's such a shame he can't return.'

'Do you know if they ever found those missing medical notes?'

'They haven't yet, as far as I know. If they have, it's unlikely that they'd tell me. No one knows I'm helping him out so why would they? I'll check though. Why do you ask?'

I hesitate for a moment, wondering if I'm betraying a confidence by discussing this with George.

'Clive has an old arm injury. He can't remember how it happened and I just wondered if it has any relevance… Apparently he didn't tell the doctors about it because he didn't think it was important.'

George rakes a hand across his day-old stubble. 'I'll see what I can find out, but I doubt an old arm injury is connected to his current problems.'

'It would be great if you can. Clive seems a bit down after returning to the allotment because it didn't bring everything back to him, or rather hasn't helped him forget.'

There's a moment where we both contemplate the situation. For the first time I take in the fact George isn't in his uniform. He's wearing jeans and a plain grey T-shirt. We're practically twins with what we're wearing, but I realise in good time that it would be totally uncool to point this out.

'Do you want to stop for some lunch?' I ask, wanting my stomach to settle down. 'I brought us both some food. I figured we would want to battle on.'

'You weren't wrong.'

I find the packed lunches I've made. As George has organised everything else, I have a multitude of snacks to support our efforts: crackers, vegetable crudités, boiled eggs (the shells very carefully removed in their entirety) and cheese slices. It's a random mix, but I like to keep my diet in balance and there are no complaints from George. Because we're at Clive's, I realise the main thing that should be in this lunch is pickled onions. He might tell me off for not adding any. We'll probably come across a stash when it comes to sorting the kitchen.

It isn't long after refuelling that we're both back to packing up our respective rooms. After I finish the other half of the cabinet, I move on to a sideboard. The top is covered in trinkets that I take off and wrap one by one. Inside, I discover paperwork files in boxes. At least this is one section that'll be easier to sort. I slide out a box that looks like it contains recent bills. The next contains insurance paperwork. Another looks like important documents to do with the house.

The last box is wedged at the back of the cupboard and is awkward to grasp. I use both hands to get a purchase on it and manage to tug it out. It's an old shoebox full of photos. Some old back-and-white ones, others full of colour.

It's only on finding the shoebox that I realise for all the items in the room, there aren't any photo frames displaying images such as these. Some of the pictures are visible without me poking around and I take a moment to see if I recognise Clive in any of them. None are recent and with at least thirty years and a full head of hair having passed by, it is hard to tell if any of the men are him. I stop myself from wondering if they are more charity-shop finds by taking the shoebox lid from the bottom to place on top. It's not my business.

A single photo drops to the floor.

I grab it and go to place it with all the others, but I can't help myself... I have to take a look.

There is nothing on the back other than the brand name of the company that developed the photos printed over and over again in small text. When I turn it over, it's a beach I don't recognise. The picture is in faint colours that indicate it has faded with age. There's a couple grinning widely, each with their arm around the other's waist. The man is undoubtedly Clive. Even with the fading colours, his crystal-blue eyes are unmistakable.

This is a precious photo, I realise. One that hasn't been looked at for years.

But does it mean anything? Is it just a coincidence that this one is caught up under the lid of the box? Or has it been hidden away from the rest for a reason?

I decide to put it safely on the top of the other pictures and tape the lid shut. It's there for Clive to find when he unpacks his things.

After stopping to take my pulse, I continue well into the afternoon and evening, all the time fixated on that box of photos. I can't help glancing in its direction. Is it possible to find the impossible? Is Nancy sitting in that box?

Chapter Thirty-Eight

Clive

The nicest thing about staying with Tess was not being alone in the evenings. Clive didn't need to find a way to occupy himself when there was company and the option of watching a film. Since moving in, he'd learned Tess put a lot of hours of work into the café that was below her flat and she often referred to it as her love and passion. She wasn't looking for another love (having been badly hurt by her ex-girlfriend) and that was why she was enjoying looking on Keisha's behalf.

This evening she was demonstrating to him how she'd been selecting dates for their friend over the course of the experiment.

'What's it called again?'

'Tinder.' Tess settled two mugs of hot chocolate on the coffee table for them both and re-joined Clive on the sofa. She'd gone to the effort of making them with the café's machine and the drinks came complete with luxurious whipped cream and fluffy marshmallows. What a treat!

'Why do they come up with such random names for these things?'

'It's the start of a spark. I guess that's where the name came from.'

'Can a spark really occur from seeing a picture?'

'There's normally some messaging involved.'

'Do they know it's not Keisha talking to them?'

'Yep. I let them know I'm setting up blind dates for her. It doesn't take much to work out whether they're a creep or not. If they start asking to see pics of me and whether I'm up for a threesome, I know it's time to block them.'

'Golly. It sounds so unromantic.' Clive picked up his mug and enjoyed its warmth. Tess had added some salted caramel syrup from the café and along with the added whipped cream, it gave the drink a delicious dessert-like quality.

'What are you planning for your recruitment process then?' Tess asked.

'Now don't get me wrong. I'm sure the way you've been going about it is exactly how things are done these days. I was just thinking that if we planned an event and advertised it, we could get them to give us a few more details beforehand by writing a letter.'

'A letter? Do you mean via email? I don't think anyone knows how to send one on paper these days.'

'I really hope the art hasn't been lost. We can't just have Keisha there, either. We'll have to have other women as well.'

'Of course.'

'Are you going to take part?' Clive asked.

'Not if you want the café to run at the same time. Besides, as you know, not all of us are looking for a man. Some of us want a woman in our lives. We'll have to do that next time.'

'And one for us golden oldies. We'll have to see how much money it brings in for the café and whether it's worth continuing.'

'We can make it ticketed with a drink and a slice of cake included. That way we know we have a set amount coming in and any extra is a bonus.'

'Excellent idea. You never know. We might help more than just Keisha to find love.'

'If we help Keisha find love, we'll have performed a miracle.'

For some reason, thinking about her at that moment made Clive want to take his pulse. They'd obviously been spending far too much time together.

'Right, let's get the ball rolling and write down our plan.'

They spent the rest of the evening ironing out the details. Clive was enjoying doing something that he hoped would help Keisha. Even if it didn't help her find love, it would help get her to the end of the hundred-date challenge. It was one tiny way of doing something for her, knowing the enormity of the task she was helping him complete this weekend. He thought of her and George working away together at his house. They were both such generous spirits.

The thought made him realise that if they were setting up an evening to help Keisha, it wouldn't hurt if George was there participating. He just hoped that, when he asked George, he'd also be willing to take part. Because if there wasn't a spark already, wouldn't it be great if this was the thing that created one.

Chapter Thirty-Nine

Keisha

It's pitch-dark by the time we leave Clive's house. The hours have slipped by without me realising and the sky is a canvas of black, barely visible clouds hiding the stars. It's only the moon that is managing to shine brightly.

'How are you getting home? Did you drive?'

'I don't have a licence. I walked here.' I surprise myself by letting out a little laugh. 'I didn't realise it had got so late.'

'If it weren't for all the boxes taking up the space, we should have thought about camping out. I'd give you a lift, but I can only offer a backie on my bike. My dad dropped the boxes off, but he's out for dinner this evening so no chance of a lift back.'

'Don't worry, I want to get home. I know Lucy wanted rest today, but I'm hoping to see her in the morning at least.'

'Of course. Well, let me walk you home.'

It wasn't a short walk, but I wasn't going to give up the offer of an escort. Otherwise it would be a taxi and Southampton prices are so ludicrous I only ever use them if it's an absolute necessity.

We're over a mile into the trip back without having spoken. It's strange that I've managed brief conversations about Clive's things throughout the day, but now I'm suddenly completely stuck on what to say. There are a multitude of questions on the tip of my tongue, so many things I want to know. I should tell him about the photo, but I find myself wanting to know about him. I want to know the places he's travelled and about the people he's helped by volunteering. In the end I only manage to stumble out the thing that intrigues me the most.

'What made you come home from your travels?'

'Time and roots.'

I throw him a perplexed look. 'I take it you don't mean your hair roots?'

George laughs and I marvel at how, for all my nerves, I'm beginning to feel at ease with this man.

'No, roots as in I needed to establish myself somewhere. I'd been away for too long. What was going to be a jaunt turned into five years. Then my mum was poorly for a while and I felt too far away. I knew it was time to come home.'

'I'm sorry your mum was unwell.' I stop at saying anything about my parents. He doesn't need to know my mum passed away when I was a baby or any of the tragedy surrounding my dad.

'The good news is she got better, but once I was home I knew I wanted to stay. Not with my parents forever, mind. I'm saving up to try and get my own place. What about you? Will you always live with Lucy?'

'As long as she'll have me.' I laugh, knowing we should have cut the apron strings years ago, but as we haven't, we're likely to remain that way for as long as we can.

When we're near to approaching home, George takes off down the hill on his bike. So much for chivalry. When he's out of sight, I begin to feel guilty for all of the dates I've walked out on. Maybe this is how it feels… like their stomach has been taken out from underneath them.

Not that it worries me… Walking home solo doesn't scare me. I've done self-defence classes and I'll take a bet on being capable of weirding out the worst of weirdos given the right circumstances.

As I think about such possibilities, George is back, macho-wheeling his way up the hill. *Definitely* showing off. Perhaps it's some strange alpha-male display. The hill is at quite a gradient and it requires a good level of athleticism to not fall off. Still, even if it is what he was attempting to demonstrate, I'm not going to fall for that. Am I? My stomach feels like it's made of marshmallow with its response to everything that is going on.

He comes to a halt when he reaches my feet as if he is testing whether I'll jump.

'What was that all about?' I have to ask.

'Dinner,' George says, as he hops off his bike and produces an open cone of chips at the same time. 'I thought we should prob-ably eat.'

As soon as I taste a hot, salty chip, my theory about George being odd switches to me concluding that he is an absolute genius. For a woman who doesn't eat takeaways, this second lot within a week reminds me why people indulge in them. This chip is the yummiest thing I've tasted in a lot time. I try not to think about the salt content.

I hold a fry up to the sky to see if it matches the crescent of the moon. It's something I used to do as a child. Any time we indulged in alfresco chips, my dad and I would try to match them up to something: the shape of the waves or a windbreaker, the moon or a wonky chimney pot. It makes me realise that I've not done this in my adult life. Not wanting to dwell on the past, but next to George, in this moment, I carry on. The chip isn't a perfect match, so I eat it and try the next one and the one after that. Rather than ask me what I'm up to, George joins in. It takes a while, but we soon have two chips that are the same shape as the moon.

Once I say goodbye to George, I head to bed. On my dresser, I place the two crescent-shaped chips.

If anyone looks close enough, they might think it was meant to be the shape of a heart.

It's one of life's simple pleasures, but making Lucy a herbal tea the next morning really defines the meaning. Her not being here has made me more aware of how much I love having her about, even if she is a klutz at times. She's my klutz.

'I could get used to this you know,' she says.

'And so you shall, for a while. But no milking it.'

'Do you want some help today? At Clive's?'

'No milking it, but no overdoing it either! You need to take it easy now you're back home.'

'Spoilsport! I want you to fill me in this evening.'

I leave Lucy with everything she needs and instructions to behave. Hopefully I won't need to start adding Post-it notes around the house.

On the way to Clive's, I decide to pop in to the café to see the man in question and find out how Tess is getting on with having him to stay.

As the café isn't open yet, I join Tess in the kitchen as she carries out the morning prep.

'Oh my God, that's so romantic,' Tess declares when I relay the details of the previous day. It is early, but she is busy making a Moroccan lamb tagine ready to serve on the specials menu. She opens later on a Sunday, but many of the local residents come for a delicious lunch.

'What's romantic about that?' Getting sweaty and dusty doesn't strike me as romantic in the slightest.

'You shared a cone of chips by moonlight. If you ask me, that's the pinnacle of romance right there.'

'There was a lot more to the day than that.' I glance towards the door that leads to the stairs and the flat above. 'Is Clive okay?'

'He's fine. He doesn't like to get up until what he calls a more sociable hour. I don't blame him, but this place needs an early bird like me to run things. Does this mean the search is over then?' Tess asks.

I think about the photo. About how I'd not been searching for clues, but it revealed itself to me anyway. 'The search for what?'

'The love of your life. If you've made it to date number two with George, can we wipe the board clean and call our experiment a success?'

'It wasn't a date. We're just helping Clive. The board can remain.'

'Spoilsport.'

'You're the second person to say that today. I'm only making sure *you* don't have your heart broken when your fantasy matchmaking doesn't work out.'

'We'll let the search continue then.'

'Is there anything I can do before I set off?'

'You can wash up those few bits for me, if you don't mind?'

'Of course not.' It seems the least I can do seeing as she's supplying me with much-needed caffeine this morning.

As the water runs, the sound gives me the chance to whisper to Tess. I decide I need to tell someone about what I've come across.

'I found an old photo. It was hidden away. It must be at least fifty years old. It's Clive when he's younger with a woman. I can't help but think it's Nancy.'

The relief of sharing the discovery is immediate. I know Tess will provide sensible advice.

Tess stops what she's doing, the prepping of ingredients no longer important.

'How would we find out if it's her?'

'I don't know other than showing Clive. I don't think that's a good idea, though. He's had enough heartache. If it is her, what would seeing it do to him? There's nothing to indicate it is Nancy, but I just have this feeling. I know I have a preference for accuracy, and I wouldn't normally consider my so-called sixth sense, but I think it wins out this time. I think we need to try and find out some more.'

'Didn't the police rule out that Nancy ever existed?'

'They confirmed that Clive had never been married. I'm not sure if that means she never existed.' I stop the tap to save the washing-up bowl from overflowing, our whispers no longer muffled by the sound of running water.

'Would you be happy for me to see if I can find anything out?' Tess asks. 'My uncle Gary works in genealogy and he might be able to discover a thing or two.'

'If they didn't locate a marriage record, I doubt you'll find anything. But I guess that's less harmful than triggering anything Clive's brain might be hiding from him. I'd suggest looking into deaths. Maybe we can find out what happened to Nancy.'

There is a creak of floorboards from the stairs and we both respond by returning to our tasks, our cheeks flushing.

'Good morning. More than one early bird today I see. I thought I could hear chirping.'

'Morning, Clive,' I say, taking his jovial manner to mean he hadn't overheard what the chirping was about.

'I've just been filling in Keisha on the speed-dating idea and she thinks it's great. She can't wait for our event,' Tess says.

I can't?

'Oh, that's great. I was worried you'd think I was meddling. I only came up with it with your best interests at heart,' Clive says, before starting to help with wiping up.

'It's very kind of you.' I'm not completely sure what he's on about. I just hope he will think the same of our meddling if he ever finds out.

Chapter Forty

Clive

Clive was enjoying his role as organiser of the speed-dating event. If nothing else, these few weeks in limbo had given him a number of varied new hobbies and pastimes to enjoy.

Tess had managed to convince him that being open to email as well as written applications would make the event more popular, especially in the age bracket they were aiming for. That had seemed to be a good move as so far only one applicant had used 'snail mail' as Tess liked to call it. For this event, they'd opted for a twenty-five to forty age range. Clive had requested people send in their particulars (age and so forth) and a paragraph about what makes them happy. The answers had included spending time with family, lying in a field staring up at the sky and eating a whole tray of doughnuts, and were giving him lots of ideas for how to spend his time. In the email inbox they'd set up especially, he had enough male applicants already. He was two short on females and had had several enquiries about whether they were going to do events for other age groups.

It hadn't all been down to the newspaper ad and the posters that he'd put up locally. Some of the interest had come from the Facebook event page that Tess had set up. Between them they'd done very well and Clive was currently on Tess's computer narrowing down who should be picked. Even though it should have been first come, first served, he was attempting to play Cupid by selecting applicants who he thought Keisha would be compatible with. Although, did he want to be accurate in his selections if really he wanted to set her up with George? Not that he'd convinced the lad to join in yet. He'd not seen him, George working flat out on his days off to help pack up the house for Clive.

By the time Clive had finished the administration, he had seven male candidates for the speed dating, and five females, not including Keisha. If they weren't able to get any more women on board, they could always make one of the stops a date with a cake. After all, no one wanted to cram in a slice of cake with a new date watching.

In a moment of distraction, Clive typed 'new allotment holder' in the search bar like the internet might somehow hold the answer. Of course all it brought up were practical guides on how to start up the hobby. He deleted the words and wished he could get rid of the niggling idea that was still lingering.

To rid himself of those thoughts, he decided to call George.

'How's it going, lad?'

'We're getting there gradually. You've got so much stuff! How long have you lived here?'

Clive had to think. It was another one of those facts that should be like a reflex, but he was having to stop and recall. 'All my life. It was my parents' house. I was born there.'

'An entire lifetime of treasures in that case.'

'A lifetime. Yes.' Clive guessed so. 'I had something I wanted to ask you.' He needed to get back on track before he forgot why he'd called in the first place.

'What's that?'

'Tess and I are hosting a speed-dating event at her café. It's to try to create a bit more revenue for the business. I'm one man short and wondered if I could persuade you to take part. I'll pay for your ticket as a thank you.'

'You don't have to do that.'

'There's cake. I'd do it myself, but I'm far too old and we'd get complaints.'

'What kind of cake are we talking about here? Because if it's red velvet then I'm sold already.'

'Tess's red velvet cake is the best. I'll make sure that's one on offer.'

'When is it? I'll have to check my rota. If I'm free and we're finished here, then I'll step into the breach. With cake as payment.'

Clive gave him the details of the event that was planned for the following Friday evening, and crossed his fingers. He just had to hope that George would be able to make it. There was really no way Clive could be the stand-in.

Chapter Forty-One

Keisha

For once, Lucy is doing as she's told. She's following the guide the dietician gave her to a T. She's sticking with softer foods such as soups and drinking the milkshakes they've given her to bulk out her calorie intake. Even Rob isn't having to nag her and I've not come close to printing out a label.

Seeing her being so compliant is a testament to how poorly she's been. It's visible in all her movements. She's slower, having to pace herself, reserving her energy. We start going for daily walks around the block like Clive did with me and on the seventh one, I'm beginning to notice a difference. Lucy is coming back to me.

'How are your investigations going?' she asks. I've told her about the mysterious photo I found singled out from the others.

'Tess's uncle knows all about genealogy and is looking into it for us. To be honest I think I was getting my hopes up. There's nothing to say it is her.'

'Is there anything else you can do to find out?'

'George is checking to see if they've located the other medical records, but that's not likely to help with Nancy. It might explain why he can get muddled at times. I just hope it doesn't show up anything tragic. He's had enough of that.' I know that's my fear and why I'm reluctant to delve any further into the past.

'I can't wait to get back to work and meet him again.'

'It won't be long. Hopefully you'll feel up to it soon. I can't wait for Clive to be able to treat you to afternoon tea.'

It's good to see the colour in Lucy's cheeks as we walk and laugh about the fact the lab now has a full tea set including vintage sugar tongs.

The buoyancy of seeing Lucy recovering carries me all the way to the dating event this evening even though I'm absolutely dreading it. One date is bad enough, but eight in a row seems like too many. Despite Tess and Clive's reassurances that this will make it easier than running off, I'm not so sure. At least my way I get to stick to my routine. I get to take my pulse afterwards. I get to leave the room to save any awkwardness. I have no way of knowing how I'll cope with this new style of dating. I won't be able to run to the bathroom in between each one without appearing to have bladder issues and if I take my pulse constantly it will look odd – even odder than usual, that is.

The only comfort is the fact I'll be at my table, in my comfort zone. I get there suitably early so that I can eat and have a drink with me ahead of anyone else arriving.

'Are you feeling okay?' Clive asks. He's carrying out some final touches. At the moment he's adding a red rose to a small vase on every table. It doesn't quite go with Tess's sparkly unicorn theme, but at least they're not adding glitter to flowers.

'Is it bad to say I'll just be glad when it's over?'

'Just think of the hassle this is saving you. You're knocking eight crosses off that chart in one go.'

Clive has me well and truly sussed. He knows I'm only here to help reach the end of the challenge. Getting to number one hundred is the only way I can put an end to this infernal experiment. In some ways, however much I think Tess is wrong, now we are near halfway through I almost want her to be right.

Other people start to filter in. The women are shown to tables whereas the men are being led to a bigger side table by Clive. When the event's due to start, the men pick a number out of a hat to determine which table they go to. As systems go, it seems a fair one, but I can't help but notice the pieces of paper are different sizes. I fight the urge to request they cut them all to the same size and do a redraw. It really isn't going to make any difference.

I stare at my coffee. I don't want to make direct eye contact with anyone. My nerves are jumpy and I have no idea how that will affect taking a reading. I attempt to measure one discreetly before anything starts, and as I expect my resting heart rate is up.

Tess calls everyone to order. The men are chattering like comrades planning their attack. The whole thing makes me feel uneasy.

I figure, at this moment, that I don't have to stay. If it feels like it's all getting too much, I can leave at any point. The door to the outside world is just over there. Just steps away.

Tess issues instructions on how the evening will unfold. The ladies don't need to worry about moving and will be able to remain where they are. The gentlemen will join their first table and then will work their way clockwise around the room every time the bell rings to indicate their time is up. Each date will be three minutes.

'Would the gentlemen like to go to the table number they picked out and your first date will start.'

For the first time I spot a wooden spoon on the table that isn't usually here. It's poking out of the menu holder and has the number three on it made from a series of love hearts. I'm certain it's a bargain charity-shop find that between them they've jollied up for the event.

My first date mumbles so badly I'm not sure if his name is Fred or Algernon or Phillip. It might be all three as I've asked him to repeat it twice and both times it sounded like something completely different.

He starts with the killer question: 'What do you do for a living?'

'Look, if you're going to be doing seven more of these, don't start with that question. I mean, it can be such a conversation killer. What if it's something you don't like or something you've never heard of? You need to start by finding a common base. Talk about hobbies. Talk about your pets.'

Fred Algernon Phillip then spends the rest of the three minutes trying to find out what my occupation is by asking roundabout questions. 'Are your hobbies related to what you do for work? How many work colleagues do you have? Do you drive to work?'

Dates two and three may well have been twins. If they aren't at least relations then they certainly got ready together. They ask almost identical questions that are perhaps meant to be offbeat, but they lose their quirkiness when they both go with the same opener of: 'What's the worst movie you've ever seen?'

It's oddly like having an interview with questions that are designed to try to catch me out.

By the fourth date, I decide there's absolutely no point in continuing to take my pulse. My heart rate is up, not because I've come across the love of my life, but because of the stress I'm currently under. Admittedly, though, that isn't making me want to run away like I thought it would. Instead, it's a surprise to find I'm on the verge of enjoying myself.

It's quite nice to be able to see others around the room having dates as disastrous as I am. For the first time I pay attention to some of the other women. At the table beside me is a beautiful Asian girl who gives me the brightest smile when I catch her eye. 'Please tell me it gets better,' she pleads, before greeting her next date with the same wide smile.

It's George. How have I not noticed he's here? He's one table ahead of Franco Phillipe three-names.

My next date arrives at such a slow pace it's as if the action of having to move from table to table is fatiguing him.

I glance at George and our eyes meet, but he's busy chatting to my beautiful table neighbour.

'Hi, I'm Edward. Do you come here often?' My date chuckles and offers his hand to shake.

For the rest of the three minutes, conversation continues easily with this Edward. On the whole, he is nicer than many of the forty-five dates I've previously been on. If I were to slip to the toilet now, he seems gentlemanly enough to actually notice. But the comfortable ease with which I'm managing to chat to him is partly down to my mind being elsewhere. For the three-minute date and the remaining three that follow, I'm mostly focussing on George and why he's here.

When the bell for the final date goes, my heart skips a beat. There's a long pause, as if time slows down, until George lands in the chair opposite me. Foolishly, I miss the opportunity to see if my heart jumps.

'Rather conveniently, Clive didn't mention you would be here.'

It's more awkward than the seven previous introductions I've encountered. 'He didn't say you'd be here either.'

'Is this what they class as a set-up?'

'I'm sorry I'm a wasted date,' I say.

'Don't apologise. You're the poor girl who spent most of last weekend with me. I can't imagine you want another three minutes.'

'Oh my gosh! Is he your ex?' another table neighbour asks, clearly not busy enough with her date.

The prying question shocks me, and in a rare moment of spontaneity, I decide to shock her back. 'Yes, he is. But as you heard… he can't last three minutes. It's why we can't be together.' I'm not sure what has got into me, but it seems like the correct thing to serve to someone who has been listening in to what should be a private conversation.

'Incorrect,' George says, playing along. 'It was three minutes, twenty-seven seconds at my peak. But if you will time me and put that added pressure on me…'

I can't help but laugh at George's retort and the look of shock on everybody's face within listening distance.

'Maybe we should try again. Maybe if you think you can make the full three minutes and thirty seconds, there's a chance for us.'

More of the daters are listening in now.

'Will you throw the egg timer away for me? Will you take that pressure off? I'm just not sure I'll ever be able to perform to that length unless I can do it without knowing how many more seconds I need to go on for.'

'I will. But only if you'll come with me now and prove to me that you can go the whole three minutes and thirty seconds. I don't believe you, you see.'

'For you. Anything.' George stands up so quickly that his chair topples over. 'Take my hand. We must make this our mission.'

Tess is watching, the bell hanging loosely in her hand, neglecting her role as timer.

I take George's hand, knocking my chair over in the process. 'Here? Or shall we wait until we're home?'

The look of horror on Tess's face is enough to make me want to chortle. But I manage to keep a straight face.

'Let's get home, darling. I'm so glad this brought us together again.'

I don't manage to glance back at any more of the expressions, instead rushing out of the café holding on to George's hand and we manage to rush to the end of the street before falling into peals of laughter.

'Honestly, who does that?' I can barely breathe, our little production having made me laugh so hard.

'I'm glad we made her blush.'

The laughter is continuing to tumble out of me and for the first time in my life I appear to have a stitch from the activity. It's the closest I've ever been to spontaneous and there's a freeing quality to it. One that I like. I can hardly believe it.

'And I'd just like to point out if we ever—' George pauses, the giggles beginning to ebb away. 'Well, it would last a whole lot longer than three minutes and thirty seconds.'

It's my turn to blush. 'I should bloody well hope so.' Because for all my failures in finding a boyfriend, I know plenty about how that part of a relationship goes.

'Do you want to go and grab some dinner? I'm famished. I think we've missed out on the awkward post-date cake eating.'

'I'd love to get something to eat. Maybe a sausage so I can measure it.' I say it with a smile and the laughter from the evening bubbles out of both of us again.

Technically speaking, it's the first time I've ever found myself flirting and I laugh some more at how appallingly bad I seem to be at it.

Chapter Forty-Two

Clive

After the resounding success of the speed-dating night, Clive had spent the rest of the weekend helping Tess out, planning another event and wondering how things had gone. He was eager to see Keisha and catch up. He wasn't sure if he'd ever find out if George lasted longer than he'd so loudly proclaimed, but the fact that they'd left together hand-in-hand, even if it was in jest, was a darned sight better than any of Keisha's previous dates. And much better than any eventuality he'd been hoping for. It had also made a good icebreaker amongst the rest of the daters after the couple's dramatic exit.

Tess had made a nice profit, especially when people had stayed on to network (if that's what it was classed as these days). Clive and Tess were already planning the next speed-dating event, this time for an older age group, in a couple of weeks' time, followed by some LGBTQIA evenings.

On Monday, he took the short walk to the lab. Keisha had spent the weekend with Lucy and, as this was Lucy's first day back, Clive popped into his favourite Polish store to get some supplies. First he selected an iced sponge cake that looked delicious and then the chocolate and pink wafers that were proving so popular.

Keisha was busy on the phone when he got there and with no sign of Lucy, he busied himself with the usual duties he tried to tackle on a Monday afternoon. First was a quick clean of the kitchen surfaces and the fridge if it was needed. Then he replenished the biscuits and he'd started getting the cake on a plate when he heard someone arrive.

A young woman entered the lab and Clive had a glimmer of recognition. 'You must be Lucy! Nice to see you again,' he said.

'I certainly am.' Lucy gave Clive a broad grin and took him into a welcoming hug. 'Anything she's said about me isn't true.'

Keisha was still on the phone.

'You get yourself settled. What can I get you to drink? Have a seat and I'll bring it over.'

Lucy took off her coat and kicked her bag under the desk. 'I'll have a tea with lots of milk and three sugars. I've heard all about your hospitality skills.'

'All good things I hope.'

'They certainly are.'

Lucy took a seat and Clive made sure he set everything out perfectly before taking it over.

'Everything okay?' Clive asked once Keisha finished her call. She looked grey. That horrible ashen colour people turn when they've been told something horrible.

'It's so lovely to have you back,' Keisha said, embracing her friend in a long hug.

Clive didn't miss that she was deflecting the question.

'Who was that on the phone?' Lucy asked.

'It was George. Just something about the study.'

'Did you have fun on Friday night?' Clive bravely ventured. Perhaps the colour draining from her face meant love's young dream was over already.

'Was that whole evening set up purely to put more crosses on my board?'

'Yes, eight in one go. Not bad, huh?'

'So you weren't just trying to set George and me up?'

'It seemed daft not to invite both of you. I thought you might have told me off if I'd mentioned it beforehand. I didn't want to make it any more nerve-wracking than it already was. You both seemed to handle it with good humour.'

'I think we had to in the end.'

'So I'm not in trouble?'

'Not today.'

'And is everything okay between you and George?' Clive tried to gauge Keisha's reaction.

'Is there some kind of romance going on here that I need to know about?' Lucy took the side plate and cake fork Clive offered, ready to receive her piece of sponge.

'George and I are just friends. Same as when he was date number forty.'

'You've dated before?' Lucy asks. 'How much have I missed since I've been ill?'

'It wasn't a proper date. It was arranged by Tess, but it was after we'd met on the ward so he only came because we had Clive as a common interest. Not because he actually wanted to date. He came to the café to talk to me about Clive. It was then that we vowed to help. It was when we became your guardians, I guess,' she said, looking at Clive.

'Guardian angels, you mean. I don't know where I'd be without you both.' Between them, Keisha and George had managed to box up all of Clive's belongings, which were now in storage. An estate agent had been over to take pictures once Clive's paraphernalia was safely out of the way. Now they were just waiting for a sale and that would be another thing sorted.

'That's a darn sight more than what usually happens in a fortnight here. I'm never leaving this place again,' Lucy declared, while spraying a few cake crumbs over the floor for good measure.

For the rest of the afternoon, Clive did everything he could to make sure Lucy was okay. She was a complete contrast to Keisha, far more relaxed, and as a result, far more haphazard. But also keenly astute, taking note of all the small changes he'd made.

'People can hear your smile. Good one, Clive,' she noted when she took her only call of the afternoon.

Keisha seemed far away and, most unlike her, she kept checking her phone. She was doing so more frequently than she took her pulse so that was saying something.

The first of the afternoon's study participants arrived and making tea was good therapy as always. The talk of George was making Clive think about the flat he was going to be moving into soon. He'd put in an offer, which had been accepted, and now all the various searches were done, his solicitor had said he was in a position to go and sign for it, but he'd been delaying. He'd been convincing himself it was because of the attitude of the salesman. After the treatment they'd received when they'd been shown round, he didn't want to make it easy for them by handing over all the money they required. But there was a difference between attempting to teach someone a lesson and shooting oneself in the foot. If he didn't get a move on he'd be in danger of losing his new home. There weren't any others near his beloved allotment so it would be foolish to miss out on this one.

It wasn't that stopping him, though. It was the fact he couldn't work out what had gone wrong there. Perhaps if he spoke to the new allotment holders they might remember what he didn't.

Clive went to talk to Keisha about it and noticed she'd hardly touched her cake. It would have gone dry by now. 'When you get a chance, can you see when George is free for me? I'd like to visit the allotment. Maybe spend a few hours there sorting it if the weather is nice enough.'

'Is this another attempt to steer me towards seeing George? Because you do know you can contact him from the mobile Rob got for you if you want to.'

'I don't know how to use that fandangled thing. Whenever I attempt to do something I end up doing the wrong thing.'

'If it's not a ruse, I'll send George a message and see when he's free.'

'Thank you,' Clive said. 'Is everything okay? You looked a bit pale when you were chatting to him earlier.' Lucy was busy whistling into the fridge and it seemed a convenient time to ask.

Keisha gulped and nodded. 'They might have a case study number six for me.'

'Well that's good, isn't it? Unless they're allergic to beetroots of course!'

'Yes, it's great.'

'I guess they'll never be as good as number five though.'

'No, they won't,' said Keisha with something of a smile.

'Do you know our fridge no longer contains salad cream sachets that expired in 2015? I made a bet with myself that they would last the year out in there. You're far too efficient, Clive,' Lucy shouted from beyond the fridge door.

Keisha glanced at her phone again. 'I'm going to have to pop out. Will you two be okay?'

Lucy returned and gave Clive a look that he interpreted as meaning they were in cahoots.

'We'll be fine,' Clive said. 'I just hope you are.'

But it was hard to know when Keisha was already on her way.

Chapter Forty-Three

Keisha

It's not my heart I'm worrying about at the moment. It's my head. It feels as if it's going to explode. Clive's missing medical notes have been found. George phoned to let me know and, right now, he is taking the opportunity to look through them before they are shared with the police. I'm waiting to hear from him. To see if there is anything important that I need to know.

When a message pings on my phone it puts me into a spin.

Nancy is real.

In an instant my head pounds as I read and re-read the text trying to make sure that Clive doesn't see. It takes a while to process that it's from Tess, not from George.

It doesn't seem possible. Tess has it wrong. Autocorrect is surely to blame. I leave Lucy and Clive in the lab and pray that it'll all be okay.

My heart is drumming hard against my ribcage, as if I've pushed myself too far on a run. Trying to keep myself calm and not give away that anything is up is a hard task. So much so that I know it can't wait and I choose to leave.

As soon as I'm round the corner and sure I'm far enough away, I call Tess. 'What do you mean, Nancy is real?'

'My uncle Gary has got back to me. He knows his stuff when it comes to looking at family history and all that jazz.'

'Right. And?'

'There is no record of Clive getting married, like the police said.'

'So how come you're telling me she's real?' People don't tend to appear out of thin air, as far as I know.

'That's where having an uncle who knows what he's looking for has come in handy.'

This filtering of information is agonising and if it wasn't for the fact it's a phone conversation I'd have been pulling at the collar of Tess's shirt to tell me what she knows.

'He looked at other information to establish Clive's family tree. When he searched the electoral roll for Clive's property, one of the years there's a Nancy registered as living there.'

'What? I don't understand. So he was married?' My hammering heart upgrades to a judder.

'No, that's the thing. She's not registered as Nancy Ellington. Her name is Nancy Fuller. They weren't married. The electoral roll is only taken every four years so it's only a snapshot. She isn't on the roll before that or the one after, but that year she is registered there. Clive's father, Keith, also lived there at the time. Clive's mother had passed away a few years before and Keith died a few years after this roll was taken. Since then, it's only ever been Clive living there alone.'

'Wow. Was your uncle able to find out anything else? Did Nancy pass away as well?'

How sad that Clive has gone from being surrounded by people he loved to being totally alone. Not only did his parents die, but if his fractured recollections are true, Nancy also passed away.

'He's still looking into it. Those records are a bit complicated as they don't always give a true indication of things. If somebody has been confirmed as deceased, then it's indicated on those records. If that hasn't happened, it isn't clear either way. If she has passed away, it just means it hasn't been formally verified. Equally, she may still be alive.'

'So we don't know?' It's hard to decide whether I'm experiencing hope or hopelessness. Nancy *is* real. Or in the very least, she isn't imagined. But as Clive's 'hallucination' has indicated she's dead, what are the chances of her being alive? His dream must have been some kind of supressed memory. My mind's scrambling to keep up. How will poor Clive feel if he finds out?

'There're a few other avenues he's going to look into. He'll get back to us in the next day or two.'

'Clive's medical records have been found. George is going to take a look to see if there is anything important,' I say, even though stringing together a sentence is almost impossible.

'Maybe they'll tell us something about Nancy.'

'Hopefully.'

There is a knot in my stomach pulling tighter than ever before. I wonder if it's how Lucy felt when she was poorly. I brush a hand over my pulse point, but for once it's to feel my scar, not to take my heart rate.

I ask myself, would I want to know? If we find out the truth about Nancy, should we tell Clive? If the events surrounding my scar weren't as clear as the light of day, would I want to remember?

'Don't say anything to Clive,' I finally say to Tess. 'I think we need to establish a few more facts and then decide what to do.'

What we have in our hands is a time bomb, and I for one have no idea what to do with it. As far as Clive is concerned, Nancy has already died. He imagined her being killed only to be told she isn't real. It will be a cruel blow to tell him that we were all wrong. That in fact she does exist, but died long ago.

He doesn't need to suffer all over again. Nobody does.

Chapter Forty-Four

Clive

For the rest of that day, Keisha was preoccupied. Clive noticed she didn't take up the offer of biscuits later in the afternoon and focussed solely on her computer, leaving Clive and Lucy to get to know each other a bit better. Already he knew she was all heart.

The good thing was that Keisha had managed to speak to George and he was able to drop him off to visit the flat and the allotment the following day, which soon came around. It was a relief to get there, George checking he was okay before waving goodbye.

Clive had wanted to get his head round this next move some more. He was at the point where everything was in place to exchange and complete. All he had to do was give the go ahead. But he was stalling and said he wanted one last visit to double-check some measurements. That wasn't the real reason though. He wanted to gain some sense that he was doing the right thing and hoped a further visit would do that.

Inspecting the flat for a second time, Clive was aware how bland the space was. It was also tiny compared to the home he was used to, but this was his best bet, wasn't it?

Clive traced his way around each of the rooms once again, trying to garner more enthusiasm for the space. It reminded him of the sleep lab. There was everything that he would need, but that was it. It was a tick-box home. All the practicalities that would make life function were there: a place to wash, a place to cook, a place to sit, a place to sleep. There was nothing fundamentally wrong with it, it was just lacking that sense of home.

It was something Clive was going to have to get used to though. Plenty of people his age ended up in places they didn't consider home. And his old house wasn't home any more either.

'All okay here?' The overenthusiastic salesman was back, even though Clive had asked for some time alone.

'They don't put much colour in these places, do they?'

The salesman glanced around. 'It's a lovely blank canvas, isn't it? They do it deliberately so whoever moves in can add whatever personal touches they like. You can have it painted whatever colour you prefer.'

Clive wondered how odd it would look if he locked himself in the bathroom. He wasn't too worried about coming across as rude. Not only had this man not listened to his request of leaving him alone, the touch of condescension in his voice was almost too much to bear.

'I'm an old man. I'd much rather it came with those added touches.'

Rather than wait for further patronising, Clive set off for the other thing he was here for. He'd been lucky that George had agreed to drop him off here before his shift. He had a shorter one today and would pick him up at the allotment in about five hours' time, if he stayed that long. Clive was using it as an opportunity to have a proper day at the allotment. Visiting the flat was just an added distraction.

'I can get some numbers for reliable painters and decorators if you need.'

Clive was being followed and, unfortunately, these days, he wasn't really able to pick up the pace.

'What I needed was to admire the space without interruption. Perhaps then my vision might have been given the opportunity to explore its full potential. As it stands, I haven't conjured up any colour palettes so I'm off.'

'Apologies, Mr Ellington. Call me as soon as you'd like another look.'

Outside, more signs of spring had started to appear: daffodils blooming along pavements, tree blossoms starting to flourish. It was Clive's favourite time of year. The time when the plans he'd made over winter could be put into action. Because of the drama of the past few weeks, he hadn't decided what he was going to sow where and what he'd like to grow the most this year. Today he'd be able to make some more concrete choices.

If nothing else, he wanted to prep some of the ground. There were bound to be more weeds than his friendly allotment neighbours would have been able to keep at bay. His flask of tea and the gorgeous lunch Tess had provided him with should see him through an hour or two of physical work. The rest of the time he planned to firm up his decisions in his notepad and if the mood took him, he'd head back to the flat and cogitate some more, like he'd hoped to before he was interrupted.

As he approached, the view of the allotments was clear from the road, only a wire mesh fence separating them from the world. He liked that system. It kept people out, but it didn't stop them from seeing in or Clive being able to look out. He liked the frequent conversations he had with passers-by as they went about their day. He had prime position for chatting to the public, being the first slot. Perhaps he'd catch a few familiar faces today. Heading in, the first thing everyone passed was Clive's composting section that he'd built next to his shed. He added everything to it from tea bags to potato skins. There was some quality compost waiting for him at the bottom and he'd need it this year if he was going to grow some gladioli again. Wandering round to his shed, he was going to be pleased to get started: the beginning of a new season.

He spotted two thistles that had worked their way onto his patch and were set on taking up residence. Certain weeds were more stubborn than others, so they were his first challenge for the day. Clive opened his shed and popped his things away, deciding that once the first thistle was out of the ground it would be tea-break time.

There was a great pleasure to be had when he trod on the fork and the prongs glided into the earth. It was even better when he was able to get his gardening gloves dirty as he finished the battle and pulled the root from the ground. Thistles never liked to come out easily and it was always satisfying to be rid of them. Not that he'd usually let them advance this far.

When the second root was out, he stopped for lunch. Tess had packed it and told him it was a surprise. Clive half expected glitter to fall out as soon as he opened the Tupperware. There was parcel upon parcel in there. He unwrapped two home-made Scotch eggs, a small tub of home-made coleslaw, another one that contained cheese and crackers, a salad and crusty freshly baked bread. It was a feast fit for a king and for this quiet portion of time he was going to enjoy being that king. Everything he needed was packed in there: cutlery, butter, a sachet of salt and pepper. It struck Clive that this was another way to bring in some income for the café. Packed picnics for the weekends. He knew some fishermen and other allotment holders that would delight in a lunch like this. The small jar of piccalilli relish confirmed that it would be perfect because Tess always thought of everything.

Thinking about Tess, Keisha and George made Clive's stomach churn. Would these new parts of his life, and these wonderful people, still be there when he moved away from them? He really hoped so, but he'd lived through enough cycles of life to know that nothing ever stayed the same. If only he could remember all the cycles he'd been through.

Clive found himself raising two fingers towards his neck. It didn't take him long to locate the pulse he'd been feeling for. Was it odd that it made him feel connected to Keisha? It was strange… Now they weren't working together every day, he found he was beginning to miss her. That her odd habits had become endearing. That after a while he'd come to recognise the changes in her heart rate as well as she did.

Right now, he'd love to know if her heart was bounding along at its average of fifty-nine beats per minute. He wondered if it ever pattered differently when she was in George's presence or was he completely off the mark about that match? He'd love to know what was happening there, but hadn't wanted to pry any further.

Clive's pulse was thready and not as solid as he would have imagined. Taking another bite to finish his Scotch egg, he then checked his watch to take an official recording. Some beats seemed to be weaker than others, to the point he wasn't entirely sure that his count was accurate.

Forty-five beats.

From what he had observed over the past few weeks, that seemed a bit low. It always depended on what was normal for that person though, Clive recalled Keisha saying. If only he was able to remember what his normal rate was. Still, he felt fine. Especially thanks to the splendid offerings of the picnic he was enjoying.

In a second layer, he found his pudding. A slice of Dorset apple cake that smelled heavenly and tasted even better, the tartness of the apple balanced out by the sweetness of the cake. Hopefully that would bring up his pulse if it even needed to be higher.

He checked one more time, pressing more firmly to make sure he didn't miss any beats. He was sure he hadn't caught all of them last time.

He was right… Fifty-seven.

That seemed more reasonable. But even once he'd finished counting he kept his fingers there, feeling for something.

What was there was a memory. It was lightly balanced under his fingers, scrambling around, trying to make its way to the surface. It was there and then it wasn't. One of those tip-of-the-tongue moments that was hovering just out of reach. He was having so many of those of late.

He knew it was something to do with being ill. A recollection of when he'd become poorly at the allotment, perhaps? That would be a useful memory to recall. He'd hoped remembering being picked up by the ambulance here would cancel out the false memory that he had. The one he could hardly bear to think about.

Under his fingers was his light pulse, barely there. And that was all he was able to remember… Something that was barely there. It was no use to him at all.

Chapter Forty-Five

Keisha

I like to be confident in my decisions. As someone who tends to look at things analytically, I can normally work out what to do for the best. Probability is a girl's best friend.

But what to do when there is no way to know what the outcome will be? When we are entering uncharted territory?

I feel bad that Clive has gone to his allotment without knowing that we're all meeting up to talk about him and what we've found out between us. But a chat at the café seems the best way to proceed. Once Tess places drinks on the table for Lucy, George and me she sits down and joins us.

'Tell them what you told me about what you read in Clive's records,' I say to George.

He takes a moment, stirring three sachets of sugar into his black coffee.

'Clive had a prolonged stay in hospital in his twenties. They thought he was attacked at the time. He had a head injury resulting in significant memory loss.'

'What does that mean?' Lucy asks.

George shrugs. 'At the time he was unable to remember what happened and had short-term memory loss. I'm not sure if it has any significance now, but it might explain why he often gets muddled.'

'I haven't told George or Lucy yet,' I say to Tess.

'Told us what?' Lucy says, dunking her biscuit into her tea. A second later the soft half plops into the mug.

'Tess got her uncle to look into some things. He's a genealogy specialist.'

'There was a Nancy living at the property with Clive years ago. But she wasn't Nancy Ellington, she was Nancy Fuller. It might tie in with the memory loss George is talking about.' Tess lays a list down on the table. Five phone numbers. Five Nancy Fullers.

'Hang on,' Lucy says, trying to salvage the biscuit with a teaspoon. 'So for weeks Clive has been going on about his wife that everyone says isn't real, but now you're saying she is? Newsflash!'

'We think so,' Tess says.

'What do you think we should do?' George asks.

I realise I want to be closer to him. I want to be next to him, rather than opposite. It's quite the revelation to have amidst a meeting that's full of them. It's been building up, but there it is. On the other side of the table is a man who makes my heart flutter.

'How can we be sure she's one of these?' Lucy asks, pointing at the list.

I'm not feeling for my pulse right now, not when breathing is hard enough.

'My uncle said they might not be,' says Tess. 'But he's not found any record of a death. It doesn't mean there hasn't been. She also may have married and changed names or moved out of the area.

The only way we'll find out is if we ring these numbers to see. If they all say they don't know Clive then at least we know we tried.'

'It seems so implausible,' George says.

Lucy is still busy retrieving her biscuit with her spoon.

'It certainly does,' says Tess. 'But Clive isn't able to tell us the full story. The only way we'll get that is if we talk to Nancy. I know I want to hear the other half of Clive's life.'

I pick up the piece of paper and rub a finger across the names, as if somehow I'll develop telepathic skills that will lead me to knowing which of these women to call first.

'I'm just worried that we're opening up a can of worms. Shouldn't we just be telling the police?' I ask.

'They didn't come up with anything. And they'd be duty bound to tell him if they did have new information. At least if we do this we're preventing any more potential hurt,' George says.

I opt to be the one that makes the calls. I feel like I'll be more in tune with the potential responses, as if it is possible to listen to the heart from afar and know what it is saying. I decide to approach the list from top to bottom, practical as ever. I stand behind the counter to make the call as if that somehow gives me protection from the anticipation that's pulsing around us.

'Do you know a Clive Ellington?' is the question I settle on as an opener.

'This is not the garage. How many times do I have to tell people?' is the response from the first call.

'I'm sorry. What's this about? I'm just heading out to the gym,' is the second. From her voice I can tell she's far too young to be our Nancy.

After those unwelcome responses, I'm getting ready to throw in the towel. This isn't my puzzle to solve. But I know I need to at least get to the end of the list, to try to find the missing piece.

On the third call, there is silence.

'Hello, did you hear me? Are you still there?' I ask.

I hear a swallow and a faint cough from the other end of the line.

'You *do* know Clive Ellington.' I mean to say it in my head, but the truth is those words need airtime.

'I've been waiting a lot of years for someone to call,' the faint female voice says from the other end.

Chapter Forty-Six

Clive

A few hours at the allotment had made Clive feel considerably better about the prospect of living nearby again. The past few weeks had been full of uncertainty. What Clive had known to be a happy life had been turned upside down.

Even now, weeks after it happened, Clive didn't think he would be able to wander back down that short road to his old life, knowing what he'd imagined there. It was still trapped in his mind and it was so vivid it was heartbreaking.

Instead, while Clive waited for George to pick him up, after receiving a message to say he was on his way, he was making the last of his plans for the allotment and what he hoped to grow over the coming weeks.

He was opting to go with some quick-to-grow items that he knew Tess would be able to make use of: lettuce, radishes, spring onions and the like. He was also going for some staples that he enjoyed: potatoes, white onions, shallots, carrots, beans and peas. In addition he was also going to have a go at growing peppers. He'd never tried to grow them before, as the soil conditions might not be the best for them, but as they were something Tess used regularly, it was worth giving it a try to see how well they did. It was an experiment of sorts so Keisha was bound to approve. Thinking of Keisha made him add beetroot to the list. He was beginning to feel a lot better and, along with the company he was keeping, the juice regime seemed to be helping. He planned to start making his own once the trial period was over to keep up the health benefits he was experiencing.

His plans were a thinned-down version of what he usually went for each year, but as he was late to start and he was still recovering it seemed sensible not to overdo it. Getting the allotment straight again would keep him busy enough.

He brushed a hand across the paper of his journal. He'd done his best to remove the rest of the torn page with a Stanley knife. It was only obvious there was a page missing if one was to really go searching for it. He still didn't understand how or why that had happened. It was most unlike him, but he'd just have to blame it on being unwell, like so much of what had occurred. It was going to be one of life's mysteries. One he was going to have to ignore.

George beeping his horn confirmed as much. Locking up, Clive cast one last glance back at his patch of land. His corner of the universe was at least here to keep him going.

Chapter Forty-Seven

Keisha

This must be what cheating feels like. I'm sweating from every pore and more nervous than I've been for any of the dates I've been on.

The usual comfort I gain from being in my usual spot at the café isn't present today. If anything, it's making me more fearful. What if Clive stumbles across this moment? He's at the lab working with Lucy and she knows she needs to keep him there, but what if he says he needs to pop to Tess's flat for something?

I'm concerning myself unnecessarily. Clive won't be turning up while this meeting takes place.

The meeting that shouldn't be possible.

'Do you think she's chickened out?' Tess is pacing and busying herself with more tasks than usual: checking the sauce bottles, refilling the salt cellars, dusting all her precious unicorns.

'I wouldn't be surprised if she has. I'm not far off chickening out myself.' I have two fingers on my radial pulse and the rhythm is jumping about in the way I've always imagined it will when I fall in love on the spot. This is something different though. It's what it feels like to be dealing with a love that isn't mine.

'Don't walk out,' she says. 'Then I'd have to talk to her and you're Clive's friend.'

'So are you,' I point out, realising we're both anxious. George is at work, but it would have been too many people if he was free.

'You're right. I'm going to close the café. I don't want her to arrive and then for me to have to go off and serve customers. We both need to hear Nancy's story.'

Tess turns the sign to close the café and writes a handwritten note about being shut due to unforeseen circumstances.

'Won't that put her off when she arrives?' Though I'm beginning to think, like Tess has already suggested, that Nancy might not be coming.

'Maybe. I'll change it.' Tess opts for a note that says: CLOSED FOR A PRIVATE FUNCTION FOR NANCY.

Over the past few days I've gone over all sorts of scenarios as to why Nancy hasn't been part of Clive's life. It is a puzzle with too many missing pieces to make sense of. I'm really hoping the meeting with Nancy will see that picture made whole.

'Do you want another drink or anything to eat yet? I need a coffee even if I've had enough to make me jittery.'

'Yes, please. Coffee for me too.'

I glance at the door, where light bounces off one of Tess's glittery unicorns. The effect dances off the wall like a disco ball, as if it is an illustration of all the jitters bouncing around the room.

For a moment, the movement mesmerises me, making me forget for a fraction of a second why we're here. So when the door does open, I jump. I'm standing without meaning to and I nearly scare Tess enough to drop a mug.

She catches herself at the same time I do and we manage to stop ourselves from screaming at the frail lady entering the café.

'Thanks for the note. I've never had a café open exclusively for me,' the woman says, breaking our silence.

I gravitate to Nancy, and put out a hand, hoping to make up for our initial shock at her arrival. 'I'm Keisha. It's so lovely to meet you.' I've come a long way in a few weeks when it comes to meeting new people. And somehow, I feel like I know Nancy.

She has a sparkling smile. I realise it's partly down to dentures, but there's also a warmth that comes with it. It's not something I normally notice, but she has an aura. A glow that is radiating from her small frame that's not much over five foot tall. Her white hair is cropped short and she has blue-framed glasses that suit her. It's not a surprise that she has a patchwork handbag.

'I'm Tess. A friend of Keisha's. Can I get you a drink? I'm making us a coffee. We thought we could have lunch after a chat.'

'I'd love a hot chocolate,' Nancy says, and it makes both Tess and I smile.

I know all I'm doing is staring and I'm thankful that Tess is providing some direction. Somehow I manage to guide Nancy to a seat and take my own, continuing to stare as I go.

'You must be Clive's daughter then. I've always wondered what happened with his life. I'm glad he went on to find someone.' There's a pleasant tone to Nancy's voice as she wishes the man from her past happiness.

I shake my head. I don't want any confusion. It's confounding enough as it as. 'I'm not Clive's daughter. I'm not even a grand-daughter. Clive doesn't have any children.'

'Oh. I always rather hoped he would.'

I should clarify further, but I'm desperate to know about Nancy. 'Can you tell us a bit more about you? How did you know Clive?'

'It was a long time ago. It's fairly complicated.'

Tess arrives with the tray of drinks, each of them with a couple of Biscoff biscuits in the saucers. The added sugar is definitely welcome.

'We've got time to listen,' I say, hoping to encourage her confidence. She doesn't need to know that really I have to get back to work.

'Can I ask who you are? How you've come to know that I was part of Clive's life?' she asks.

I realise that's also fairly complicated to explain.

'I met Clive because he was put forward for my PhD study. It's following the progress of patients who've been diagnosed with broken heart syndrome. My study is looking at the benefits of beetroot juice in someone's recovery. It's high in nitric oxide and, anyway…' I realise I'm in danger of boring the poor lady. 'Broken heart syndrome, otherwise known as takotsubo cardiomyopathy, is a rare heart condition that normally occurs as the result of a shock or trauma. It causes a temporary weakening of the heart. In Clive's case, it happened because he believed that his wife, Nancy, had passed away.' I decide to spare her the full details of what his hallucination includes. She turns grey enough without being told he thinks she has been murdered.

'Nancy?' she repeats, as if it isn't her name that I've said.

'Yes, Nancy. He thought just prior to being unwell that he was married to a lady called Nancy. When it was looked into, it turned out Clive didn't have a wife. He's been told it was all because he was delirious and we thought the same until we looked into the history of his house. That was when we found out that a Nancy had lived with him. We believe that's you.'

Judging by her reaction it has to be. She has taken a napkin from the table ready to use as a tissue.

'Did he really say Nancy? I didn't think he'd ever remember me.'

'What do you mean?'

Nancy takes a moment to compose herself, removing her glasses so she can dab her eyes.

'Clive and I were never married. We were engaged, but the wedding never went ahead because of what happened. He was only twenty-four. We'd been courting for several years when he had a head injury. It changed everything.'

'If you don't mind me asking, what happened?' Even though there are pieces slowly slotting into place, I still don't understand the whole puzzle.

'Nobody really knows what happened to Clive at the time. He was working at the post office temporarily as a clerk after leaving the army. In the afternoon, on his break, he headed to the bank for some personal banking. The assumption is that a gang of some kind thought he had a substantial amount on him and mugged him. He'd been depositing a small amount towards our wedding, nothing from the post office. He managed to wander home after the attack, but his injuries were significant. There was obviously more than one person involved. He shouldn't have been able to walk anywhere. They hit his head at some point and for a long while they weren't sure if he was going to make it.'

'Did they ever find out what happened?'

'No. Clive's memory was completely wiped. He had no recollection of the recent years before. And certainly no memories of what happened.'

'And no recollection of you,' I say, as if I'm lifting the lid of a coffin and revealing a ghost.

'Not at all. It was a very hard time. For all of us.' Nancy's eyes glaze over as if she's gone to another place and time and it's only the tears that are forming keeping her present.

'Can I ask a question? Feel free not to answer if you don't want to,' Tess says.

Nancy involuntarily shudders. 'Go ahead. In for a penny, in for a pound, I guess.'

'The reason we discovered you were real is because we found your name on an old electoral roll for Clive's address. If you weren't married, why did you live there? In those days it was different, wasn't it?'

'That'll be the hard time I'm referring to. Clive's injuries meant he needed a lot of care. When they wanted to send him home, he wasn't able to look after himself fully independently. His mother had passed away a few years before and his father wasn't in the best health. His dad, Keith, suggested that I come to live with them to help. It was an opportunity to get him better and hope that in time, he'd remember me. It took over a year, and in the end he got back on his feet, but those first twenty-four years and any memory of me were gone.'

'He didn't fall in love with you all over again as you nursed him back to health then?' That's how the movie would play it out.

'I only stuck with it as long as I did because I was holding on to that hope. Sadly, the injuries had turned him into an angry young man, frustrated by his condition. He only ever saw me as a carer. He genuinely thought his father had employed me to look after them both. When his dad passed away, I helped make the funeral arrangements and as Clive was much better and able to cope by himself, he sacked me.' Nancy gave out a little laugh at that. The absurdity of it clear to anyone listening. 'I took it as my cue to leave. There was no point continuing to cling on to a relationship that ended the day he was injured. It broke my heart, but it was the only thing I was able to do.' Nancy clears her face again, the napkins disintegrating with the number of tears being shed. 'I'm sorry.'

'We should be saying that. This must be quite the shock,' I say, wanting to extend a hug across the table even though I never do hugs. The pain this lady has been through is palpable, reaching out through the years.

'It is a shock. In all that time, he never called me by my name. I never thought I'd hear him say my name, let alone think that I'm his wife.'

'Would you like to see him again?' I need to find out. Knowing that Nancy is alive changes everything. Clive doesn't need to live through the trauma all over again if she doesn't want to know. But with Nancy here spilling tears over their lost love, does it really have to be so lost?

'He's not here, is he?' Nancy glances round in a panic.

'No, he's not. I just wondered if you did want to meet up with him now you know he has some memory of you.' In my head there is a happy reunion in the future that doesn't take into account what Nancy must have endured all those years ago. 'What am I thinking?' I say. 'You must be married and have children of your own. It was a lifetime ago. I understand if you don't want to see him. He doesn't know that we've made contact with you.'

Nancy composes herself with the help of the extra napkins Tess passes over. 'I have three cats and no children. I've had a few relationships over the years, but the trauma of what happened with Clive never left me. Life can be very cruel and I think I was always scared of something like that happening again. Tell me, what does Clive remember of me?'

'To be honest, I'm not completely sure. The problem is it's been very muddled. At first, he thought that you'd been living together as husband and wife. But as he was told that he'd been hallucinating, and that was what I'd been led to believe too, I've not really probed him on the matter. As it had upset him in the first place, I didn't want to upset him further, particularly as at the time we didn't think you were real.'

'So what he does remember isn't a true account? He might have plucked my name from thin air with no real memories of what I was to him.'

'I do think he knows who you are. I think there are fragments of your life together that he remembers and that are coming back to him. He told me about the first time you both met. He refers to you sometimes as if you lived together. Now we know you have been part of his life, it makes far more sense.'

I realise that I don't want this lady to walk out of here and never have the chance to meet Clive again. I want her to have tea served from the pot with sugar tongs and pink wafers as side accompaniments. I want her to taste Clive's pickled onions and to bear witness to his unusual clothing choices.

'I very much doubt he'd know who I was. If he didn't remember back then, a few snippets of recollection aren't going to translate into knowing who I am now. It was over fifty years ago. He'll be remembering a different person to the one that is sitting before you now.'

Tess clatters her coffee cup into its saucer. 'What if there was a way of meeting him without having to tell him who you really are?'

'What do you mean?' I ask, wondering where Tess is going with this.

'The speed-dating event. If we get Clive to take part, we could get Nancy to be one of the participants.'

'What do you mean?' Nancy repeats.

'Well, if we arranged for you and Clive to meet, we'd have to explain who you were and why you were meeting up. There'd be no way of knowing if he remembers you without spelling out who you are. As he doesn't think you exist, that might be a bit traumatic. If you do the speed-dating event, it's a chance for you two to fall in love all over again.' There's a misty quality to Tess's expression as she makes the suggestion.

'What do you think?' Nancy asks me.

I run through the scenario in my head while nibbling on one of the biscuits. It melts on my tongue. If they have their speed date and there is no recognition, then nothing extra is lost. It won't be nice for Nancy, but it will give us our answer at least. If he does recognise her, then without the need for data or statistics, won't it be achieving the impossible? Is this the way to mend a broken heart?

'If you're happy to, I think we should do it,' I say to Nancy. And before I finish the sentence I know she wants to see Clive. She wants to know if the love of her life remembers the love of his.

Chapter Forty-Eight

Clive

Every task that Clive carried out these days was bringing him closer to the next chapter of his life. He was going to miss Tess's company. Her flat was a complete contrast to where Keisha lived. The front room had a Moroccan vibe with a terracotta orange on the walls and a wall hanging with tiny mirrors woven into the pattern.

Unable to settle, Clive found himself staring into one of the small circular mirrors, wishing it was some kind of porthole. While he wasn't as low as he had been when he first landed in hospital, he was still finding it hard to appreciate that life had to go on. It was hard when life hadn't worked out how he thought it would. He was too old to start over, even if Keisha and Tess were trying to convince him otherwise.

'Everything okay, Clive?' Tess asked when she caught him staring at the tiny reflection of himself.

'Nerves are getting the better of me, I'm afraid. Is there any chance we can find someone else and I can be let off?'

Keisha joined them, appearing from the café below. 'You look amazing, Clive.'

Clive adjusted his bow tie. He had made an effort. He was particularly pleased to have found the burgundy velvet smoking jacket. It wasn't an everyday outfit so he'd been thrilled that this would be an opportunity to wear it, but now he felt fussy and over-dressed. 'Is it a bit much?'

'Not at all. It's completely you.'

'Can't I just go back to being a host? I'm well past finding love.'

'You made me do it and this whole thing was *your* idea. We're not going to force you, but it really would be a shame if you didn't. Be brave.'

After some consideration, Clive got rid of the bow tie and undid the top button of his white shirt. It wasn't going to help matters if he fainted.

'Everything's sorted. People should start to arrive soon. Come down when you're ready or we'll give you a call,' Tess said.

For the first time, Clive understood why Keisha needed her emergency exit for these occasions. The nerves he had building up were making him want to combust. This was well outside his comfort zone and he hadn't realised it would be until it had come to getting ready. He spoke to women all the time: in his old job at the post office, passers-by at the allotment admiring his plot, the volunteers at the charity shops he frequented. He was in the business of being pleasant to everyone he encountered. So the prospect of talking to six ladies in a row shouldn't have been a scary one. But the fact that these were dates made it a different prospect altogether. The charm he usually liked to believe he possessed was standing at the exit ready to run, waiting for him to follow.

'It's time,' Tess yelled up the stairs.

Clive checked himself one last time and wandered down to the café. Everyone else had already taken up their places at their tables. He realised it would be a bit different from the event with the spring chickens. They had made a few adjustments to the plans, including that each date would be five minutes rather than three and it was in the afternoon rather than the evening.

'You're on table two, Clive,' Tess said, an impish expression on her face he'd not seen before.

Keisha was also looking at him differently. Perhaps it was how he'd looked when he'd set her up with George.

Clive's date was already waiting for him and the room was void of conversation, as if it wasn't allowed before the bell had sounded.

As soon as Clive had taken his place, the sound of the bell they'd been waiting for went and the nattering began.

'Sorry to have kept you,' Clive said, feeling as if the whole room had stalled because he'd waited to be called down the stairs.

Out of the corner of his eye he spotted Mrs Baldwin. He didn't know whether to be pleased to see a familiar face or whether to be concerned this was a set-up. It would serve him right if it was after what he'd done with Keisha and George. He wasn't going to be rude to the lady opposite him, though, and start talking to someone else in the room, even if she hadn't replied to him yet.

Clive took her in fully for the first time, wondering why she'd not yet managed a hello.

'You don't need to apologise.' She almost choked on the words as if something was stuck in her throat.

Clive gained the distinct feeling he did need to apologise, he just wasn't sure why. 'I'm going to anyway. I know it's a terribly British thing to do, but I'm a gentleman, so I'm sorry.'

Now they were talking, Clive took more note of the lady across from him. She had blue-framed glasses that had a great snazzy design along the arms. They enhanced her features: white hair, high cheekbones, beautiful eyes that were almost violet.

Of course that might have been down to some anti-reflection coating on her spectacles, or the fact his apology had made her eyes gloss over.

'You look beautiful,' he said, truly meaning it, and for the first time noticing that they were matching. She had a burgundy velvet top on that could have been purchased as a matching item for his jacket. 'We match,' he said, euphoric at the notion.

'We do! What are the odds?'

Clive leaned in, taking one of her hands in both of his. He wouldn't normally be so forward, but there was a familiarity he wasn't able to explain. It must have been the burgundy velvet.

'I'm Clive. It's lovely to meet you.' There were only five minutes. He reckoned two must have ticked by already. He didn't want to waste any more.

'I'm Nancy,' she said. More composed now. Her nerves must be dissipating as well as his.

'Nancy,' he repeated. 'I knew a Nancy once, I think.'

The Nancy he knew had come into his life and left again too many times for him to know if she were real or not. She would drift in on a memory, the taste of a well-baked pie or the faint smell of gladioli. One minute she would be there and the next she would be gone. The recent thoughts of her, the ones that seemed real… He'd dismissed them all. He'd been *told* to dismiss them. But still, he hadn't been able to shake them.

'How are you finding this?' Clive asked, forgetting all the things he'd planned to ask.

'Surprising,' Nancy said, twiddling a bracelet and glancing at that rather than him.

The links of the simple gold chain sparked something in Clive. Something he *was* able to catch hold of for a change.

'Are you *my* Nancy?'

The gloss became formed tears that puddled in the corner of her eyes. 'Am I?' she asked.

It was hard to process what was going on. His Nancy had died. And then he'd been told it was nonsense… Made-up memories caused by illness. It wasn't possible, and yet…

'I think you might be.'

Was she? There wasn't a true representation of what Nancy looked like in his mind. When he thought he'd found her, he didn't get a look at her face. What existed of Nancy was a feeling. A knowledge that he'd been completely in love.

'I am, but it's been fifty-five years.'

'So long?' he said, his voice catching in his throat. He found tears rolling down his cheek, matching hers to create another set.

Nancy nodded, making feeble attempts to wipe away her tears.

'What happened?'

'I can't.' Nancy shook her head.

Clive still had her hand in his and cradled it closer to him, like it was a precious gem. As if by holding on to it, he'd capture the essence of this moment. He didn't fully understand her upset, and yet the tears were pouring and in contrast he was experiencing a sense of euphoria. He wasn't sure what the exact word was… He'd never come across one that was the exact opposite of mourning. But he was being filled with joy. Bursting with it, in fact.

'It doesn't matter now, does it? Can we start from this point with our matching outfits? Can we make these five minutes count?' If Nancy wasn't so upset, he'd propose on the spot. He didn't want the rest of the five-minute dates when he'd found the love of his life on the first table.

'I need to take a moment. Just some fresh air,' Nancy said, as she got up and headed for the door.

Clive didn't know how to react, so he turned to Keisha in the hope she knew some of the answers.

'How did you…? What did you…?' Clive's sentences were running away from him before he was able to complete them. This was impossible.

'We weren't sure if you'd remember her.'

There was a frustration building up in Clive. The grumpy old man who'd been in hospital was returning. 'Why didn't you tell me? My God. She's alive. And no one thought to let me know before I sat down on a table in front of her for *five* minutes. Don't you think fifty-five years of loss deserves more than that? No wonder she's upset.'

'It was my idea,' Tess said, before Keisha was able to explain.

'We honestly weren't sure you'd know who she was. We thought it was better to see if you realised rather than tell you.'

The explanation was baffling, but then again so was everything in Clive's life at that moment. He'd spent a lifetime carrying on with his routines, knowing something was missing, but not able to find what it was. Now he knew. And she'd just walked out of his life in tears.

Unlike the dates he'd observed Keisha have, he wasn't going to let the chance of true love walk out on him. He wasn't about to miss an opportunity in real life by scrolling through posts on Facebook.

'I've got to go,' Clive said.

But as he reached the street outside and tried to work out which way Nancy had gone, there was a chance that he was a lifetime too late.

Part Four

The Left Ventricle

This is the thickest chamber of the heart, responsible for
pumping oxygenated blood back to the body.
In other words, it's the beginning of a journey…

Chapter Forty-Nine

Keisha

I can't respond. I should be responding, but my fingers are pressing up against my neck, willing the jumping to go away.

This isn't how this should be working out.

'Go!' Tess implores.

Every conversation in the café is on a pause, with people staring at me. They're all wondering what has just gone on and I want to tell them how badly I've mucked up. About how despite my years of study, I don't know how the heart works at all.

'I'm going to call George,' Tess says, when I don't respond because I'm too busy counting how many beats per minute my heart is running at.

Too many is the simple answer. I don't need to be doing this right now. It's a waste of time. It's preventing me from existing in the moment.

Even though the second hand of the clock I'm staring at hasn't reached twelve, I stop short of taking a proper recording. For the first time in my life living is more important than checking I'm alive.

'I'll call George,' I say. 'I've created this mess. I'll explain it to him.' I want to be the one who speaks to him, knowing he'll understand.

Forgetting to take a coat or anything practical, I leave Tess to host the rest of the speed-dating event now the disruption is over.

The delay of attempting to take my pulse is only fifty-three seconds. Clearly too many as I'm unable to locate any red velvet jackets to follow outside. I was hoping it would be like the first time I lost Clive and he was sitting outside the café. That he'll be slightly out of view and easy to find.

I call George. Crossing the road, I'm careful to pay enough attention to not get run over.

'Are you free? Can you come to the café?' I ask as I glance every which way to try to catch sight of Clive or Nancy.

'What's happened?'

'Clive met Nancy.'

He knew that was the plan, but somehow it needs clarifying.

'And?'

'I think I might be responsible for their hearts breaking all over again.'

I cry at that moment. Unexpected sobs take over. They say lightning doesn't strike twice. And yet here I am… Living proof that sometimes one scar can cause another.

Chapter Fifty

Clive

There wasn't a sign of Nancy. Oddly, it made Clive think again that perhaps she was a figment of his imagination. That he might be caught in the middle of another delirium episode.

As luck would have it, he managed to hail a taxi and asked it to trawl the surrounding streets to see if they were able to catch sight of her. The taxi driver was very accommodating, following Clive's instructions as they both kept their eyes peeled for the woman in a top the same colour as Clive's suit.

'Your wife, is it?' the driver asked as he turned another corner.

'Almost.' Clive wasn't sure if he was talking about then or now. 'Can you take me to the Guildford Gardens allotments? She might head there.'

He thought there was a vague chance she might go somewhere familiar. But in all honesty he didn't know where Nancy would have headed. He knew nothing of her life and if she wasn't able to fill him in he wasn't sure he wanted to hear it from anyone else. Certainly not at the moment when he was trying to process what was going on. At least if he went to the allotment it would give him the chance to try and remember again.

As it was late afternoon when he arrived at the allotments, it was busier than it had been on his last couple of visits. He wasn't in allotment attire, but being the first shed past the entrance gave him the chance to slip away before anyone noticed him. He didn't need to have a conversation about whether someone should plant mange tout right now.

Equally, as he slipped past his compost pile and round into his shed, he didn't know *what* he needed right now. In a lot of ways a good cry would do him some good, but there was too much shock in his system for any tears to come loose just yet. It would be nice to go back and live those five minutes all over again. If he'd have known from the start, if the recognition had been instant, he would have been able to express how much he loved her. As he breathed in the musky wooden scents of his shed, he hoped it would be calming, but it only made the loss more acute.

Now all he was left with was wondering where Nancy was. Would he ever see her again? Were those five minutes the only ones he would get?

At least he knew she was alive. That those scenes his mind had created were complete fabrication. The body. The blood on the carpet tiles. The mark on the door. They were all made up.

His brief moment of gathering his thoughts in his shed were cut short when he realised, suddenly, he'd come to the wrong place. Any memories he had wouldn't be here. They'd be back home. It was finally time to go back.

It was only a five-minute journey without the wheelbarrow. Guildford Gardens were just opposite, but it was one of those roads that looped around and he needed to turn the corner before his home would be in sight.

For a hopeless moment he was filled with optimism. Was it too much to believe she might be standing there waiting for him?

But as the house came into view, she wasn't there. Not at the garden gate or the front door. The optimism left him like a wave that had found its way out of his empty chest and he wondered if there would be any heartbeat at all given how he was feeling.

There were two routes into Clive's house: the front door or the side entrance. He had a key to both; he'd been carrying them round all the time like the intention had always been to come back here despite him being afraid to do so. He opted for the front door, too afraid that using the side entrance would spark off flashbacks of the horrific event that had seemed so real.

For a moment, Clive forgot that Keisha and George had been busy clearing out the place. Over the years the house had started to get a little cramped with all the trinkets he had purchased. He was a bit of a hoarder at heart and if something spoke to him, generally it came home with him. The place was bare now, stripped back to what it originally was like. His parents hadn't had the same fascination that Clive had and the collection was entirely his. The carpets and the furniture were still there though, much of it original to the time his mother and father had been alive.

Even the thoughts about his parents, especially his mum, made him realise… He remembered.

Not everything. Nowhere near everything. But enough. The years that he often referred to as the grieving years were coming back to him piece by piece.

What he needed to do now was go to the spot that had haunted him. The place by the kitchen counter where he thought he'd found Nancy bleeding. Having seen her alive and well would hopefully stop that nightmare from taking over.

The first thing he noticed was the carpet was different. Not from the last time he'd been here, but from the memory in his head.

And it *was* a memory, he realised, all of a sudden. But not one that involved Nancy. Instead, it was him…

It had been Clive there bleeding, nearly dying from the injuries to his skull and the wound on his arm. The scar that he only made up stories for, the true recollection lost.

But this… This was a truth hidden amongst a lifetime of confusion.

Standing there in the kitchen, he had the flashback he'd been afraid of, but not the one he thought he would have.

Clive held his head as he remembered being hit there. There were three of them, and every one of them was happy to beat him to a place close to death. The cut on his arm was caused by his fall to the ground. He'd sliced it along some railings with the force of falling and the skin was lacerated as if someone had taken a knife to him. It had been followed by kicks and punches before being left for someone else to discover.

Only he hadn't remained there like someone more orientated would have done. He'd risen and stumbled his way home. It wasn't a feat someone barely conscious should have been able to manage, and yet in his injured state, he'd made it home.

His recent delirium was no such thing. It was a fifty-five-year-old memory. It hadn't been Nancy lying there dying, it had been him. It was the day his world had faded to black. It was only today that he was remembering it had once held colour… Violet eyes he was afraid he'd never get to see again.

Chapter Fifty-One

Keisha

The fact that George is a nurse and has seen many people broken is a comfort. I can't get a hold of myself and I'm not sure I ever will at this moment.

It's not helping that my upset is affecting my rational thought process. I'm not sure what to do now that locating Clive hasn't been as simple as walking up and down a few streets. I've even checked in the nearby charity shop to ask if they've seen him.

George cups my face with his hands once we're in his car and dabs away my tears with a tissue.

'Look, I know you're worried, but you need to think positively. For all we know they might have taken the opportunity to book into a local hotel to make up for the past fifty-five years. We just have to hope he can last longer than my three minutes if that's the case.' George smiles an impossibly beautiful smile. 'This doesn't mean that it's all gone terribly wrong.'

'I know, it's just…' I don't know how to tell George I'm worrying about history repeating itself. Not in an eloquent, clear way at least. 'His heart.'

'Hopefully his heart is ticking by fine, even if it is in shock. Right, now let's work this out. Where would Clive have gone? Do you know Nancy's address? Is there any chance he could have gone there?'

'No, I only have her phone number.' The sentence makes me realise how my thought process is malfunctioning. 'But I have *his* phone number. I can call Clive!'

I don't know why I didn't do that first before running along nearby streets. Being able to get hold of Clive is why we got him a mobile in the first place. As it starts to ring, I wonder if he'll answer. I can't shake the images of him having collapsed somewhere nearby out of my head. I know what can happen to a heart under stress, one that's unable to cope with the shock it's been exposed to. It's hard to imagine anything else when you've had first-hand experience of what happens.

Every time the phone rings at the other end, it increases the pressure on my heart. The seesawing of it with each swell and release is pushing down into my stomach cavity with each trill that doesn't get a reply.

'Please answer.' I look to the sky as if I believe that's where some source of hope is at. 'Please let him answer.'

'Hello. Have I pressed the right button? Can you hear me?'

I thank the clouds and any entities beyond them.

'Clive, where are you?' A few tears of relief spring from me, the panic yet to subside.

'I'm at the house.'

'The house? Which one?'

'Home. I decided it was time to come home.'

'You're at the flat? Or the house?' I'm not sure why I need to clarify, but the part of me that knows Clive is never going to be able to return to his home can't quite catch up with what he's saying.

'I'm at my house. I needed to come home. I needed to see if I remember.'

'We're coming over. I've got George with me. Don't go anywhere.'

'Is everything okay?' George asks once I've hung up.

I'm crying without checking how much of a mess I am. There are tears streaming down my cheeks. I take a moment to wipe my face to make sure I'm passable, although I'm no doubt well past that point.

'Clive's at his house. I should never have agreed to this happening.' I feel like I've opened a can of worms and it's not one where I'll ever be able to put the lid back on.

'Don't go trying to blame yourself. Nancy was happy to do it. Nobody knew how it was going to go. Consider it an experiment and hopefully it won't take much clearing up.'

'I just feel like I've let Clive down. He's my friend and I chose to do it this way rather than tell him.'

George takes a tissue from the pack I'm holding and dabs my face some more, the flow continuing.

'But you did it for the right reasons. I imagine you've been the best friend that Clive has ever had. You and Tess have done everything you possibly can for him these past few weeks. He might not have any daughters, but he seems to have gained one or two. Possibly three if we count Lucy.'

'And maybe a son, too,' I say, considering the role George is playing in Clive's life too.

'Well, no.'

'No? You've been a major help. You're about to drive me to his so we can make sure he's okay. I think he'd consider you in that way.'

'Still no. If you're an honorary daughter, I can't take up the role of honorary son. It would be far too incestuous.'

For the umpteenth time, my stomach flutters in George's presence. 'What do you mean?'

For the first time, I notice how George is looking at me. I realise how things between us have shifted. I'm comfortable enough to ugly cry in front of him for starters.

'I can't do this if you're my honorary sister,' George says. He leans in and kisses my lips. One small, sweet gesture, as if he's unsure of himself.

'Oh,' I say. It's shock that's making my response so inadequate and lacklustre. For the dating experiment, it turns out Tess and Clive are right. It isn't always the heart that responds first. It's every part of me that's been wanting this to happen, while never for a second realising that George might feel the same way.

'Sorry. Wrong moment. Forget that happened.'

'I don't want to forget.' Not when Clive has lost a whole lifetime of love because of memories escaping him.

If Clive forgetting the love of his life for fifty-five years was going to teach me anything, it was that in the very least, I need to embrace mine.

I kiss George the way it really should be done. Even though we need to make sure Clive is okay, for a minute or two, nothing else matters other than the feel of George's tongue brushing against mine. It's reminding me what it is to be alive. It's making my heart jump at last. It might even be helping it heal a little.

'I don't want to ever forget a moment like that,' I say when I break away.

'Me neither,' George says before kissing me again for good measure.

I can't help but think about the old adage that everything happens for a reason. That without meeting Clive, I would never have met George. He wouldn't have become my go-to person in case of emergency.

Going to find out if Clive is okay is going to be so much easier with George by my side. And we'll get there. Soon. Once we manage to stop kissing.

Chapter Fifty-Two

Clive

Clive was filled with emptiness, which was a strange oxymoron of a position to be in. If his house being cleared of many of his possessions wasn't enough to cause it, then the knowledge of what life had allowed him to miss out on definitely was.

He thought of the many meals he'd had alone. Of the walks for one. Of the theatre trips with a solo seat. He'd passed through the years convincing himself that it was because he was happy by himself, and he was. Because he'd not realised there was a love that he'd left behind. But the more he thought on it, the more the nice memories were surfacing. Those pies he'd remembered were ones she'd really made. Those complaints about his mucky wellies were true. A lifetime ago, he *had* grown the gladioli for her to enjoy.

There was a knock at the door stopping him from dwelling further for now. It was Keisha. She sprung in, giving him the biggest hug of his life. The first one he'd ever received from her.

'I'm so sorry. This is all my fault. I should have told you that we'd found out about Nancy and that there's more to your history than we'd originally realised,' Keisha said, adding that George was waiting in the car to allow them some time by themselves.

'Nonsense. How is me being mugged a lifetime ago and then becoming a muddled, but somewhat more enlightened, old man ever your fault? There's no one to blame here other than the misfortunes that life sometimes dishes out to us. I just wish I'd remembered some of this sooner.' There was still something niggling away at him.

'But Nancy. I should have told you. We just weren't sure if you'd remember.'

'I didn't at first, but then that knowledge was there again as solid as a rock. I really hope she's not too upset. Are you able to call her? Check she's okay?'

'Can I take your pulse first? I want to make sure we aren't setting off another episode.'

'Go ahead.' Clive took a seat on the sofa and offered Keisha his wrist and doing so reminded him of her scar – the one she'd never spoken of, but with which he knew their connection had been created. 'We don't want another bout of broken hearts. Are you ever going to tell me about yours?' He gave the heart tattoo a gentle brush.

Keisha glanced at her scar and it was only then Clive noticed she'd been crying. It would seem they were all a tad broken-hearted today.

'I've never told anyone, you know.'

'I know. You don't have to tell me either, but I've remembered what caused mine. And what caused me to become ill this time.'

'Really?'

Clive nodded as he observed Keisha carefully counting his pulse and only releasing his wrist once she'd taken a recording.

'All okay?'

'Your heart rate is perfect. No changes to usual despite the afternoon you've had.'

'It has been quite the afternoon.'

'Do you want to tell me about it? Do you want to tell me what you've remembered?'

Clive swallowed. He knew both their stories needed to be shared. 'I can't say it's completely clear yet. I only seem to remember fragments.'

'Fragments are fine. I don't think you can ever force the mind to remember. If that was possible, I'm sure you would have made those memories arrive much earlier.'

That was true. If Clive had remembered Nancy earlier he would have acted on it far before the eve year of his eighties. 'Are you braced for this?'

'Only if you're braced to hear my story afterwards.' Keisha sat next to him on the sofa, the room barren without its many trinkets.

'Of course.' Clive held Keisha's hand as if they would steady each other along the way. 'My mind has really jumbled a lot of things over the past few weeks. It's an improvement on the lost knowledge that I'd been living with, but it means nothing is as clear as it should be. What the doctors put down to delirium was on the most part, but it was delirium based on true events that I'd long since forgotten. Coming back here has made me remember some things, but not everything. I know what sparked it, though… When I was at the allotment, I met one of the new allotment holders. I knew there was something familiar about him, but I didn't know what. That's why I wrote that note. I was trying to remember. It was only when

I was on my way home today that it came to me. He was one of the attackers. He had aged, obviously, but he had a tattoo on his forearm that I recognised straight away. A mermaid with anchors all the way along her tail. Recalling that brought everything back in an instant. All those missing years returned as jumbled memories that I'm still only beginning to make sense of.'

Keisha smoothed Clive's palm, her expression aghast, as he continued.

'When it happened all those years ago, I somehow managed to stagger home. I collapsed in the kitchen and nearly bled out. I have a feeling it was Nancy who found me. It was her that had a life entirely changed that day and she's had to wait fifty-five years for me to remember who she is. To know that she was the woman I loved and wanted to spend the rest of my life with.'

'Oh, Clive. Has it really taken seeing who did this to bring it all back?'

Clive nodded sagely. 'It would seem life has been cruel enough to let that happen.'

'But we know about Nancy now. It can be different.'

'Don't go spouting anything about second chances. You saw how upset she was.'

Keisha tightened her grip on Clive's hand. 'If I'm honest, I'm surprised she was so prepared to go along with the idea. I think she genuinely thought that you wouldn't remember her and it was just a way of closing that chapter for the final time.'

'And now who knows where that chapter is heading. Now tell me, before we lose our chance. What is this chapter of your life you've never told anyone about?'

Chapter Fifty-Three

Keisha

I decide to take my pulse on finding comfort from taking Clive's. It gives me a chance to feel the scar and decide if I really want him to know. The secret I've based a lifetime on and yet kept totally and utterly to myself.

'I've broken a heart before,' I say, knowing it to be true in every sense.

'How so?' Clive asks.

As I peer into his crystal-blue eyes, I realise that it's easy to tell a soul that has borne the same responsibility. And even though it is neither of our faults, it still feels like it sits squarely on our shoulders. The burden of it all too difficult to take.

'I caused this scar myself.' I have a feeling Clive knows that already. 'I was fifteen and I decided I wasn't able to carry on. I'd always been bullied for being different. For being odd. I thought everything would be better if I wasn't about so I tried to take my own life.'

'And what happened?' Clive's voice is gentle as he asks the question.

The part about trying to kill myself doesn't make me sad. At the time I thought I was being practical without realising how it might make others feel.

'I never got to finish the job like I planned to. It all got much worse.'

'What could possibly be worse than wanting to kill yourself?'

'Getting caught trying to kill yourself.'

'Surely that's not a bad thing. That must have stopped you from giving yourself a matching scar on the other wrist.'

They are fractions of a moment. They are events that occurred in such a short timeframe. But all these years on I'm unable to forget them. Unlike Clive, who wasn't able to keep hold of his memories, I've been unable to push mine away. I'm not sure if I can voice why the other wound never made it to my wrist.

'It was the worst thing,' I say, discovering that I'm not crying, but finding it hard to breathe. I focus on the empty mantelpiece. I think of all the trinkets that are no longer here – a lifetime of other people's memories.

I don't want to say it out loud, but I realise that in some ways, it might be like a removal. It's mine, but by letting it go it will become someone else's.

'My dad found me. He knew I was struggling and came back from work early. I was in an empty bath, trying to be considerate of the mess that I would make. He came in and saw what I'd done. He grabbed the phone and started calling for an ambulance.'

I take a breather. Remind myself that perhaps never sharing this memory is what has made me hold on to it. 'It wasn't as bad as it looked at that point. I'd bled a lot, but it pooled rather than poured, but Dad was busy telling me all the reasons I should stay alive: that I was the most intelligent person he knew, that being different was a blessing. He listed all the reasons I was great, all the things I would go on to do. That I would be a great scientist once I'd finished studying at university. He told me *he* was the only person I needed to listen to. Not the bullies who didn't understand who I was or what it was like to be the odd one out. He didn't take a breath as he spoke to me and when he did, there was nothing but fear in his eyes.'

I can see it happening now as I talk about it. As if it wasn't over fifteen years ago, and instead only yesterday. The terror in his eyes as he fell to the floor, still clutching the phone. The knowledge that the urgent phone call wouldn't be for me. That we now needed it for him.

'It was takotsubo cardiomyopathy. He died from a broken heart. It wasn't me who died as I planned, it was my father. I tried to save him, and bled all over him as I tried, in vain, to make his heart work again.'

Clive moves his hand, wrapping me in an embrace, and I realise I'm crying now, the same as he is. There aren't just two people in this room. There's a lifetime of ghosts and memories and make-believe spinning around us, laughing with glee at the way they've defined us.

'Please tell me you remember everything your father said. Please tell me that your memory hasn't ruined the best parts like mine has?'

'I do,' I say, realising that perhaps it is his words rather than his death that I've been focussing on all these years. 'He said to follow my heart beyond all others.'

'And have you managed that?'

'I've certainly followed hearts.' A small smile manages to curl my lips. I know more about hearts than most people and yet they are still such a mystery.

'I know you've done everything you possibly could for mine.'

'I had to. I've never admitted it to myself until now, but in not being able to save my father, I knew I had to save someone. My life wouldn't have been complete without achieving that. You were my chance to mend a broken heart. I think that means I've followed my heart, even if it was choosing to look after someone else's. I think there's a need to know that I can follow my heart and it will all be okay.'

I think about Nancy and how things are turning out. It isn't like they were shacked up in a hotel like George's suggestion. It isn't like I can banish the missing years that Clive's mind has given him.

'Is it okay?' I ask, needing to clarify that *we* are.

'My dear Keisha. It may have escaped your attention, but you are the dearest thing to have come into my life for many a year, even if you don't like pickled onions. I will never be able to thank you enough for everything you have done for me and I need you to understand that for as long as I'm about, I'll be there for you. Not just in the lab helping out, but in whatever way you need. And while you are doing perfectly fine in most areas of your life, I do rather feel you need me for advice in interior design, in the very least.'

I hug Clive, realising that I haven't been returning his embrace in the way that I should. It might be crossing all the study–participant boundaries, but he is more than a friend. He's become my mentor, a father figure in the absence of my own.

'I'd suggest I should give out tips on dating as well, but as we know, it turns out I'm much worse at it than you. My first one in over fifty years and she ran out on me!'

I pull away from the embrace and clear my face. I blush when I think about the kiss with George.

'I might not be in need of dating tips any more…'

'Really?' Clive clears his eyes with his hankie and the twinkle is back.

The doorbell rings.

'That's probably George now. He'll be wondering if we're alright.'

I've been in the house a whole half hour without realising. I get up and somehow I feel lighter. I'm not about to stop checking my pulse every half hour, but I'm going to try to look to the positive. Look towards the future, rather than focus on the past.

'I'll get it,' Clive says.

'Don't say anything,' I say.

'I never would. The story of our scars are our secrets. No one else needs to know unless we want them to. Only you get to decide who to tell.'

I contemplate that for a moment while I follow Clive to his front door. Even though I've never told anyone else until today, it doesn't mean that I won't. When the time is right I will tell George and Lucy and Tess. I know they'll understand why it's a part of myself that I find hard to think about. A place where I normally only ever find blame that I've laid at my feet. A broken heart that I caused and wasn't able to save. I need to remember I've been trying to make up for it for the rest of my life and every day that I accumulate a set of statistics, I'm helping save someone. It might not be the pounding on the chest or the attaching of probes that George and his many colleagues carry out, but I'm finding out what I can do to help one heart at a time.

'George and I kissed,' I whisper to Clive, just as he's about to open the door. 'Don't tell him I told you that either.'

'I knew it!' Clive turns and offers me a quick wink. 'I'm so pleased for you.'

I place a finger on my lips to make sure he knows to keep schtum and I smile, glad to have something to be happy about in amongst our despair.

I smile even more broadly at George once the door is open. Despite all the emotion of the day, I have an overwhelming desire to jump his bones. It's not my most ladylike thought, but for all the first dates I've been on, I'm feeling very ready to dive in at the deep end and hope that it involves a duvet and a bed and some more kissing.

'I'm rather regretting packing away your tea bags,' George says to Clive.

'I could do with a cuppa,' Clive says in agreement.

'And you do have a guest,' George says, as he steps aside to reveal Nancy.

Chapter Fifty-Four

Clive

Clive and Nancy were having to make do with water in glasses. For so many years he'd prepared for this moment without realising and when it came to it, he didn't have a doily in sight. It made him sad to think that the seaside-themed items he'd been collecting weren't being put to good use at this moment.

George and Keisha had made their excuses and left them to it. Now he was at a loss as to what to say, other than apologising for the lack of resources and the many years that stood between them.

'It hasn't changed much here,' Nancy said, making small talk.

Of course. She *had* lived here. Only not ever in the way it should have been, the way he would have liked. The version where they'd continued to take dance classes together through the years. The way his recent delirium had made him believe it had been.

'It had changed a bit. I've collected hundreds of trinkets over the years, but George and Keisha kindly boxed them up for me because I was thinking of moving. You'll be glad you're getting to see the less cluttered version.'

'I would have liked to have seen your things. Are you still planning on moving?'

Clive glanced round the kitchen diner where they'd positioned themselves once the kids had gone. After everything, this room didn't hold the fears he'd thought would be here, that he'd thought would haunt him. 'I think I should move back here. I think I was wrong to be so rash about moving. I've been wrong about a lot of things.'

'None of that was your fault, though.'

Clive nodded agreement. It was cruel that his mind had wronged him. That his past memories didn't hold a full representation of the truth. But perhaps that was a blessing. He would take a bet that young Keisha would pay to forget what had happened to her.

'I guess all we can do now is enjoy the present. I can't change what happened or the hurt it caused, but I can start doing whatever I can to make it right. What I thought was a dream, I have the chance to make reality.'

Clive wasn't sure if it was the right thing to do. There were many ways it might go and many other people would err on the side of caution. But if life had taught him nothing else, it had taught him to be bold and brave and unapologetic.

By the time he got down onto his knee, he really had to hope Nancy didn't run away, as there was a strong possibility he was never getting up again.

'The sun may have risen more times than I care to count since we could last class ourselves as a couple. I know what happened was more than a storm cloud. But you are the reason I know what love is. And even though this is fifty years too late, Nancy, will you marry me?'

There was the possibility he should have waited for this moment and built up to it. Taken her to a dinner, a dance, or a walk in the countryside. But life seemed suddenly very short. It was an easy decision not to wait.

Nancy moved her hand towards her neck, a move so in keeping with how Keisha would take her pulse, that for a moment, Clive thought Nancy was going to do the same. Was his proposal enough to break her heart?

But rather than take her pulse, Nancy hooked her thumb around her necklace, pulling it out from under her top.

'There's just one problem.'

'What is it? Other than the fact I can't get up.'

On the necklace was a ring. It was beautiful and had a patchwork of small stones – emerald, ruby, sapphire, diamond – in the shape of a flower. It was exactly the kind of thing he'd choose. In fact, it was exactly the ring he'd chosen.

'I said yes the first time, so technically we're still engaged.'

Epilogue

Keisha

Three Months Later

It seems that life is proving to me that it's never too late. Even with probability completely against them, here I am at Clive and Nancy's wedding. Not only that, it appears that at thirty-one, it's not too late for me to become a bridesmaid for the first time.

I'm not even upset that it's a burgundy patchwork dress. Not when I'm matching Tess and Lucy and two of Clive's great nieces, who are over all the way from Australia. They go nicely with the burgundy velvet outfits that Clive and Nancy are wearing from their date that saw this reunion happen. They also match well with the flowers inside St Saviour's Church where they've decided to hold the wedding: a local church they've both visited over the years, but never knowingly crossed paths.

The past few months have provided Clive's life with a massive amount of repair. It's been the same for me. It's funny how sometimes we can see the scar, but not know the cause. How a process, like the beating of a heart, can seem so simple and yet be so complex.

'What a glorious summer day we have to help us all celebrate this wonderful union, the longed-for joining of Nancy and Clive,' the vicar says, leading us through the beautiful ceremony.

I enjoy the ceremony so much that I dare to miss a heart-rate recording.

'I do,' Nancy says, and by then there is not a dry eye in the small church.

Everyone here knows their story. The local paper is covering the fifty-five-year engagement. Even PC Doyle is at the back sobbing his heart out. Clive's original cold case is now solved, with the help of the allotment CCTV and a confession, the suspect being an allotment holder making it fairly easy work.

I smile at George in his patchwork jacket in his role as best man. It turns out that Clive's infamous jacket wasn't a charity-shop find. It was in fact a creation of Nancy's, who still has quite the flair with a sewing machine.

Later, we head for afternoon tea at Tess's café. Every vegetable in the spread has come from Clive's allotment, as he now supplies Tess's Treats regularly with his produce. There are quiches, potato salads, pickled onions (of course), couscous and stuffed peppers. And the puddings are delicious things like rhubarb fool and summer berry meringue and a three-tier wedding cake made by Tess herself. Clive and Nancy have obviously let her choose how to decorate it because it is a triumph of unicorns and edible glitter. There are hundreds of other places they could have had their reception, but they wanted it to be here. At the place where they re-met, and as a thank you to all of us for helping them find each other again. It's the perfect venue. I even get to sit in my favourite spot.

Clive delivers a beautiful speech, declaring the only thing that could have been more surprising is if Nancy announces she's expecting.

One more sentimental part in particular speaks to me. It's when he says: 'The heart is more complex than I've ever imagined. It has the ability to remember, but also to forget. It can love to the point of bursting. And I feel so privileged to have had my heart burst, not once, but over and over again. I cannot tell you how much love I have for the people with us today, knowing we wouldn't have found each other again without your help.'

It's only later, when Clive and Nancy are attempting to teach us all how to dance, that I get a moment with Clive.

'Now, we finally get our dance,' he says, as he takes my hand and brushes a finger across my heart tattoo. 'Follow my lead,' he says, like it was ever going to be that simple.

I stand on his foot within two moves. I take up an unreasonable amount of his time as he tutors me through the next three songs until Nancy has to ask for her groom back.

It makes me realise that we'll never be able to make up for the loss of time. But as with all things, we must look to the positive…

Life, in the same way it can grind us down in despair, can also give us unexpected gifts of hope.

A lost love found…

A broken soul healed…

A heart so tiny it can't even be heard on a Doppler yet.

George and I are waiting until after the honeymoon to let them know they're going to be grandparents.

That brings us back to Part One – The Right Atrium – the start of the story. The beginning of the beat of a heart. The chance to start all over again…

At some point in the future, when someone looks to see what history we left behind, they will see on the electoral roll that Nancy Ellington does live with Clive Ellington. Fifty-five years after Nancy Fuller couldn't live with the stranger she loved.

And around the corner, over the road from the allotment, Keisha Grant moves into Guildford Gardens with George Palmer, into a blue-painted house with a colourful interior, influenced heavily by their most frequent visitor, who no longer drinks tea alone in his allotment shed when they're home. And for the next three electoral rolls, another name will join them as their family grows. Fortunately, all three children end up liking pickled onions.

A Letter from Catherine

Dear Reader,

This story has come from a special place in my own heart. The initial idea stemmed from reading an article about broken heart syndrome. Having previously worked in cardiology as a physiotherapist, I was surprised to come across a heart condition I'd not known about and immediately thought there had to be a story in it.

The other reason this story is special is because some parts are reminiscent of my own nan and grandad. After my much-loved grandad (who was an allotment holder) passed away in 2012, my nan missed him dearly and often voiced the fact she would like to join him. I wrote this story for her, a love story in reverse, if you like. She passed away and joined him not long after I finished writing this book. They first met at a dance like Nancy and Clive, and I like to think that my grandad still has two left feet and they are once again reunited.

If you did enjoy the book, and want to keep up to date with all my latest releases, just sign up at the following link. Your email address will never be shared and you can unsubscribe at any time.

www.bookouture.com/catherine-miller

I hope you loved *The Missing Piece* and if you did I would be very grateful if you could write a review. Every one of them is appreciated – I'd love to hear what you think – and it makes such a difference helping new readers to discover one of my books for the first time.

I love hearing from my readers – you can get in touch on my Facebook page, through Twitter, Goodreads or my website.

I know recently we have all collectively been going through tough times and I hope this story has brought with it the sprinkling of love and hope that life often requires.

Love, happiness and thanks,
Catherine x

katylittlelady
katylittlelady.author
katylittlelady.com

Acknowledgements

This book wouldn't be what it is without having asked some people for help in their field of expertise. Firstly, I would like to thank my friend, Dr Will Nicolson MBChB, PhD, MRCP, University Hospitals of Leicester NHS Trust. He has provided invaluable help with Keisha's job and her PhD study to make this as accurate as possible. For anyone who wanted to know, here is the outline of Keisha's study that Dr Nicolson came up with, that I'm sure, if it were real, would make it to the *British Medical Journal*:

Title:

Mechanistic insights into the pathogenesis of takotsubo cardiomyopathy: the synergistic role of nitric oxide

Summary:

Background:

Takotsubo cardiomyopathy, colloquially known as broken heart syndrome, has a clear stress trigger in around seventy per cent of cases. However, the mechanism by which the stress causes the characteristic cardiac features of apical ballooning and ST elevation remains unknown.

Studies have indicated a pivotal role for a surge in catecholamines and have demonstrated higher circulating levels of catecholamine in patients acutely presenting with takotsubo cardiomyopathy. But stress is a frequent part of the human condition and it remains unclear why a particular individual on a particular day is susceptible to developing the myocardial inflammation and associated oedema termed takotsubo cardiomyopathy.

Nitric oxide has a key role in causing the vasodilation of blood vessels and recent studies have shown that dysregulation of nitric oxide exacerbates heart failure and arrhythmogenesis.

Hypothesis:

Dysregulation of nitric oxide explains the susceptibility of an individual to a surge in catecholamines causing takotsubo cardiomyopathy.

As you can see, Will went above and beyond, creating the study that would see Keisha requiring candidates to drink beetroot juice. I've weaved this into the story as much as possible and I have every faith that Keisha would go on to do her study in full. If not, as this is as authentic as it gets, it may well be Will and his colleagues doing so. Any mistakes in the translation of facts to fiction are mine.

On the genealogy side of things, I need to thank my uncle, Malcolm Austen. In the story, Tess refers to her uncle as the 'genealogy specialist' and it is in fact something that I have grown up with. For as long as I can remember Uncle Malcolm has had a keen interest in family history and is the current chairman of the Oxfordshire Family History Society, amongst other family-history groups. His knowledge has filtered through over the years so I know some of the technicalities involved with searching family history and worked out how to fit it within the plot. Of course, having an expert uncle did mean I was also able to clarify I had these things correct, even if they are unlikely.

I don't normally base my characters or story on real people or places, but in this story, the allotment is based on my grandad's and the home is the one he and my nan lived in all their lives. Because it was my way of bringing them together while they were apart, those places were in my head as I wrote the story. I'd like to thank all of my family for all the happy memories we've had there and hope they continue in future years.

I finished this book just ahead of what would become a particularly hard period of time for all of us. Covid-19 was unexpected. For every book I've written I've always meant to say a thank you to some of the healthcare workers involved with looking after me and my chronic eye condition. I'd like to extend a thank you to Mr Nigel Hall and the staff at the Southampton Eye Unit who have been looking after my eyes since I was twenty-one. I'd like to thank my GP, Dr Boddeke, and all the staff at Cheviot Road Surgery. I'd also like to extend a special thank you to all the staff working on F8 at Southampton General Hospital, caring for the Covid-19 patients during this time. They ensured messages could get through when we weren't able to visit my nan during her final hours. Never have I been more thankful for the kindness of strangers.

This book, as always, has had lots of support from friends and family. The revisions would not have happened without my girls, Amber and Eden, my partner, Ben, and my mum, and not forgetting Tara the dog. I'd also like to thank some of my extended family and friends: Brian, Sarah and Shane, Uncle Malcolm and Auntie Lesley, Rosie and Jen, Emily and Kaiden, Vee, Don, Ryan and Angela, Sarah, Stacey, Kat and Chrissie. I'd also like to extend that thanks to some of the writing organisations I'm involved with: the RNA Southern Chapter group, the RNA, the SoA and, of course, my fabulous bunch of writing friends: The Romaniacs.

I'd like to thank my agent, Hattie Grünewald, for always steering me in the right direction and my editor, Christina Demosthenous, for doing the same. They are a dream team along with all the supportive staff at Bookouture and The Blair Partnership. Thank you for helping me run with my ideas and seeing them through to the final version.

Lastly, a thank you to you, the reader. It is such a blessing knowing that so many are enjoying the stories I write and I really hope you've enjoyed *The Missing Piece* as much as I've loved writing it.